DOC ARMSTRONG: SUBURB AT THE
EDGE OF NEVER

DOC ARMSTRONG: SUBURB AT THE EDGE OF NEVER

LARRY BLAMIRE

Bookaroonie Press

ISBN 978-0-692-63781-4

This is a work of fiction. Names, characters, places and incidents are the product of the author's imagination and any resemblance to person or persons living or dead, or events or places is entirely coincidental.

This book is dedicated, with love and pride, to my wonderful brilliant sons Cory and Griffin. Because adventures both silly and serious should be handed down.

PREFACE

If the success of my film *The Lost Skeleton of Cadavra* is measured by the enthusiasm of its fans then it is very successful indeed. I've said it before: our fans are the greatest in the world—smart, funny, and passionate. They're also some of the nicest people I've met, both virtually and in person. And they seem to want more of "Skelly," so I was very glad we were able to give them a sequel, *The Lost Skeleton Returns Again*. However, the idea of these characters coming to life in prose form was quite recent.

A couple of years ago I had a sudden urge to mess around in Photoshop and create a "vintage" paperback cover that paid tribute to the great Doc Savage covers from Bantam, painted by the amazing James Bama. I plopped *Lost Skeleton* protagonist Paul (who looks like me) in there as "Doc Armstrong," adapted the distinctive Doc Savage typeface, added wear and tear for an authentic look, and ended up with a spoof that was very nicely received by fans on social media. So much so that one led to another, and then another, until they became kind of infectious. Before I knew it, I had ten; each cover subtitle riffing a Lost Skeleton reference.

They were actually a bit painstaking but so much fun that, after several months, I made another batch of ten.

Sometimes I was inspired to accompany them with a mock-excerpt, a page or less, as though lifted from the actual book, if there had been an actual book. I found myself really getting into this over-the-top mixture of pulpy prose and absurdism. It flowed quite naturally.

These faux passages were also well received, and people started asking me to make an actual Doc Armstrong book. The idea appealed to me, and I thought about it every so often, but I just wasn't sure when I could get around to it. Timing is crucial for me, and it just wasn't right, so I had my mental valet park it round the back (you should all get one).

Spring 2016. A new Doc Armstrong cover image came to me for some reason, and I started working on it casually. It wasn't quite like the others, wasn't a Doc Savage spoof—oh no, oh no, my friend. One late afternoon I happened to head outside and froze at the sight of a gorgeously ominously cloudy sky. I quickly took a couple of pictures. Days later I realized it was the perfect background for the new cover: a lowering sky behind Doc Armstrong.

Then this story started flying at me, like chipped beef flung at toast. Next thing I know, I'm writing my first novel.

The process was interesting. At first, I depended on index cards (as I've sometimes incorporated in screenplay writing—thank you, Syd Field), but I ended up only doing that at the beginning and end of the book. Sometimes I'd write on the computer, sometimes scribble in a spiral notebook. Changing venues seemed to keep things fresh.

The strange thing was that, except for a very general idea, I really didn't know where the thing was going. I would just stop and outline every so often. I knew very little beyond two or three chapters. Yet I knew that what I was writing was heading somewhere. I never had any doubt. It was not unlike driving at night and trusting beyond what the headlights showed. It all felt right. When I started, I estimated thirty chapters, and that's exactly what it turned out to be, which I think means that I have chapter prescience.

One of my favorite things about writing in any form is that satisfaction of finishing a day's work, finally letting your mind relax, and immediately having the next sections unfold, faster than you can write them down. That was the case here. I will never understand the creative process. It might as well be cottage cheese as far as I'm concerned. Or public hatstands.

I've written plays, screenplays and short stories, but one unique and fascinating thing I noticed with a novel was the sheer density. It's too much to remember. This book would not allow me to recall what I had written on a day-to-day basis, except the general thread. The bits and pieces, details, throwaways, were like a byproduct of a trancelike state.

My films have an odd blend of elements, but this story was a golden opportunity to paint with broader strokes and combine even more things I love: movies, mystery, adventure, 50s scifi, pulp, horror, television, absurdity, surrealism, pop culture in general and a hint of satire. Every so often I asked myself if these diverse elements would gel into a cohesive narrative (although I used smaller words). Was it too much? Was I constantly switching gears. Would it be a smooth ride? Could my novel induce nausea? I never wanted to hurt anyone.

Well, I knew better than to dwell on this, so I trusted my instincts and continued to write the book I wanted to read. Like it or not, that's what it is. I would read a whole series of these if there was one. I don't know what that says about me.

Another thing I liked about writing a novel was my budget. I went crazy. I spent mental money like it was flypaper. Wait'll you read the extravagant sets I didn't build, and the amazing special effects that are in my brain (and soon, yours).

Now I should provide some context. This story is set following the events of *The Lost Skeleton of Cadavra* and *The Lost Skeleton Returns Again,* as well as the events following those, as laid out in the finished script I wrote for *The Lost Skeleton Walks Among Us* (not yet produced—an oversight we hope to correct in the near future). While there are numerous references to the first two films, I was careful about revelations concerning that exciting and epic third saga, thus have avoided spoilers (which I personally am not fond of).

If you are among the deprived, or depraved, few who have not seen the first two films I urge you to seek them out, as it can only enhance your reading experience, as opposed to merely hancing it.

Will there be more? That's pretty much up to you.

I'm hoping yes, because I've already started jotting down notes. I mean I can't turn back now.

Larry Blamire

September 27, 2016

CONTENTS

Chapter 1

HOME: THE WRONG WAY TO GO

B. "Bunny" Bretterspitt, "Hare" to his friends (sometimes "O'Hare" or "Rabbit Pal") was well liked. He was outgoing, easygoing, and many other types of what are considered some of the nicer goings. But the sad truth was, the guy just never had a green thumb. Except for that time he was a kid and sampled some of his mom's good kale pie when she wasn't looking. Other than that, Bunny just never had a reason to know even the first thing about vegetation of any sort, not to mention growing things. Fortunately, he kept this minor embarrassment to himself, so it did little to undercut his likability in the neighborhood.

It is, however, more than likely the reason he chose "manufacturer of fine industrial sand" as a career, and not "grower of fine broccoli." Let's face it, nothing is farther from the lush, moist world of greenery than sand. And B. Bunny had never once regretted his choice. Until now.

As he strolled home from the Blendview bus stop, a convenient three blocks from his quiet suburban home, he had the strangest sensation of something he could only think of as "shrub awareness." Not just shrubs—trees and grass. And hedges, especially hedges. Suddenly he was noticing just how foliage-rich his little Blendview neighborhood was. He would have to make a point of commending everyone at the next Blendview Homelivers Association Meeting. Normally those meetings were boring, and he rarely had anything to add, being easygoing and other goings, but B. Bunny had no doubt this carefully dropped bon mot would spice things up.

As he continued, B. Bunny tried thinking about sand, as he usually did on his way home, the day's trials and tribulations lingering with him, just as they did with every other poor soul who tried not to bring his work home with him. But, in his weary mind, those pale (or tawny), fine and gritty cascading granules that had become his life were replaced by the stems and blades and petals and leaves whose world now seemed to overwhelm him. How could he have not noticed it all before? All that green?

He was about three houses from his own now and, despite his distraction, B. Bunny did what he always did: cut through yards to save time. He walked a tricky line coming home at the time he did, and he knew it. Any lollygagging or pussyfooting, the two gagging and footing things B. Bunny most frowned on, would mean missing the beginning of his favorite television show, *Tigerbeat*. And the kids never liked having to explain what had happened thus far. It just wasn't the same. Plus they'd all miss even more things during the lengthy "catch up."

Besides, he confessed to enjoying the *Tigerbeat* theme song and opening credits with its oddly-angled shots of unusual upholstery. He even sang along on occasion (though he'd never in a million years admit around the water cooler at Fine Sand and Granulated Dirt that he actually knew the words).

Now, as he moved through the yards, B. Bunny noticed that his newfound flora awareness began to take on a decidedly narrowed focus.

Hedges. He had never noticed so many hedges before, so many perfect round hedges. Didn't they come square?

Wasn't that the natural condition of a hedge? Weren't they born rectangular? They usually seemed rectangular, often enlisted for barrier duty, like a wall or a fence, only made of leaves. For the first time he found himself admiring what must surely be a delicate manipulation of greenery; such precise surgery to result in so impressive a ball of leafy goodness.

B. Bunny paused. Something had gone skittering through the congregation of round hedges before him. They stood there, this especially noteworthy grouping, looking for all the world like a village of leafy green huts about belt-high. What would skitter through there? Probably one of the neighborhood cats, he thought, maybe a squirrel. Maybe the latter fleeing from the former, Bunny laughed in his mind.

Well, thought B. Bunny Bretterspitt, won't catch my favorite show by staring at a short uninhabited hedge-village. And, with that, the reasonable man pressed on. Cutting through those fine leafy balls would take him right to his house, and the slippers, meal and TV that eagerly awaited his arrival.

Again, the skitter, just ahead of him. B. Bunny paused. That was a large cat. Maybe it was two cats, one on the other's back. That suddenly seemed ridiculous, and this time B. Bunny Bretterspitt found himself laughing out loud by himself, just like the time he got his own bald head covered in cake. Great winkers, you almost never heard of one cat riding on the back of another, and he was fairly certain *that* was in the circus, and even then only on special occasions. And, anyway, why should this make him stop and risk missing his favorite show? Stupid cat acts. They sure get in the way sometimes.

The head B. Bunny now shook was the head of a very foolish man, he thought as he once again grasped sanity by the shoulders and proceeded on his path. Walking all the way around those silly but picturesque bush balls could cost him that jarring first upholstery shot in the credits, and the announcer's words, "Whenever you fail geometry, let no one hear you cry." But this man of fine granulated grains was made of sterner sand. He would plow straight forth with the heart of a thousand rock crushers.

Suddenly, B. Bunny was between the tightly-growing globes of green and there was no turning back now, unless he were to turn around and go back, which he never would. How could he face his wife, his kids, his dog, his TV show? No. This was something he had to do. He had to face the skittering. In life, we must face the skittering head on, and he knew it. Besides, it was probably just some chipmunk that never missed a meal. He chuckled, suddenly imagining that chipmunks had formal sit-down dinners at regulated times. That would be one for the books, if he ever had books.

The steadily building guffaw stuck in his throat and, denied freedom, threatened to back up on him. The skitter again. Louder, closer, bigger. Now B. Bunny was scared. He did not know what he was scared of, but he was scared and, without further hesitation, not only did he speed up his winding meander through the hedge village, he increased his pace. Only a few hedges remained between him and his house and *Tigerbeat*. Lovely blessed *Tigerbeat*—he must write to them. Write to the show, the producers, the sponsor, tell them how much he enjoyed it, how much it meant to him. He had never done that. Not enough people did. And this was its second season. Ungrateful son of a gun. How could he live with himself? If he could only make it through these hedges he would do that first thing. Thank goodness he had come to his senses in time to rectify this egregious and selfish oversight. As soon as the show was over—

According to a neighbor across the street who happened to look over at just the right time, the last that was seen of B. Bunny Bretterspitt was him circling around the far side of one of the round hedges. The witness later swore that, as B. Bunny walked around it, he seemed to get shorter and shorter and shorter until he was completely lost from view. Until there was nothing to come out the other side.

Chapter 2

HOME: THE RIGHT WAY TO GO

The man navigated the short round hedges with the assurance of a man who understood pinball, the science of shiny balls. Doc Armstrong tended to move like a fluid through Earth's doors and empty spaces. It had always come easy to him, this moving. Sometimes he imagined that all of the air was a vast ocean for him to swim through, like a carp or a fish. The analogy only stopped at their intelligence. Doc had more. So much more.

The house stood quietly, as though it couldn't talk, as though untouched by civilization or time, except for the other houses and yards that made up the quaint suburb around it. It was his house. Doc's house. He entered.

"My, someone has certainly embellished the food table," he chirped spryly to the pretty strawberry blonde who turned to him, fully aproned.

"Leave it to you to make lunch sound special and complicated, Mr. Word-User," chuckled Betty, his wife.

It was true. When it came to talking, sometimes Doc

Armstrong was like the Mayor of Wordtown, a quality Betty found as endearing as it was annoying. She didn't let her annoyance show, however, as it was petty and minor and really only pointed out how much she still had to learn about speaking. Maybe it was herself she was annoyed with. A thought for another time perhaps, when there was less lunch happening.

But Dr. Paul Armstrong, scientist, adventurer, doer, seemed distracted today. "What? Oh, sorry, honey, I was thinking about round hedges."

"I wish your thinking about them would sometimes lead to your trimming them more when they need it."

Doc took her in his arms. "Heh. You know perfectly well I forget to trim things."

"Let's just be glad I don't, or think where we'd be."

"I don't want to, believe me." He turned and moved towards the window, eyes lasering the perfect balls of waist-high bush populating the backyard beyond.

Betty noticed him staring out. "Why are you thinking about hedges now, Paul? You've never thought of them before, as far as I know."

"Well, we never do really know, do we. We can never truly be sure if a loved one is thinking of hedges. No matter how close, no matter how well we think we know someone."

Betty pondered this, but not for long as she continued about her kitchen duties. In this case it was preparing some lunch, which Doc usually looked forward to as his wife only worked with the finest foods. Today, however, despite hurrying home from the science store to enjoy a healthy repast, the beloved man-of-science just seemed distracted. Distracted by common leaf bushes.

"I don't know, Betty. Just... something today about their round perfection... so perfectly round and full... like a maze for mice who don't even know they're mice..."

Something in his voice made Betty look at him, even more than usual. Some foreign note. Not French or Armenian, just something different in his tone. She hadn't seen him so distracted before, so mesmerized, at least by landscaping. In fact, nothing short of atmosphereum had so captivated the respected rockhound; a sensation Betty herself knew all too well. Just the memory of it, and the terror of a certain living skeleton, brought fresh shivers to the well-trained housewife. Well, she wouldn't try to figure it out now, she thought. There were plenty of other things to figure out, and Betty remembered her old saying when it came to mysteries: pick your baffles.

"Well, that lunch isn't about to eat itself, Dr. Paul Armstrong," she chided gently, as though to shake her own head of lingering ghosts.

Like an impatient bullfighter, Doc suddenly pulled away from the lure of the window. As though second nature, he slid a chair out from the kitchen table, allowing just the right amount of clearance for him to sit in it and still reach the things he needed food-wise. Wasn't the first time. Wouldn't be the last.

As she placed a plate of "sandwich in sandwich-bread" as she liked to call it (a Paul favorite), Betty brought up the odd man she'd seen lurking about the neighborhood lately. She had mentioned him earlier, but Doc had yet to see the mysterious stranger, whom she described as having a "macaroon-shaped head," which of course could describe most people, as Paul so cogently mused. Her first use of that vivid description had launched him into a week of research, resulting in a scientist with a far better understanding of cookies, and round edibles in general. For that alone he was grateful.

Doc made a mental note to inquire of the neighbors, see if they'd also seen this strange fellow with the round head. Mental notes had become a given with him, though he was pretty sure it wasn't something he'd invented. "Not this time," he mentally chuckled. Paul had barely finished chuckling mentally when Betty sprung another doozy on the topnotch test tube toter.

"I almost forgot. City Brad came by."

"City Brad who was once Jungle Brad, brother to the late Ranger Brad, now a police detective, but still brother to the late Ranger Brad?"

"That's the one," confirmed Betty as she started washing the dishes with her trademark aggressiveness. "He was sorry he missed you, but I told him it was nothing personal."

"Absolutely not, and thank you for that. I never know what or when people might come by when I'm out. My being out doing something is never a reflection on them. It simply has more to do with not knowing everything in the world at the same time. But I don't want to get off on a science track. What did City Brad want, Betty, did he say?"

Betty answered without missing a beat of her task at hand. "No, but he did say he had something he wanted to show you. Oh well."

"Well, I'm sure if it's important he'll stop by later."

"Paul Armstrong, that's exactly what he said he would do. I mean, those were his words *to a T.* A large and very clear letter T. Sometimes you spook me to a haunted brain, and I even know it's just you. My husband."

Doc simply smiled and took another bite of his breaded sandwich. There was no witchcraft here, no black magic on his part. Just a simple deduction, what he liked to call an "educator's guess." But, no reason to give away all his trade secrets. If Betty wanted to think he had some mystical guessing powers, where was the harm? Besides, he had started giving Betty science lessons, and the ability to guess things intelligently was bound to come out at some point. Until then, he would just sit back and enjoy it, like a lizard basking in some good news.

And on that resolution, Doc brought his now empty plate, freed once again from the excruciating weight of its bread-bound burden, to the sink where it would join its imitation china compatriots in the furious struggle between soap and Betty's hands (and had Doc been a betting man, there was little doubt which his money was on). As he did so, his eyes, almost small keen animals in their own right, once again went to the kitchen window and, unhindered by something as feebly transparent as glass, to the green yard that lay beyond.

And then it hit him. Like a man at a clearance sale,

Doc froze there, unable to do anything else, eyes riveted on the pristinely manicured globes of leaves.

He was almost certain those hedges had been square just yesterday.

Chapter 3

A BEAUTIFUL DAY IN THE NEIGHBORHOOD

Doc cursed himself. At least mentally. He almost never cursed himself out loud, but he didn't mind keeping it mental. Oh, not objectionable stevedore or waitress language, mind you. More of the milder scientist type swearing, involving quarks and photons and isosceles things.

He was not happy.

Sure, one might argue, Doc Armstrong's head was filled with enough stuff. It was already pretty crowded in there. The science he knew alone could fill two large barrels, yet there it all was, crammed in Doc's human head, and he seemed pretty fine about it, just walking around like a person. And yet...

He still expected himself to know about so many other things, things he didn't even take in school, like making candles, or hiding. Doc's very upbringing reflected this: this dedicated striving for perfection, bordering on obsession, even as a child. He began tying his shoelaces too tight at an early age to force more blood up into his brain. He trained himself to never step on the cracks in the sidewalk: a sure sign of weakness, and possibly dangerous. Young Doc was opening and closing an umbrella while most kids were still trying to reach their suspended crib mobile. By age ten, Doc could count to seven thousand four hundred and sixty-two. He read the works of Blitt and Throwber, and could recite all of Tonninner's Seven Rules of Casement. While other kids began throwing things, Doc was happy to start looking up at stuff that was high up.

After graduating fourth in his class at the Institute For Scientific Science Studies, he began sweeping at observatories just to pick up the random meteor dust. He was integral in Dr. Peefisch's Half-Drawn Camel Studies and assisted Bort in the Rumination of Song Field Biting Resonances. While still at Caskell he helped Schieperbetternopper develop the Oval Ox Separator, even while helping Doskler prove his famous "Mallowbit" Theorem. Striking out on his own he made a splash by creating a calculator as big as a stadium.

One would have thought that earning his doctorate in meteography would have specialized him. But Doc was not content with that. He started reaching out into other sciences, something he still continued to do. His book on multiple personalities, *The Crowded Necktie,* became a best seller, and his studies of alcoholism in frogs were legendary.

So it was no wonder that Doc Armstrong had high expectations of himself, even though he was himself. And being constantly aware of everything around him was but one expectation, no matter how distracted he was by his science work, like the proverbial "accent-minded professor." And let's face it, thought Doc; gardening and landscaping were two things he could not afford to ignore. Not them.

Since they virtually surround us.

But ignore them he had, thought Doc, and woefully so, like the girl at the party that stays on the wall. The smartest stone-scoper in the world and he didn't know a topiary from a top hat. When it came to Doc, no one was harder on Doc than Doc. Sometimes Doc wished Doc would let up on Doc. But he couldn't afford to. Not and still be Doc.

So it was no surprise as he moved through the backyards adjoining his that he gazed about with rejuvenated interest, like a newborn who just realized it doesn't know stuff.

How could so many previously squared-off hedges, mostly rectangular, some acting as fences, have been trimmed to such perfect roundness, practically overnight? Could there be a paper here? Doc loved it when there was a paper, loved doing papers, and it was a while since his last one: Acrobatics in the Animal Kingdom Involving Cantaloupes, inspired by his recent South American adventure.

Was it possible that Dr. Paul Armstrong had stumbled on evidence of a kind of... superlandscaper previously unknown to science?

He had barely started this afternoon stroll and was already seeing signs that the phenomenon was prevalent. Every yard he cut through so far showed clear and distinct clues indicating recently rounded hedges, and no evidence was more compelling than the round hedges themselves. Thus was step one of an Officially Documented Doc Armstrong Scientific Study (or ODDASS) confirmed: seeing something. Now for step two: confirmation. In other words, he would ask the neighbors. For only with corroborating testimony, gathered under the strictest of laboratory conditions, could Doc move on to step three: telling everybody about it.

His first inquiry would be elderly Mrs. Toaspy. It made sense for several reasons, plus he was already in her yard. He noticed she seemed to have about an even number of rectangular and round bushes. Doc had stooped down and was closely examining a particularly circular hedge when a querulous voice interrupted.

"Did you lose something, Dr. Armstrong?"

Doc rose to see Mrs. Toaspy herself standing on her front porch with an eggbeater in her hand.

"Mrs. Toaspy, you surprised me."

"Oh, it was nothing," she replied confusingly.

"I was just about to come and ask you some questions, but you saved me a knock on the door," grinned the scientist.

"Well, you can always use it later," offered the older neighbor. "I'm guessing it's about that science you love so much."

"You know, I invented that eggkiller you're holding," smirked Paul, unable to resist.

Mrs. Toaspy stared at her eggbeater like she'd never seen it before.

Inside, she offered Doc a cup of garlic tea and a plate of crispy crones. He passed on the latter. The tea, however, was welcome, as it would keep his mindwheel churning, ever churning.

As indicative of his kind, Doc wasted no time in launching right in, asking Mrs. Toaspy if she'd always had so many round hedges, to which she replied that she didn't know she had any hedges. Showing her the yard seemed to refresh her memory and she indicated that, in fact, a new landscaping company had been around, going door-to-door, trying to drum up business. She recalled turning him down, however, as she preferred to putter about herself, cutting anything even vaguely green with massive shears, which seemed to relax her.

Suddenly, a disconcerting thought hit her. "Dr. Armstrong, you don't think this new landscaping company came around in the middle of the night and trimmed my hedges without my knowing it so that I could get out of having to pay them do you? That would be insidious. Could anyone be that vile?"

The thought seemed to both infuriate and disturb her, though Doc had to admit he was having trouble grasping the woman's logic.

"Mrs. Toaspy, do you recall the name of that company? Did he leave a card?"

"Oh. Think he may have. Let me check my card drawer." And with that Mrs. Toaspy opened up a drawer that must have been filled with hundreds and hundreds of business cards. "Now, let's see... Maybo-Bell Knocker Cleaners, Hampstam Refrigerator Rehearsals, Oakerdyne Music Listeners, Billet Boys Brand Bungalow Bookends, Wakefellow Knipe Dog Songs, Crinton Boare Baby Lozenges, Eldu Electric Bracelets—"

"Mrs. Toaspy, that's okay. If you happen to come across it could you please give me a jingle?"

"On the phone?"

"Preferably."

Doc was about to leave when he had a thought. Thoughts sometimes came to Doc Armstrong like tiny presents to a hamster. "Say, Mrs. Toaspy, one last thing. That salesman for the landscaping company—did he happen to by any chance have a head like a macaroon, or any other kind of delicious cookie?"

The elderly neighbor thought for about two minutes with barely a sign of life. Before Doc could intervene and ask if she needed help, she turned to him thoughtfully.

"You know... funniest thing. Now that you mention it. After he left I had a strong hankering for a snack. And I did, as I recall. I went and had a delicious snack. Right after he left." Then she shook her head. Hard. "But I'm afraid he didn't look anything like a cookie. In fact, it was one of the things that disappointed me about him."

Doc was no stranger to the power of suggestion, having almost jumped off a water tower himself once. He knew his question had been a leading one, and that the most likely reason she had wanted a snack just then was hunger. The science man left there with no harder evidence than when he had arrived, with no hard evidence.

Moving to the yards adjoining the other side of his house, Doc found himself at Algo Reeter's place. He had skipped his next door neighbors, the Armstrongs' close friends Kro-Bar and Lattis, aliens from the planet Marva who were now settled on Earth as human Earth couple Hildon and Clackie Pottadew, since he knew they were not home. He would be seeing them soon anyway, so he knocked on the Reeters' door. He was not even bothering to examine the hedges any more, having already come to the conclusion, through scientific observation, that the round ones clearly dominated the neighborhood.

Just then, before anyone could come to the door, Doc's scientist senses began to tingle just a little bit, indicated by Doc's almost subliminal catlike whine, pitched just above the senses of most humans. Someone was approaching.

Ducking down, fittingly enough, behind some hedges, Doc waited with a stillness learned from his many hours living among the Patahoyo Tribes of East Boolinia where he wore fruit on his head for a year. The crackle of twigs and leaves grew steadily louder as someone approached, and one particularly loud branch snap caused something within the hedge beside Doc to suddenly go tearing off. But before the scientist could figure out what it was...

"What are you doing to my hedge, Doc Armstrong?"

Doc looked up to see Algo Reeter staring down at him with a pair of large and quite formidable clippers aimed right at Doc's neck.

"Oh, hello, Algo. I didn't know it was you," said Doc.

"Are you the one who's been rounding off my squares? Somebody's been rounding off my squares," the large sartorial engineer grunted towards his hedges. He preferred that title to tailor, as it felt more rugged and outdoorsy, even though he worked indoors and was a tailor.

"No, Algo. No, I'm not. In fact, that's the very thing I've been investigating. On my own time."

"Are you going to stand up?"

Doc stood up.

Algo, his defenses lowered at the sight of a friendly face, not to mention a scientist he respected, related to Doc Armstrong his visit from a door-to-door salesman trying to get him to hire some new landscaping company. It confirmed Mrs. Toaspy's story, as well as Doc's suspicions, though any possible motive still escaped him at this point; the rock-hunting brain wizard needed more to go on.

"Tell me, Algo, did this salesman by any chance have a head like a macaroon?"

Algo thought about it for only a moment, though, as Doc observed, it was a moment pregnant with fondness for a good dessert. "Not that I recall. He was just kind of average really. Funny you should mention it though, because, come to think of it, there was another fellow I've seen lurking around here lately, had a large head that reminded me of an almond-flavored cookie."

That description was close enough for Doc. It sounded like the macaroon-headed stranger and the man from the landscaping company were two different people. He watched as Algo, huge shears in hand, went about trying to square off the now-rounded bushes. Doc's heart went out to his neighbor. It seemed an almost futile yet valiant effort on the part of the burly apparel-bender.

"That someone would do such a thing and not charge for it indicates either a sick and twisted mind... or someone with a motive we have yet to fathom." Doc's calm resonant voice was like a motor, a confidence engine that set people at ease and let them know they were not alone, and it was also entertaining.

Algo grunted. "Maybe someone just likes roundness. A whole lot," he ventured, unwisely wiping his sweaty brow with his hedge clippers.

Doc shot him a look that might have felled a lesser tailor. But this one had some beef on him and was able to withstand the sudden neck-whipping ocular assault inflicted by the noted labhound.

"Out of the mouths of babes," thought Doc, but only to himself.

Doc Armstrong still did not have the name of the landscapers, the new company that looked like the likely suspect in the phantom hedge trimming. Doc thought about using that as the file name for the case, "The Adventure of the Phantom Hedge Trimmers," though he still wasn't sure there was a case, and it was hardly an adventure at this point. More a kind of wandering-around-talking-about-hedges. He would probably come up with a more apt name when he knew more.

Unfortunately, Algo had not accepted a business card from the salesman, given his aversion to things that are handed, and so Doc was no less closer to having the company's name than when he started trying to find out the company's name.

At the last two houses he found people not home, which of course meant that he actually hadn't found them at all. He found a lack of them. And lacks of neighbors would certainly not help his investigation, which he realized was still in its infancy, though the idea of changing and burping an investigation amused Doc to no end.

One of the families not home was, in fact, the Bretterspitts who, he surmised, must be out on a family outing, which they normally did out of doors. That B. Bunny loved his outings. This did not help Doc who, for a scientist, was striking out like a ballplayer.

So when the weary investigator arrived at the Perrilsons, it was with little hope of obtaining a business card or a company name.

He found a lot more than that.

Chapter 4

WHEN IS A CHAIR DELIGHTFUL?

The Marvan sat stock still in the comfortable overstuffed chair. So studied in his pure stillness was he that, back on his home planet Marva, he might have been mistaken for an exhibit of Earth life in one of the "Life on Other Worlds That Aren't Marva" museums.

The truth was, the alien formerly known as Kro-Bar *could* pose for such a display, for such was the typical Marvan efficiency of his incredibly fast adaptation to the strange and curious ways of the third planet from Sol. For Kro-Bar was now officially Hildon Pottadew, Earthman. And his wife Lattis, former woman-of-the-stars, was now Clackie Pottadew, a typical Earth housewife with all those telltale housewifely ways.

Perhaps not so typical. Fit in as they might, unsuspected as they were, they still had some things to learn: the quirks and foibles, oddities and follies, of these people so much less advanced than the technologically superior Marvan race. Take his current preoccupation, for instance.

Kro-Bar, while appearing to be in something of a trance in the overstuffed Earth chair, was in fact testing out something he had heard recently, from the very lips of one of the humans he was studying.

Their best friends were the Armstrongs, who lived right next door. In fact, they had already shared several adventures together, forming a strong interplanetary bond of friendship. This friendship, as Earth people called it, resulted in regular and numerous visits between the two houses, often for the purpose of enjoying a meal together—a practice that resulted in the visits to the Pottadew household dwindling exponentially, possibly due to Lattis's unfamiliarity with the mysteries of ovens and cooking. At least, that was Kro-Bar's theory, judging from some of the faces Betty made, decidedly unpleasant in nature, unseen by Lattis, but spied by him, despite the Earth woman's attempts to conceal them.

It was this very Betty who had made the remark that led to Kro-Bar's present study. She had said, quite simply and quite unabashed, "My what a delightful chair."

The words did not seem to affect Lattis, but they reverberated in the pragmatic Kro-Bar's head for days afterward. Of the two, he tended to be the one to hold onto things and agonize over them—particularly things he did not understand. Though Lattis did this too, it was not nearly to the extent that he did. Which was extreme.

Since landing on Earth, the three most terrifying words Kro-Bar had heard were "the chair recognizes." So he already had his guard up when it came to chairs. This one was supposed to be delightful and that did not sit well with him.

Finally, born of sheer frustration, sheer stubbornness and sheer ego, Kro-Bar decided to set aside some time on his day off from the Earth office to find out exactly what was so delightful about that chair. He had settled into it shortly after breakfast when Lattis went off to go shopping, and he was still in it hours later, that afternoon.

So far it had not delighted him.

The really aggravating part was that Betty hadn't even sat in the stupid thing that evening. Never did. She had merely looked at it, felt its arm, smiled and dropped her devastating remark, willy-nilly, without thinking of the consequences, without a care for anyone else, apparently. As fond as he was of his best friends, he found they could be a little callous at times.

These long hours in the chair wearied him, and he almost dozed off at several points; a humiliating prospect for a Marvan in the middle of an experiment. Kro-Bar blamed the innate comfort of the overstuffed chair for allowing this drowsiness and relaxation to nearly overtake him. The cursed thing really was comfortable. Fortunately, his will, like his Marvan mind, was strong, and he was able to overcome the embarrassing sensation.

What was so delightful about this blamed furniture? Why? Why this piece? Why not their modular sofa with its endless brain-twisting puzzle of dizzying "sections," seemingly devised by an evil Earth mastermind. And those inexplicable "hassocks"—surely they were the work of Earth's cavemen, back in some distant primordial time when furniture confusion ruled the land.

He began hoping against hope that Lattis would come home so that he could at least talk to someone, complain about this chair and its carefully veiled delight, commiserate about Earth inferiority and its preoccupation with pleasure and comfort.

Feeling a perturbed aggravation that bordered on panic, Kro-Bar gathered himself and strove to revive the masterful analyst who had first undertaken this problem. He would employ reason. What did the chair do? What did it actually do? Nothing. It just sat there. It sat there, and he sat there. Everybody involved was sitting. Where was the delight in sitting? Where was the delight in anything having to do with this stupid chair? It was, as Kro-Bar now surmised, not a delightful chair at all. It was a stupid chair. It was a stupid chair that he had been tricked into sitting in for an entire day by a callous Earth woman who had no more regard for the Marvan sensibility, than Kro-Bar had for that of an ant or a duck. Let *her* come over and sit it. That was it. Next time the Armstrongs came over, likely for one of those card games Lattis never understood, he would force Betty to sit in the blasted thing, in the clever guise of sharing the delight! Yes, he would share the delight! That would show her—

Lattis walked in and Kro-Bar screamed.

Lattis stood there for a full minute, holding bags of Earth shopping that she had obviously traded for, using the Earth money Kro-Bar was given at the office. Deciding he was not injured—physically at least—she continued to a table where she put the bags down.

"That chair is delightful," remarked Lattis.

Kro-Bar stared at her in silence a moment. "It is a comfortable chair," he admitted.

"I can tell because you were in it when I left. Look, I bought twenty-four drain stoppers," said the Marvan woman, taking out twenty-four drain stoppers.

Kro-Bar made scoffing noises that sounded a bit forced. "Does my wife truly think I have been sitting in this single chair the entire time she has been out? Surely, a foolish notion from one so intelligent and Marvan as you. Why, in truth, I have been in hundreds of chairs since you left the house… One chair, indeed…"

"Yes, my husband," Lattis replied, with that familiar tone she often used while going through her new things.

Kro-Bar watched her emptying more goods, mostly members of the clothing family, and found he somehow could not stand the lack of attention. "Well, if you must know, my very nosy wife, I have spent a very fruitful day off, studying and pondering the Earth customs. You would do well to emulate my example."

"Does my husband josh me, as they say? I have been out shopping with millions of other Earth women. I'd say I have these customs down pretty blamed good, as yet another Earth person might say."

"Yes, I am sure you know so so many of the Earth customs, my woman. I am so sure you do."

His condescending tone now clearly rankled her. Lattis slowly put down the frilly nightgown she'd been holding up in front of her. "Does my Kro-Bar imply that there is a habit of the Earth race that I am not yet familiar with? I know you are dying to tell me."

Kro-Bar looked smug now, like the proverbial glennip that absorbed the eupox through its veddick. "Perhaps you *are* familiar with it, Lattis, I really do not know. I know you have been earnest in your Earth studies. I have been very proud of your progress."

"Come on. Let me have it, my husband. What custom am I unaware of?"

"Well, there are, of course, many such curious habits of the race whose home we call our own."

"Yes, yes—"

"I refer to one that I, in particular, witnessed recently that is, shall we say… not what you'd call one of the more common—"

"Yes, yes—"

"I refer, of course, to that curious Earth trait of walking around the far side of one of those peculiar round shrubberies until, upon growing shorter and shorter, the person simply… vanishes."

Lattis stared at Kro-Bar, purposely devoid of expression as she tried to read him. Unless he was fabricating it entirely, Kro-Bar had piqued her interest. He knew it, and took it as a sign to continue.

"Never, I might add, to come out the other side."

Lattis still stared. Had Kro-Bar looked any smugger he would have collapsed in on himself. He went on, insufferably. "Why, not only is such a thing commonplace here, but I saw our neighbor B. Bunny Bretterspitt do it just yesterday, across the street. With my own eyes."

He could tell now that she had absolutely no idea what he was talking about. This pleased him to no end. For several seconds he said nothing, choosing to enjoy the feeling of superiority. Rather, it was Lattis who broke the silence.

"Oh. Hedge melting."

Kro-Bar shot her a look. Despite her dry understatement, he didn't believe her. Still…

"You invented that. You don't know the name."

"Don't I?" Lattis released a little mirthless chuckle. "Betty—you know, Betty Armstrong? Why, she showed me that the very first month we were here. I only regret that I forgot to share it with you, in our new 'Earth sharing' kind of way. I do hope that you can forgive my oversight."

There was a long pause as they held each other's look, like gunfighters in an interplanetary game of chicken. It was Kro-Bar who broke the spell. "Oh, *hedge melting*. I thought you said *inch milking*, which of course refers to the dairy farming of certain tiny worms."

Lattis was about to call him on it when she stopped herself, suddenly afraid he might be right, despite the fact she'd made up the term. What if it *was* a real Earth thing? She couldn't take a chance. She'd never live it down. Instead, she chuckled amiably. "Right. I see our mix-up now."

"What Earth people call a *merry mix-up*," said Kro-Bar jovially.

They both laughed, as they had learned to do, in that carefree foolish way effected by Earth people.

"Yes," chuckled Lattis. "And all because neither of us knew the other already knew about hedge melting!"

"Have you ever heard of anything so absurd, my wife?"

Their laughter was building. "It's like a television program," snorted Lattis. "We are like a television program!"

They were having a good time now. At least to some extent. Some of it was clearly forced.

"Maybe we *should* have a show," blurted Kro-Bar. "We could bring them some delight, that is for certain."

"And all we need to do," continued Lattis, "is take one tiny misunderstanding and perpetuate it, ad infinitum, for humorous purposes."

They continued laughing for another hour.

Chapter 5

NOT EVERYTHING THAT GOBBLES IS TURKEY

The Perrilson house was the last one on Doc's street, sitting right at the end of the corner, which was why it was last. Paul and Betty didn't know the Perrilsons really well, as they were five houses away and it was too far to yell, but their few encounters had found them to be both pleasant and amiable. And as Betty often said, "More people should be pleasant and amiable. Pleasant and amiable is not a bad thing to be. If more people were pleasant and amiable, maybe the world would be a better place." Except for the overuse of the term "pleasant and amiable," her husband found that a pretty solid rule.

As Doc neared the Perrilson yard, he began to once again note the abundance of round hedges, though there were still some rectangular ones. He also noticed something else.

As he got closer, he began to see a vehicle parked on the side street, hidden by the house. It appeared to be a panel truck, plain, typical. As he got closer he could make out lettering on the side, the word *Landscaping*. Realizing he'd need to get closer to read the name of the company, the action-scientist ducked down and started to move furtively through the yard. Doc was able to go furtive at a moment's notice and often practiced when they threw dinner parties, suddenly ducking low and squat-walking or slithering along the floor until a guest spotted him. The indispensability of this exercise more than compensated for the embarrassed explanations.

Doc moved from hedge to hedge, nearing the corner of the yard. As he did, a sound came to his attention. A snipping sound, but somewhat loud, like giant barbers going to work on the gods of Mount Olympus, who certainly must have needed a shave or trim now and then.

Hedge clippers. Big professional ones too, if their rhythm and resonance was any indication. Someone knew what they were doing.

Doc approached the corner of the house like an attention-hungry seal after a beach ball. His keenly attuned ears, or "shelled listening holes," as he liked to call them, determined that there were exactly two landscapers at work on the other side of the house. But he needed to get closer, not just to see exactly who they were and what they were doing, but to get the name on that van.

He decided he would use the round hedges to his own advantage. Crouching down low, he would move through them with the ease of a puppeteer's hand slipping into a puppet. The spaces between them were pretty tight, barely allowing room for his passage, but he was well hidden.

As he squirreled through, the ominous and repetitive snipping grew louder. He was around the corner now, closer to the landscapers, managing to stay hidden below the tops of the waist-high globes of green that were turning into such a mystery.

Suddenly, Doc realized he no longer heard two clippers, only one. When had the other clipper ceased? Doc cursed himself for not being more alert. Then he cursed himself for cursing himself again, which was becoming a bad habit. He needed to stop moving and chance a peek.

With the cautious trepidation of a novice stage mom, he slowly lifted his head above the top of his leafy cover.

There was a landscaper, in white coveralls, snipping away with grim determination. He was turned just enough so Doc could see part of a rough-looking face, like a rocky cliff, with natural steps, and a nose broken so many times it could talk. These were no ordinary gardeners, if this one was any indication. But where was the other? On break? Fired for cutting an incorrect leaf? The absence of the second snipper made Doc uncomfortable and he carefully ducked back down.

As he did, the sound of one shear snipping stopped. Doc froze. With the chutzpah of a three-legged chair manufacturer, Doc slowly ventured his head up for one more peek, though his head wasn't too sure about it. The sight made his pupils freeze. The smash-nosed cliff-faced man was nowhere to be seen.

The silence due to the sudden lack of clipper snips was disconcerting and put the lab coat warrior on his guard. Though often on the threshold of science danger, Doc frowned on firearms, literally making angry faces at them. He felt it was wrong to take human life, be it person, animal or mineral.

Instead, he sometimes carried a weapon of his own devising. Looking like some kind of kids' outer space blast ray gun blaster, his *science gun* shot a specially devised ball of super-compressed gas, developed by Doc, which had the effect of creating an instant feeling of euphoria in the would-be attacker. Thus the name U4Eon. It had worked flawlessly, coming to his aid many a time, though he had to remind himself to keep it away from Betty.

He had not thought to bring it with him this time, however, having set out to merely inspect some curious neighborhood bush pruning. Now he wished he had.

Doc had no more time to contemplate wishing he had done things, however. He turned instinctively, coming face to face with a large pair of garden shears that was headed right for him. This must have been landscaper number two. The fellow behind the shears was a human weasel, completely chinless, unless you counted his Adam's apple. His tiny rounded teeth were set in a ferret-like grin, though ferret grins had yet to be been proven.

Doc ducked just as the big blades scissored the air where his neck had been, cutting the helpless air in two. The scientist felt the breeze from the blades as he quickly undulated through the close-set hedges like a mink threading a grizzly bear party. Ahead of him, sudden rustling brought him up short, and he peeked around the bush to see Smash Nose Cliff Face crawling towards him, hedge clippers first. Another sound made him turn to see Weasel No Chin, quickly crawling at him from the other direction, shears out. The effect of the two crawling, blades first, made Doc think that he was being stalked by two crabrats, crabrats bent on his destruction by crude but effective means that would make a medieval gardener beam.

He Who Studied Rocks darted the only way he could, busting through the hedge balls like a birthday present escaping a piñata. Once through, Doc scrambled on all fours through the maze of greenery. He could hear the crabrats snipping their way through, and could tell by discrete sound location that they had split up. One of them, probably Weasel, was countering to head him off.

If there was one thing that Doc Armstrong had never liked, it was cat and mouse games where he was the mouse. He preferred it where he was the dog.

That in mind, he abruptly doubled back on Smash Nose Cliff Face like bad acid reflux. The thuggish gardener was so surprised at the sudden amount of scientist in his face, that he didn't have time to pull back as Doc jammed a short thick stick into the closing scissors, right at their deadly fulcrum, effectively jamming them. So startled was Smash Nose, that he had no time to block the two quick jabs to the face, courtesy of Doc, leaving him no choice but to crumple to the ground in an unconscious heap.

But some further instinct kicked in for Doc, some inner voice developed by years of exposure to a radioactive element know as danger, that told him not to turn on the TV and kick back just yet. With the celerity of celery in a cyclone, Doc snatched up the jammed hedge clippers and whirled around, just in time to use them catch the giant chopping shears of Crabrat Weasel No Chin as he shut them on what he had hoped would be the middle of Doc's neck. The blades chopped hard with a sobering *claff* or *chiff* sound, and the two men, scientist and weasel, found themselves in a metallic gardening gridlock.

Before each opponent could weigh his options, before another breath was even forthcoming, a frantic rustling noise ripped through the rotund hedge beside them. Both froze at the sound, Doc from curiosity, Weasel from fear: cold, wide-eyed, death-is-your-uncle-so-how-is-your-pineapple-Minnie-has a-pot-on fear. The last time the scientist had seen that was in the eyes of a waiter taking Kro-Bar and Lattis's order at a French restaurant.

Before Dr. Paul Armstrong could figure out what was going on, Weasel, formerly Crabrat Weasel, but no longer wielding "claws," was up and flailing towards the parked panel truck like a pinwheeling fool. He was quickly followed by his Smash Nose partner, now finished with his unconsciousness, and hightailing after him.

Doc heard the doors of the panel truck slam and the engine start, and he could just see the top of the vehicle as it quickly pulled out.

But the scientist's focus was elsewhere. The rustling thing, much larger than a squirrel, and far stranger, was again moving through the brush. It seemed steady, calculated, its movement reminiscent of something furtive and cautious, like a tax accountant. Perhaps something more dangerous. That's what Weasel and Smash-Nose thought.

Doc's subliminal high-pitched whine rose on the air, threatening to wake every dog in the neighborhood. But a far more abrasive and chaotic sound cut that short. It was a gobble. Not like a turkey's gobble, but faster, higher-pitched. It came from within the hedges, and Doc tracked its movement with the rustling thing that now pushed through.

It seemed to be circling him.

A car door slammed, nearby. A police car, unmarked. And a policeman, equally unmarked.

Walking towards Doc was plainclothes detective City Brad, the Armstrongs' friend and ally. And the skittering in the bushes was gone.

Chapter 6

CITY BRAD'S TIMELY VISIT

Betty emerged from the kitchen carrying a large tray with a pot of coffee, a pot of tea, a plate of tiger cubs and hatty crumbles, a bowl of ripe dillquats, a plate of kitty wafers and a small dish of Bellteens. She set them down on the coffee table in the living room where Paul sat with their friend City Brad.

"Oh, thank you, Betty, but you shouldn't have gone to such trouble. It all looks so great, I don't know where to begin," quipped the Armstrongs' police guest.

"I usually go alphabetically," smirked Paul and they all laughed.

"Don't laugh, I've seen him do it. He *knows* that alphabet," assured Betty as she took a small bite of kitty wafer.

Doc had regaled them with the tale of his yard adventure, including his encounter with the gardening thugs and the mystery gobbler.

"I've heard some strange ones alright, being a policeman and all, but that one takes the cake, Doc," said the duly appointed officer of the law.

Betty misunderstood and held up the plate of tiger cubs for City Brad who looked at her a moment, but declined to take the cake, his own words to the contrary.

"Any idea what might be behind this hedge-oriented funny business?"

Doc shook his head. "I'm working on some leads, but only in my head where I keep moving things around, hoping to come up with some answers, but so far I don't really know anything, so I keep on doing it until I do. But you didn't come here twice today to hear me talk about the dangers of gardening," laughed the stay-at-home scientist as he remembered that City Brad hadn't come for that. "What brings you to Blendview during working hours, though you're always welcome here?"

City Brad took a sip of coffee and a popped a dillquat in his mouth. "You remember what I like to refer to as *The Fleming Case.*"

"Well, actually that could be one of two cases: what I like to refer to in my science journal as *The Adventure of the Lost Skeleton* and *The Adventure of the Lost Skeleton Returns.*" Each one, of course, was known for having a Fleming in it.

"Of course," smiled City Brad. "I should have clarified. I refer actually to the former case, the one in which my late brother, Ranger Brad, lost his life."

Doc grew somber. "Yes, we all recall how your brother gave his life doing the job he loved. He was a good man. And a good ranger of a man, as they say."

Betty looked wistful. "Horribly mutilated. No one should go that way."

Paul cleared his throat, hinting that Betty should drop the mutilated part, and City Brad put down his coffee as if to switch gears, though it really didn't do anything. "Because of our adventure in South America and, after that, the case you call *The Adventure of the Lost Skeleton Among Us,* I have only recently had a chance to go through my brother's effects.

"Oh, I didn't know he had effects. I'm so sorry," offered Betty as Doc stared at her.

City Brad chuckled, as though at a memory in his mind that made him chuckle. "He was always picking things up, finding this and that, in his job in the woods."

"For the Lost and Found, I imagine?" asked Doc.

"No, he kept everything." City Brad chuckled again. "I remember this one time he found some galoshes—one galosh actually."

"A single galosh?" asked Doc, intrigued.

"Yes, can you imagine?"

"Bet there was a story there," mused the scientist.

"There was. Someone had lost it."

"Interesting," said Doc, sipping some coffee.

As Betty bit into a Bellteen, City Brad continued. "Well, there I was, sorting through his things, like any person, when I came upon this."

Doc's eyes swooped like twin kestrels as the ancient parchment unfurled on the coffee table and he immediately wondered who had furled it in the first place? City Brad continued.

"At first I thought it was a gag—you know, some emotional materials for an advertising stunt, like a kids' treasure map for a new store opening or something."

"I don't think so, City Brad. Even at a glance my archaeologically-trained eyes tell me this is a bona fide member of the Ancient Family."

"Who would want to bona fie it?" inquired Betty, but Doc was already in scientist mode. He felt the parchment with the sensitivity of a trained laundress. His pencil-sharp mind reeled with possibilities. The ancient material was covered with strange writing in a strange language, as well as strange symbols and strange diagrams with strange markings and strange notations. Like a game show host with an abundance of contestants, Doc was intrigued. "I don't recognize the family as of yet, but I'm sure after we've been introduced and get better acquainted and on a first name basis, I'll have this parchment singing some sweet tunes."

The affable plainclothesman smiled. "I was hoping you would say that, Doc."

"How could you hope he'd say that, City Brad? I don't even know what family he's talking about," struggled the good-natured housewife.

Her husband gently clipped her jaw. "Why, the family of long lost curled up ancient writing surfaces, of course."

Doc winked at City Brad and they both chuckled. "I especially like how he talks about the parchment like it's a person," City Brad said to Betty. "That fills me with confidence."

"That's the part I didn't get," said Betty.

Their police friend then asked Doc what he was going to do about the gardening mystery, and if he wanted any official help. Doc declined, adding that he wasn't certain any laws were broken, and he'd rather wait until he had more to go on. He had deliberately not made much of the strange, queasy gobbling sound in the bushes, dismissing it as "just another runaway turkey." Like any thoughtful husband, he didn't want to alarm his better half.

"It's too bad you didn't get the name of that landscaping outfit," said City Brad as he was leaving.

"But I did," replied Doc inscrutably. "Just before the van drove away."

Chapter 7

COTTISILL LANDSCAPING AND LOAN

Betty was happy that Paul had taken her with him. They were only going to ask some questions at the landscaping company, but still, it would be the closest thing to an adventure for her since that last tussle with a certain dastardly maniacal skeleton, a master of booming sarcasm who shall remain nameless, namely, the Lost Skeleton.

In truth, she had wondered why her husband did not press charges, having those Smash Nose and Weasel thugs arrested for assault. But Paul (or Doc since they were officially on an adventure) thought it wise to first know more of the facts, like, for instance, if they really were employees of Cottisill Landscaping and Loan, or if they'd simply stolen a truck. He was careful that way. Doc often said, "It's better to rip the sleeves off a man's own shirts, than to falsely accuse others," and Betty always remembered that.

She was glad to see him out on a case again, what Doc liked to call a "quietus hiatus," meaning, a kind of break from non-adventuring. Not that she minded his indoor science work and rock-staring. But this really seemed to get his juke box flowing. He felt a keen excitement that kept him balanced and supercharged and, like a clown finally emerging from one of those tiny cars, Doc really thrived on that. Betty had decided long ago that, no matter what the danger, it was worth it to keep her husband on his game. Unless it killed him. That, she affirmed, would be the last straw.

Doc turned the car into a side street. The overcast day did not help the gloomy surroundings: the very heart of the warehouse district. Even on a weekday it was fairly empty, except at the end of the day when the warehouses let out. On a weekend it was downright desolate. But Doc was counting on a landscaping business being open on Saturday, traditionally a heavy gardening day. If it really *was* a landscaping business.

The Armstrong car took another turn and Doc pulled up in front of a dismal square two-story building, nestled between two larger ones. The windows looked cold and dark, hardly inviting to new customers. But the worn sign plainly read COTTISILL LANDSCAPING AND LOAN. The name hadn't sat well with Doc, right from the start. It sounded too odd, too hybrid. But then he recalled another company, Kaddell Mopping and Layout, remembering that folks were initially surprised at that unusual union of custodial and advertising services. When given half a chance, they proved quite successful. After the expected mishaps, of course.

"Maybe you should wait here, Betty," suggested a concerned Doc.

"Dr. Paul Armstrong. I haven't come this far only to come no farther than this."

Doc smiled at his spunky wife, admiring her spunk.

The glass door at the front of the building was fortunately unlocked, and Doc held it open for Betty, but then quickly clarified.

"I'm holding it open for you only on ceremony, Betty. I'm going in first. No arguments."

Betty smiled at her husband, ever the gentleman, yet ever more the protector, as if the two sides of him had waged war on Doc's shoulders, like in those cartoons, thought Betty, and his concern for her safety had won out, punching his gentleman side in the face. What *were* those cartoons?

The couple immediately found themselves in a darkened entryway with forbidding steps of concrete, like some ancient Asymian tomb, only if they did landscaping. Doors on either side looked dark so they started up the stairs. Their footsteps echoed in the uninviting building like somebody repeatedly dropping a sea lion. Holding the cold metal rail as she headed up, Betty wanted to shout out, just to break up that infernal echo with a good healthy scream and release her nervous energy, which also might be fun, particularly if Paul screamed with her. But she thought better of it.

On the second floor landing, more closed offices, then, down at the end, faded letters on the window of one door: COTTISILL LANDSCAPING AND LOAN.

Doc tried the door, but it was locked. He glanced at Betty and, in silent agreement, each knew that knocking was their only option. But, before he could work up the necessary fist required for that most popular of door greetings, the door suddenly whipped away, like a term paper in a typhoon.

Betty knew the man standing there was a stranger because she had immediately not seen him before, as soon as she saw him. He looked as heavy as he was wide, shoulders packed into his work shirt like pigs in a sidecar. He seemed to have more eyebrows than necessary, all fighting a losing battle with friendliness. But the man beamed at them with an overt amiability that belied his rouge exterior.

"Well, hello there! Why, I just opened the door to head out on my pastry break. Didn't know you were about to knock, or I would have let you knock, and happily. What can I do for you good folks about to knock?" The man beckoned them to chairs in front of his smooth and completely empty desk.

"Is this Cottisill Landscaping and Loan?" asked the couple's more scientific half.

"All day!" the man laughed. "Only until infinity. Because it's always named that." He chuckled a lot more at that. "Was there anything I can help you with that will benefit you both without necessarily benefitting me?" he asked with a decided dearth of salesmanship.

"We're after some good old American landscaping," Doc exclaimed breezily, easily matching the man's frothy good cheer.

"Well, you've certainly come to the right place. Hope you remembered to bring your yard with you—you'd be surprised how many folks forget *that* little detail."

"But, mister, sir," exclaimed Betty, aghast, "our yard must weigh hundreds and hundreds of pounds and, last time I looked, it's probably bigger than the trunk of our car."

Doc and the man both laughed.

"Honey, I think Mr.…. this fellow, is having your leg on a bit with you."

"That's right, ma'am, just a little landscaping business joke-favorite. We have certain zingers that we like to rely on and constantly use on our new clients again and again. It breaks the tension, and many other things."

"Oh, is there tension?" wondered the housewife.

"Well, landscaping can be a very personal thing," uttered the pleasant fellow soberly, "I saw a man date his own yard once. Course, he was very lonely."

"Yes, I'm sure very few customers are able to bring their lawn *in* with them," chuckled Doc knowingly, quickly grasping the tenor of the green-and-groundskeeping game. Doc's adaptive powers were nothing short of miraculous. He had once lived with a family of dung beetles for more than a year, with nothing more than a trash can lid. "So, unless you happen to have a giant six-thousand ton Rechtall earth-mover handy…" simpered the scientist obnoxiously, "which I can't imagine too many people do."

"Not too many, I'd imagine," chortled the man who still hadn't given them his name.

"Well," said Betty, getting into the swing of it, "I guess you *do* make house calls," She tittered a bit, but it trailed off when the men just stared.

"Of course we do. We were joking, of course. We come right out to your yard," stated the now serious man. "Bringing a yard here would be unwieldy."

"Oh sure, she knows that," assured Doc.

"So you folks like some of your land scaped?"

"First of all, I guess we should all meet. I'm Dr. Paul Armstrong and this is my wife. May we assume you're Mr. Cottisill?"

The man grinned, revealing gaps in his lack of teeth. "Well, you know what happens when you assume. You make an assu of m and e. Actually, there is no Mr. Cottisill. That was simply a made-up name to get us twenty-third in the yellow pages. I'm Mr. Copperscent, the manager of the company."

"Oh, okay. Could I ask a question?"

"If I can answer it," Mr. Copperscent said amiably.

"How will I know that, until I ask it?" chuckled Doc logically.

"Well, I have to admit you have a point there." Mr. Copperscent laughed at Doc's inescapable logic. "Thank you for keeping me 'honest.' Now, tell me your question, and please do ask it, I pray you."

"Well, I think your landscapers might already be working our neighborhood. Blendview? The Blendview area? I really like some of the work that's being done and, well, we'd like some of the same."

Betty wanted to blurt out about Doc's displeasure and befuddlement over the countless round hedges, but thought better of correcting him in front of Mr. Copperscent in case he were playing a "game" with the man.

"Hmmm, let me take a look," said Copperscent, removing a book from his desk drawer. "Right here I keep a record of the neighborhoods we're currently working." He perused the book with the studied focus of a soda jerk making his first extra double banana flame. "Neighborhoods, here we go... Armbend, Arspanna, Axminker, Baitypool, Billodeon, Blantwerp, Brastpott, Bremperville... No, sorry. Doesn't appear that Blendview is on our route just now. Happy to change that. Would you like to give our service a try?"

"Perhaps we could take a brochure with us, look it over?" suggested the preeminent scientist.

"Of course. You folks had your heart set on whoever's working in your area, and I know what it's like to have heartset, a serious heartset. Say, if you admire their work, try and get the name off one of their trucks."

"That's a stout idea, thank you, Mr. Cockerspin—"

"Copperskin. Copperscent, sorry. Now you've got *me* uncertain, and I *own* that name," chuckled the good-natured but uncertain Copperscent.

The Armstrongs stood up to go, and Copperscent joined them in the air above the desk. He extended a hand which Doc shook like a paddle.

"Thank you folks for stopping by. I always say, I'd rather have new folks *stopping* by, than *going* by," laughed the man who just said that.

"Our pleasure. We'll let you know what we decide about everything having to do with plants," said Doc. "Oh, one last question. I couldn't help wondering why your company is called Cottisill Landscaping and *Loan?* Isn't that a bit unusual? Mixing groundskeeping and financing?"

There was a flash of something different on Copperscent's face, something that bristled across it like a blurring centipede of mistrust. It was the first evidence of the man possibly having something to hide, that centipede was. But it was quickly replaced by the apple pie they had become accustomed to these past five minutes, like running into an old friend at an accident.

"Oh, it did say *loam,* when we first put the sign up," said Copperscent with a sheepish grin, referring to the fertile mixture of sand, silt and clay common to gardening, "but, unfortunately, at some point one of the n's fell off, so we decided to print all our literature that way. Does make for interesting conversation though!"

And, on that curious note, the Armstrongs left.

In the car, Betty saw that Doc was troubled. Doc saw that Betty saw that he was troubled, and he decided to say something about it, him being troubled. And her seeing it.

At a stop light, after stopping, he turned to her gravely.

"Loam isn't spelled with two n's," Doc uttered to the fascinated homemaker, "it ends in an *m*."

Chapter 8

SOME OF OUR NEIGHBORS ARE MISSING

Doc and Betty had barely gotten back to the house when the knock came to the door. In fact there was barely time for Betty to head to the kitchen to whip up an elaborate afternoon snack, featuring such standbys as a dish of Poltroons, a bowl of capochin sticks and a plate of Betty's baked lassovers left over from the night before.

Doc immediately went to the door with his customary answering-the-door aplomb, which consisted of him walking casually to the door and opening it. He was surprised to see one of his neighbors there, Anky Trayster—surprised, because he and Betty hadn't spoken two words to the lady. Though they *had* exchanged a couple thousand (she was very chatty).

Doc invited her in, like a boxer or a lawyer inviting a person into his house on his day off. Anky sat, and Doc offered her some of the snacks Betty had already laid out, though the woman seemed far too agitated for something as edgy as Poltroons. Doc asked her what was wrong in that soothing way he had, not unlike a parrot dealer with a first-time parrot.

The troubled Anky launched right in, as though it would help to talk about a thing, which meant that she apparently needed help every day.

"I don't know what's going on. I really don't."

"Well, I don't either, so maybe you should start at the beginning where most things start," soothed the thoughtful lab jockey.

"You're right. Sorry. How can you know anything I'm saying if I don't first explain?" And with that cryptic croissant of curiosity the Blendview gadfly jumped into a cyclonic pit of missing persons and strange occurrences, all plaguing the little neighborhood they knew and loved so well.

"Wait, Anky, please, please, one thing at a time before you pile on everything in the world. Who's gone missing?"

"Mr. Joper, for one."

"I thought he died last last year." puzzled Doc.

"That was a mistake, remember? They dug him up in time?"

Doc remembered the unfortunate *Case of the Really Sound Sleeper,* as City Brad had so accurately dubbed it. "Well, he lives alone, so that's a little harder to confirm. Who else?"

"Havey Corters. She hasn't been seen since three days ago."

"What does her husband say?"

"He hadn't noticed."

Doc instantly recalled Herber Corters' obsession with corduroy—by far the easiest material to find oneself "lost in." He could hardly blame the man. Doc himself once dissected a bowtie because he swore he saw it move. Turned out to be a "gag of the light," as he liked to call it, and a rather expensive one.

"Anyone else?" queried the scientist.

"Worst of all," choked the notorious busybody, saving the worst of all for last, as people sometimes do, though not necessarily so much out of cruelty as a need to enjoy the dramatic, even in the worst of tragedies. "The Bretterspitts."

"Which one of them?" asked Doc, recalling B. Bunny, or 'Hare,' and his wife and kids and pets.

"All of them," gasped Anky in a voice so barely audible you almost couldn't hear it.

Though this seemed a good point to go somewhere else, it was still the Armstrong living room and Anky Trayster was still there, though, admittedly, the moment seemed frozen in time as the man of science took in this new information, like an archer whose target just moved two hundred feet. Truth is, you could have knocked Doc over with a bulldozer when she told him about the Bretterspitts.

Fortunately, Betty chose that moment to pop in, waving a plate of Pitos like a snack magician. "Oh hello, Anky, I thought I heard voices out here that weren't all Paul."

The excitable gadabout quickly updated the unflappable cookabout. Betty took it with her usual aplomb, and a couple of Pitos dipped in mitre sauce.

Doc's immediate reaction, besides the characteristic high-pitched whine just audible enough for neighbors to look around nervously, was to think about giving the Bretterspitt home the once-over, maybe even twice-over, looking for clues as to their disappearance. He grimly recalled when he went hedge-hunting earlier and found no one home. Now they *really* weren't home. He wondered how long they had been missing and whether they had had time to bring anything with them, like snacks? Or were they dealing with less considerate forces?

"Anky, are you certain the Bretterspitts haven't gone away on vacation?" inquired the thorough scientist-sleuth.

"I thought about that. In fact it was the second thing I thought of, after swallowed-by-hippo," elucidated the self-appointed town crier as she pitched another Pito into her open maw like a self-training seal. "I just talked to Raddish Bretterspitt last week about that very thing. She and I were best friends, along with seven other women. She stated quite plainly that their annual getaway this year would be two weeks in the

Crottons. In fact, B. Bunny's industrial sand company was even footing part of the bill. Footing, mind you."

"Oh, how lovely," said Betty. "My friend Dootsy goes there every—"

"So you see, it can't possibly be a trip. Oh I just know something's happened to them, I just *know* it."

"Now, now, calm down, Anky. We'll get to the top of the bottom of this," reassured Doc.

"Yes, and if there's anyone who can get on top, it's my husband," comforted the neighborhood's most beloved wife of a scientist. "I don't know how many times it's seemed at its darkest, just before he lets a little light in by simply opening the right door. The one with the light in it."

"I hope so," sniffed the gabby woman, inappropriately wiping her nose with a baked lassover. "Because, when I peeked in the windows, which I did only because I thought it might be an emergency, I saw that someone had apparently ransacked their house."

Doc and Betty exchanged a glance that might have bowled over a lesser couple, anchored only by their respective hands reaching for snacks.

Again, that might have seemed like a good time to go somewhere else, but it was only a matter of minutes before the summoned City Brad was there, reaching for a capochin stick. The policeman had heard everything, and now he crunched loudly as he spoke.

"It all sounds… so very strange. There is definitely something going on here. Unfortunately, as a member of law enforcement, my hands are tied. I'm afraid we can't file a missing persons report until the person's been gone for forty-eight years."

"Forty-eight years? City… do you mean forty-eight hours?" asked the civilian-yet-well-educated Doc Armstrong.

City Brad thought a moment, dipping another capochin stick for effect. His reply reflected the selfless, sometimes sheepish, honesty of the relative novice. "Sorry, I've still got so much to learn. Seems like only last year I was still Jungle Brad."

"It was," said Doc, and they all had a laugh. All except Anky.

"Can you do anything, Detective City Brad?"

Her plea did not fall on death ears. "Don't worry, Anky. You know, I live in this neighborhood too. Well not far anyway. And I tell you this: that I will not rest until Doc Armstrong gets to the bottom of this mystery."

"I told you my husband could get on the bottom," smiled Betty, like the cat that just swallowed the pill.

Doc took the liberty of laying out the clues on the coffee table, using handy snacks that now took on a more ominous, less tasty, appearance.

"Someone, possibly Cottisill Landscaping and Loan, is trimming hedges illegally into round ones, no matter their original shape. Two of these alleged landscapers attacked me when I got a little too nosy."

"I can understand that one," winked Betty impishly.

Doc went on. " Further, a macaroon-headed man has been spotted lately, lurking about, though I myself have yet to see him."

"I myself have," shivered Betty. "And that is one cookie-headed man I'd rather forget."

"It might be wise to forget all cookie-headed men," wisely proffered City Brad. "At least, in a perfect world."

"Then there's the mysterious parchment you brought over, City Brad," said Paul, turning to his police pal.

"That's a curving ball you just threw me. What are you saying? You think there's a connection?"

"I have no idea, but wouldn't it be intriguing?" Doc was always eager for puzzle parts to all come together in rather intricate ways, like when scientists discover things around us, or inside us, that we can't see and then try to convince us they're there. To him, life was the thrill of the hunt, and the hunt was for knowledge. Smart knowledge. Betty had seen his eyes light up again and again when there was something he didn't understand. It was like Doc only understood things he didn't understand.

"Next we have the loam company with two n's. That's certainly some foul play right there, if not just a terrible sense of spell. And finally, perhaps most mysteriously, we have the hedges themselves, those leafy globes of mystery wrapped inside a topiary of terror complete with its own… gobble."

A visible shiver ran up Betty and continued into the chair she was sitting in. "Brr, that's one turkey I wouldn't care to stuff."

"Though, traditionally, the one animal we think of as gobbling is indeed the turkey," offered the zoologist part of Doc Armstrong, "there are several other species that partake of *that* particular bad habit. Like the dolphin, or the earwig, even several street vendors."

City Brad looked puzzled. "That's sure a lot of things that don't go together. Like French cooking or something. But I guess something can still taste good, even when you don't know what it is."

Doc opined that that was a good way to put it. But a plan of attack was needed and the science hero was at his best when organization was required. All his life, people had instinctively looked to him for leadership—friends, family, coworkers, some animals—and far be it for him to stop not letting them down now. It was a role he fell into like a drunk in a vat.

He asked City Brad if he could do a background check on Cottisill Landscaping and Loan. He then asked Anky to just go home and rest since she was pretty frazzled. And he asked Betty to continue to keep an eye out for the mysterious macaroon-headed stranger, knowing full well her eye was most likely way out there already, to which she happily agreed.

Doc himself would study the ancient parchment to at least determine if, indeed, it had any bearing on the present case.

Their jobs outlined, everyone felt a renewed sense of purpose and, of course, the snacks didn't hurt. They were about to get to their assigned tasks when Betty abruptly screamed and pointed.

All turned to see, in one of the windows looking out on the side yard, a large round cookie about the size of a serving platter.

But it was neither cookie nor platter. It was a face. It took a second to discern, but there were features faintly distinguishable in its crusty surface, looking as though it had been whipped with a fork prior to baking, if such a living thing could indeed be oven-born.

It was the macaroon-headed man.

Chapter 9

THE MYSTERIOUS PARCHMENT

Doc and City Brad were quickly outside, scouring this way and that for the mysterious phantom that had invaded the Armstrong living room side window mere moments before. But there was no sign of the strange figure; no small feat, considering the size of his head. Doc surmised that he had disappeared into the trees of one of the adjoining yards.

"We'll never catch that cookie-headed wraith now," surmised City Brad, impressing Doc with his use of the word wraith.

Back inside, Doc and City Brad calmed the ladies down and poor Anky decided she'd had enough for one day, though of what, she did not specify.

Betty headed to the kitchen to start dinner. She always felt that nothing could touch her while she was cooking. Something about pleasant food odors created a wall of comfort, and she sometimes saw her duty as expanding that wall to embrace as much of humanity as possible. Within Paul's scientist budget, of course.

City Brad left to do his police work, finding out all he could about Cottisill, leaving Doc to retire to his home lab for a good close look at that mystery parchment. As much as he loved going around adventuring, often employing running and punching, he treasured the moments of scientific exploration between just him and some thing he was looking at really really closely with a close-up-making device: in this case, both his magniscope and microfying glass. He would also test the object with various solutions or acids applied discretely to very small portions of the edges, without burning the whole thing up, or making a mess, which wouldn't help anybody, least of all science.

He started by laying the parchment flat and holding it down with special clamps called clamps, which was pretty much what they were. This kept the material from "rolling up" or "curling," though many enjoyed the latter in certain countries; of course, *they're* not trying to *study* the blamed thing, thought Doc. He was sure that, if they were, they would think twice about that. All he knew was, he had to lay it flat so he could examine it as it lay there. And no thing was simpler that *that*.

Next, after the complex "flattening" process, came the most deceptively simple, not to mention the least "scientific."

Doc looked at it. Looking at something, also known as "studying it," was actually one of the most important things a scientist could know about. Of course, it was also one they didn't want the public to know about, since pretty much anyone could do it. Next thing you, everyone would be running around, being a scientist, and no scientist wanted that. Doc was even careful about letting Betty in on that "dirty little secret." He already worried about her enough as it was. The last thing he needed was a wife who went around "looking at things."

What Doc Armstrong saw with those two "ocular trained ferrets" on the front of his head was what appeared to be a very old piece of writing material with strange symbols and markings, at once reminiscent of both a map and the instructions for a new kind of stereo system not yet known to man. He moved his flexible desk lamp closer for more light and his twin look-spheres went at it again. The smaller markings along the sides looked like writing of some sort: annotations perhaps. Doc groaned to himself that it was not written in English. The sad and ugly truth was that almost no one in ancient times wrote in English. They just didn't know how. He reminded himself that it took hundreds of years for the education system to come as far as it had. It wasn't right to silently chastise ancient peoples simply because they were ancient.

Doc moved a second desk lamp closer, and now the writing took on a different cast. It looked for all the world like the writings of lemmings, if lemmings could write. The scientist slowly circled the entrapped material, studying it from different angles. As he did, the odd scratchings and points and loops seemed to change. They began to remind him of tiny puppies doing semaphore, though why adolescent canines would laboriously arrange themselves in such an arcane manner, and in ancient times no less, was anybody's guess. Who would give them flags? Though it sounded cruel, Doc was forced to abandon the adorable signal puppies, as it was plainly not bringing him any closer to the elusive truth. If anything, the notion of young animals using any kind of flags at this point only seemed to muddy the waters. In which case, it was time to sift through that mud and clean out the dark obscuring particles, until that water was clear again, even drinkable. Doc cursed himself for making himself thirsty.

These were, of course, rudimentary observations at best. Doc could conjecture till the cows arrived and sat in their living room, reading torn newspapers. He could make educated guesses with the best television host. But ultimately it meant nothing without that great white shark of scientific evidence: proof. Though proof rarely killed anyone, and certainly not in a gruesome manner.

So Doc carefully began his series of tests, applying various oils, chemicals, compounds, and some things he wasn't sure of, in tiny amounts to gauge its reaction. Of course, this was not the kind of reaction one could necessarily see with the nude eye. He would hardly expect a piece of parchment to suddenly wiggle, sit up and start laughing at him while playing the banjo. That would be patently absurd, and potentially disruptive. Rather, he looked for subtle changes in the texture or color or temperature of the piece, as recorded by many scientific instruments, most of which he owned outright. This was the part that could often be laborious, as it could take in many painful hours without a single reward, save some small treat Doc might allow himself. But, more than likely, nine times out of seven, it would pay off with results that made the long hours of sitting over a thing pay off in ways a non-scientist couldn't even begin to understand, because they just weren't that bright. Such was the case here.

He began with the most obvious candidates: applying a dot of red greasepaint to see if any circus clowns had handled it—unlikely, but you never knew—and a dab of marshmallow to see what it looked like really yummy. After inconclusive results with bleach, detergent and peanut butter, Doc finally applied a few drops of coffee to one section. Though it was, in truth, accidental (and Doc cursed himself for not being more careful with his "World's Greatest Scientist" mug around science stuff. Again), it was, nevertheless, the first thing to get a reaction. A visible reaction at that. The parchment immediately discolored where the coffee spilled, not just turning "coffee brown," but starting to reveal markings that had been hidden between the visible ones.

Doc now had to be careful. Even the slightest over-coffeefication at this point might ruin the delicate and archaic material, and also they were very low on coffee, so he needed to make sure there would be enough for morning. Doc could not start a day without his coffee. Fortunately, Betty was able to confirm that there was, indeed, enough to treat the parchment and still have plenty left over for breakfast. Doc thanked her, and then made her confirm that fact seven more times. Doc needed his coffee.

Rather than spill any more with his mug willy-nilly, the veteran formula-farmer used an eyedropper which he kept handy for just such an occasion, though not usually coffee. It took the better part of an hour but it was well worth it, for, when Doc was done, the parchment was quite a different animal indeed: the incomprehensible thing was now completely covered with more incomprehensible symbols, making it even more incomprehensible. This depressed Doc.

Nevertheless, being the unflagging scientist by nature, and remembering how he frowned on the idea of the tiny puppies having flags, the weary seeker of knowledge sat and stared at the mysterious missive.

As he did, a strange thing happened. Doc started to recognize a peculiar familiarity in the object, like that old friend on the bus who looked weird now. There was something in the now-revealed entirety of the markings that rang a distant long-forgotten bell in his distant long-forgotten head. Wrestle as he might, inside his brain, with no clear opponent, but a series of mental holds that would have crippled a chimp, Doc Armstrong could not for the life of him place just what it was.

"Don't worry, darling, it will come to you," soothed the wife that stood by his side, even through the times when he wasn't quite so bright. This time she was *sitting* at his side, but the support was there, nonetheless, no matter her physical position or distance from him. Even in the kitchen, a whole room away, she still supported him. Doc put his arm around her, an arm that had known much putting-around over the years.

"I don't know what I'd do without you, Betty. And I hope I never have to find out."

"Well. It's really not like you to not want to know something," quipped the housewife known as much for her spry japes as her crunchy gingercobs. "I suppose some knowledge is better left unknown."

Paul chuckled the chuckle of a man expected to chuckle. Betty could tell he was disheartened when his snicker tapered off like the mad gibbers of a severely wounded badger. "I needed that laugh," he fibbed nobly, raising his scotch and soda for drinking purposes.

"Hey, it's five o'clock," squeaked Betty. *"Petri-phone's* coming on. How about we watch that, get your mind off things? We still have time before we're due at Kro-Bar and Lattis's."

Doc had completely forgotten they were having dinner with their favorite alien couple. "You know I like a good game show, honey, but maybe something a little less tense than *Petri-phone*. The contestant never knows who's going to call, and watching them try to stand *so still*. Frankly, I can't take any more suspense just now."

"How about *Days of the Hours?* That's on."

Doc never needed to consult their copy of TV Glance, though it was always handy. Betty knew everything that was on, and when it was on, including some of Paul's shows that she hated, like *The Lost Golfer*. She switched on the television set and, though Doc was hardly a fan of soap operas, he didn't mind seeing how the troubled folks of the fictional Danderbranch Bunt neighborhood of *Days of the Hours* were getting along, in their numerous and melodramatic conundrums.

Hopefully better than the people of Blendview, who no longer seemed in control of their own yards.

Chapter 10

MY DINNER WITH ALIENS

The alien woman feared the Earth kitchen like a thousand suns. Oh, the recipes seemed logical when you read them. But for every "take one cup of bleebleeblee and add it to the blowblowblow" she had twelve or thirteen questions. Good sound logical questions. If only Earth had microwave ovens in 1963, she lamented. How she longed for one of those babies. She knew they would have them, fairly soon—she'd seen them in Earth's future on the marvavision.

They did not want anyone, even Paul and Betty, to know they had a marvavision. Earth people were just not ready for that kind of advanced technology; they were still little tiny babies in so many ways. Most ways, in fact. So they kept their marvavision in the bedroom where no Earth people had a television (though that custom also lay in Earth's future). They used it for relaxation after a hard day's work in the kitchen, for her, or the office, for Kro-Bar.

Lattis had tried to watch Earth television. She really had. In truth, there was really very little of it she understood. So much of it concerned a violent past in which, what she referred to as, mangy-loony people exhibited an obsession with cows. And killing each other over dirt. And speed. They killed each other for speed. She realized that some of the mangy-loony shows were of a better quality than others in certain ways, like *Bannister* and *Chuck Wagon* and *The Iron Gun*. But it still presented a world that was entirely lost on her.

Game shows like *Stargirth*, *Cash Shoe* and *Name That Feeling* also left her cold, with their insufferable giddy neediness and easily performed chores, while allegedly respected dramas like *Academy Landing*, *Dr. Mileboyne* and *Soot Manor* made absolutely no sense. What was considered escapist fare, series like *Hiding Squad*, *Cut Through* and *Freighter Boy*, just seemed ludicrous. And the comedies! She could not believe how many comedies there were. *Robot Wife*, *It's That Mound* and *Dooty Datty* actually had the effect of inducing a profound sadness in her. The so-called situation comedies, like *Fit and Fitty* or *The Biting Midges*, were unrelentingly annoying. Who wanted to see a married couple bicker over foolish trifles? Who would believe that? And when she tuned in to the popular *Sandy Ryten*, all she found was a man talking. And talking. And talking.

So Earth's first housewife from Marva had to be content to watch the marvavision, on which she could view almost anything across boundaries of time and space, though Kro-Bar still managed to always complain that there was nothing good on.

Now she longed for the marvavision to take her away from this foul kitchen with all of its "cooking." The Armstrongs had been over before, and while Lattis's special brand of Marvan fondness for them could not have been any more sincere, she could not help resent Betty's seeming perfection in the ways of what was commonly called "homemaking," an absurd term since she knew for a fact that the Armstrong house had been built years before, and not by Betty. It ignited an unwanted competitive streak in the alien woman that she had not experienced before. Marvans gave up unwanted competitive streaks eons ago.

They took turns with their dinner get togethers: one week over at the Armstrong's, the next week over at the Pottadew's. The Earth housewife invariably had an elaborate and varied meal that had the men making annoying pleasure-sounds—the kind she preferred her husband to make in private, preferably with her present. She knew it was wrong to resent her best friend's success. Betty was just so good at it. And her attitude was self-effacing, humble, dismissive of lavish praise, though Lattis sometimes wondered if this wasn't for effect, or to even invite more. But it was wrong to question the intentions of one she was so fond of, and Lattis recognized the flaw immediately. She was only Marvan, after all.

Therefore, she would simply try her best, week after week, watching with the excruciating suspense of a *Petri-phone* contestant as the men took their first bites. She had to admit, everyone was always polite. They were gracious. Maybe too gracious. Even her acerbic alien husband, a man not exactly known throughout the universe for his tact. Despite this, Lattis would then launch into the string of excuses that she always had at the ready: misread labels, malfunctioning knives, explosions in the oven, dead animal catching fire, distraction by unexpected balloons... Perhaps she primed herself to fail, kind of a self-cleaning prophesy, conjectured the woman from the stars.

Mrs. Pottadew popped the latest dead animal into the oven and shut the door, hoping for the best this time, or at least second best. But Lattis was always thinking. On this attempt, she would time the cooking in Earth time, not Marvan time. She was not about to make *that* mistake a fourth time.

The vegetables would take less time, but she wanted to get the jump on them—taking no such chances as she had at the time of the asparagus disaster, or what Kro-Bar referred to as *The Discrete Horror of Green*. Within no time she had the radishes, beets and tomatoes ready to go. She had decided the color red would be her theme. Everything on Earth had a theme.

While setting the dining room table, she made certain to only put out the necessary silverware. Giving everyone fifteen forks, she realized, was nervous overcompensation on her part. There would be no such calculated, but obvious, misdirection this evening, the Marvan woman vowed; her carefully prepared dead animal would live or die on its merits alone. If it, along with its vegetable brethren, delivered no perceptible quantity of pleasure to her guests' various buds of taste, then so be it. She could but try her best.

The "jarring bing-bong of the door," as she liked to refer to it, made her jump as it always did, announcing that Paul and Betty had arrived. She immediately left the kitchen to go and let them in. From past experience, she knew there was no way Kro-Bar would get up and go to the door, no matter what he *wasn't* doing at the time. He had taken to setting himself up in his comfy chair, the very one that seemed to trouble him so lately, like a picture he had spied in an Earth magazine, carefully adjusting his props for the proper effect: the day's newspaper, which he invariably held upside down, a drink beside him that he never touched, the latest issue of *Bulb and Finial*, casually splayed and—perhaps most annoyingly—a pipe which he proceeded to immediately light upon the sound of the jarring bing-bong, like an actor preparing for a stage entrance. The pipe, of course, made him cough throughout the entire ten minutes it remained in his possession, and for a good hour after he had discarded the cursed thing. The Armstrongs were, naturally, far too polite to question him about it, or even casually comment.

So it was up to Lattis to open the door, or no one would ever come in. The Armstrongs, though they had visited many times before, at least attempted a greeting, even as they watched the Marvan woman turn quickly on her heel and beeline back to the kitchen with nary a word, once again leaving their mouths hanging in the open doorway. It was one of several things Paul and Betty always talked about afterwards, but never could get up the nerve to bring to her attention. There were just some things that would not change, and this one was relatively minor in the scheme of things.

So, the visiting couple entered and approached the coughing alien in his chair, warmly greeting him as he hastily waved them off. It was obvious they were used to this; Paul went right to the bar and made drinks, any notions of formality in this area long forgotten. In truth, the scientist had generously stocked their alcohol. Kro-Bar and Lattis didn't care, in fact they welcomed being freed from the pressures of any proprietary responsibility in the area of cocktails.

Paul whipped up martinis with the practiced eye of man who counts test tubes among his friends, knowing full well that their alien hosts would take anything handed them. Kro-Bar would nurse his, while Lattis would down hers: yet another of the things that wouldn't change.

Betty no longer asked Lattis if she needed help in the kitchen, since she usually met with a mixture of panic and confusion whenever broaching that sensitive subject. The best she could do, perhaps all anyone could do at this point, was to simply stand clear and hope for the best.

When Kro-Bar's coughing had subsided enough for at least sporadic conversation, he and Doc caught each other up on work as they usually did. Betty would either politely pipe in when appropriate, or thumb through the latest issue of *Chaise and Lounge*.

Though this was easily the thirtieth or so time the couple had visited, Paul had yet to know what Kro-Bar actually did for a living, or how he even found a job in the first place. After countless hours of conversation on the subject, all Doc knew for sure was that his alien friend: worked in an office, had a desk, had a chair, had a boss. He did find out his boss's name was Mr. Overmanner. And that during the course of his work day, Kro-Bar looked at things and occasionally wrote something down on a piece of paper, if it seemed appropriate. He also had coffee breaks. Unfortunately, none of this exactly narrowed it down.

The scientist's work was met with great interest, as the Marvan had a keen curiosity about such things. Doc sometimes suspected this was born of a certain vicarious enjoyment of the relative primitiveness of Earth science, and the fact that even the dullest of Marvans excelled in the sciences. But, if such were the case, the reserved Kro-Bar played too close to the vest to ever let on.

Nevertheless, he genuinely seemed to perk up when, at dinner, the subject got round to the neighborhood and its various mysteries of late. He seemed particularly interested in the hedges.

In fact, Paul and Betty could not remember seeing him so excited about something, and he appeared to be on the verge of bursting as Paul related his yard adventures. Finally, he could contain himself no longer, and he jumped up from the table.

"I need to show you. You will enjoy this. Lattis and I have been practicing."

"Practicing what?" asked his scientist friend curiously.

Like children eager to show a magic trick they'd just learned, Kro-Bar and Lattis stood before their seated audience, which consisted of a rather blank Paul and Betty.

"Here. Watch how well we do this," sputtered Kro-Bar.

"We have been practicing, as you Earth people would say," chirped Lattis with a smug, yet somehow impish, grin.

Paul and Betty stared, having no idea what to expect. They did that a lot around the Marvans. But they'd never seen them quite so charged up before.

Without further introduction or explanation, Kro-Bar and Lattis walked to the sofa. Paul and Betty thought they were about to witness an unusual Marvan ritual of some sort. With the self-conscious and slightly tenuous excitement of toddlers in a school play, the Marvans looked at each other, as if to say "okay," then carefully proceeded to walk around the back of the sofa. As they did so, continuing along its length, they appeared to diminish in size, which, of course, was caused by their rather obviously lowering themselves as they went, until they were last seen in a squat-walk, just before finally disappearing below the top of the long piece of furniture.

The rather numbed audience of two had no time react, or even invent an appropriate reaction, before the aliens started back the other way, in a squat-walk, slowly rising as they went, once again attaining their full height at the other end. Rather than look to their audience for any expected reactions, whatever they might be, Kro-Bar and Lattis proceeded to repeat this odd "disappearing walk" three more times, before finally turning to Paul and Betty with looks of smug contentment. So confident were they of their triumph, that there was not the slightest hint of insecurity or doubt as they waited for the adulations to roll in.

Their friends would disappoint here, sadly, as neither had the faintest clue what to do, beyond stare. It was almost a full minute before Betty spoke. She tried not to show how glad she was that she'd thought of something with which to break the awkward silence.

"Oh. Didn't Diff Stye do that gag on *The Diff Stye Show?*"

Paul was still quite glazed. "Did he?"

Kro-Bar and Lattis stared at them. "Gag?" said Kro-Bar. "Gag?" He did not look pleased. "Are you telling me that you, longtime Earth people that you are, are not familiar with the hedge melt?"

Betty looked to Doc, but it didn't help. He was still staring. "Hedge melt?" she uttered.

"Is it for us to inform you of the very customs about which you should be enlightening us?" chastened Lattis.

The aliens were thoroughly annoyed. And this right after Lattis's first passable dinner. It was nothing to write to Marva about, but at least no one was feeling ill. Doc and his wife had taken advantage of the opportunity and lavished praise, using words like "edible" and "palatable." It mattered little if those reviews were less than glowing; the Marvan housewife was in kitchen heaven. Now that all seemed to be negated.

"I'm sorry," soothed Doc, "but Betty and I have been Earth people all our lives, and we have just never heard of anything called a hedge melt."

Uncertainty shadowed the alien couple's faces and they snuck tenuous glances at each other. "My Lattis can easily confirm the pastime," offered Kro-Bar a bit pompously. "In truth, she has been well aware of it for quite some time."

Lattis looked at him, confidence quickly draining. "Well, as it happens, my husband, I had only heard the vaguest of references. Until you brought it to my attention, having witnessed the Earth peculiarity firsthand."

Her husband stared at her, now on the spot. "Well, I… have only seen it that one time. The other day. When our neighbor across the street, B. Bunny Bretterspitt, practiced it behind his very round hedges."

Doc immediately perked up and that high canine-addling whine filled the air. "When was this?"

Kro-Bar and Lattis were taken aback by their friend's sudden intensity. "A year ago," said Kro-Bar, once again confusing Earth time. But Doc had enough experience with that peculiar discrepancy to know he meant the day before.

"Please, Kro-Bar. This could be important. Explain to me exactly what you saw and, pray, leave out no detail."

A short time later the two couples from opposing galaxies were relaxing over after-dinner drinks in the living room. Once Kro-Bar had related the strange circumstances surrounding the disappearance of B. Bunny Bretterspitt, Doc filled the Pottadews in on the diverse elements of the Blendview mystery to which they were not yet privy: the furtive landscapers, the mysterious parchment and the disappearing neighbors.

The analytical minds of the alien pair took to mystery like duck to an egg cream, and Doc realized that, once again, they would be valuable allies in the fight against all things strange, except for the harmless ones. As requested, he and Betty also promised to never speak of the hedge melt.

In the hour that followed, prior to Lattis falling into complete incoherence, the four friends worked up a plan of action to confront the Blendview crisis—or potential crisis, since they all felt it was more like Crisis Eve than actual Crisis Day, when they'd be up to their necks in a crisis already well underway. At any rate, it was clearly a crisis-in-training.

It was decided that Kro-Bar would assist Doc in interpreting the strange parchment, as well as laying a trap for the mystery landscapers, while Lattis would help Betty find out exactly how many people were missing from Blendview besides the Bretterspitt family and several others that Anky had mentioned.

No sooner had they finished their plan than the phone rang. Taking the bull by the throat, as always, Doc answered it by picking the blasted thing up. It was City Brad.

He had found out some things about Cottisill Landscaping and Loan. And what he found out was interesting.

Chapter 11

TEAMWORK: LIKE WORKING IN TEAMS

Kro-Bar first setting eyes on the parchment was like a janitor discovering a pile of unused rags. The Marvan thirst for knowledge and strange-looking things was a trait Doc had become well aware of, even in the relatively short time he'd known them. He hoped that his friend might recognize something in the density of its presentation, some obscure symbol or writing, that might actually point to interplanetary origin, given the alien couple's love for space travel, including some out-of-the-way resort asteroids. But, while the Marvan was fascinated by the ancient artifact, he had little to offer, except that it reminded him of a popular brand of Earth cereal, like StaxPex, if it were flattened and squared off and left in the sun, hastily adding that he could think of no good reason to do that.

And so, the two proceeded to an appointed meeting with City Brad at Blendview's only diner, the Fussy Spoon. It was a favorite neighborhood gathering hole, as popular for its strong coffee as its equally strong pie.

City Brad was already there when they arrived, and they found him sipping coffee and wrestling with a bear claw; an odd idiosyncrasy Doc had previously observed and chalked up to therapeutic behavior to help him cope with his brother's death. Kro-Bar ordered French toast as he always did, wherever he went, including the library, because he thought it made him seem "worldly." Doc got coffee and his usual plain donut. The scientist often got a laugh among colleagues, referring to the hole as "antidough."

The Viewton police detective and ex-twin had been busy. After a little digging, it seemed that Cottisill Landscaping and Loan was owned by a woman named Senna Blue Popps, about whom he could find little. However, he did discover that Cottisill was actually a subsidiary of the Sta-Mor-Down Rug Company. This rang a distant bell for Kro-Bar who thought he might have seen a commercial for Sta-Mor-Down on TV, remarking that it made him mad and he spoke angrily to it. Doc put little stock in this, however, as he knew firsthand that this was something Kro-Bar did to all commercials.

The policeman further stated that Sta-Mor-down had been under suspicion as a possible front for money laundering, since a lot of beautifully clean money had been showing up in the vicinity. While they had no proof, for a while it was on the short list of companies with long names, like Peter Bye Bird Shoes and the Welty Drop-cloth Outlet. But the investigation was terminated when it turned out nice clean money was not against the law.

Doc thanked City Brad, who left with enough donuts for his entire shift, and he and Kro-Bar continued their investigation with a trip to the Bretterspitt house.

Kro-Bar wanted to reenact the disappearance of B. Bunny. The science man was not crazy about the idea, but Kro-Bar insisted, and he *was* an alien after all. Doc simply felt it just wasn't to anyone's advantage to risk the Marvan vanishing in the exact same way. It also didn't really add insight, watching the tall-short walk over and over again.

Nevertheless, like one of those full-sized European clock figures that come out and strike the bell upon the hour, the stubborn Kro-Bar performed the routine formerly known as the hedge melt. Except that he kept repeating it again and again. Doc couldn't help thinking he was watching an ex-vaudevillian whose mind had gone.

After twenty or so passes, Doc approached and bid his friend stop, which took several attempts. It was time for the scientist to get hands-on. With a hedge. He went behind it, like Kro-Bar had, then got down on all fours. Doc had used all fours before, but tried to only use it when absolutely necessary, kind of like a secret weapon. He scanned the small dark green leaves, and the grass and fallen twigs on the ground, but could spot no discernible clue. Ever the labman, he gathered samples and put them in his pockets to be studies later. He had no idea what properties he might find: just what in the hedge could contribute to a person's disappearance? And why should B. Bunny vanish and not Kro-Bar? Or him, for that matter? It was tight between the large carefully manicured balls of leaves, and the scientist's arms seemed to wince at the memory of the sharp branches that scratched him earlier. He made a note to see about wincing arms—that didn't sound right.

As Doc moved between them, he noticed the hedges were arranged in an alternating pattern, allowing them to mesh, almost like gears. This suddenly resonated in his very smart brain like a pingpong ball amid fast paddles. Doc stopped crawling. Finally, he felt like he might have a clue, or at least a hint of a lead to a clue. Pieces were coming together.

And for the first time in weeks he began to fear. Doc wondered how many other poor souls had shared the Bretterspitts' fate.

Seventeen, to be exact, according to Betty and Lattis's findings. So far. And they had only canvassed a third of the neighborhood. It wasn't looking good.

At first they pretended to be snopperware saleswomen, even bringing some handy snopperware kitchen containers with them ("storage so tight it could take a finger off") to complete the disguise. Lattis, or Clackie as she was known on Earth, became Pecky Ruba, while Betty would be undercover as Teetee Go Delle. Unfortunately, they were recognized and warmly greeted at the first three houses they went to, so they decided to forego the ruse. As Betty realized the hard way, it's extremely difficult to go undercover with friends, short of sporting the elaborate rubber noses neither was fortunate enough to own.

So, the intrepid twosome went as they were and continued a house-to-house survey to see who was no longer there. At each house they inquired of that person's neighbors to find out who hadn't been seen for a while, multiplying the length of their absence times their propensity for taking vacations. Betty was proud that the science training Doc was giving her sometimes had a practical use.

When no one answered a door, they asked of that family's neighbors to try and determine why they might not be home, careful to avoid belligerency or threats, since these were friends and neighbors. It was not exactly a foolproof system, and the scientist's wife knew there was a margin for error of blah blah blah—Paul could fill that in. But even halfway through Blendview, the plucky pair knew there was something very wrong. Something incredibly very wrong.

They were just starting on the east side of the neighborhood when Betty noticed something amiss. It was more of a sensation really, a feeling of being followed. By someone who might be following.

The two landscapers finished clipping and gathered up their clippers. With the furtive air of very tall chipmunks, they headed to their white panel truck parked at the corner. Looking around them like illegal glass-blowers, the two men loaded their stuff into the back of the vehicle, climbed in and pulled away.

Two other figures watched from the safety of a 1958 black Torin Streekline parked across the street. As the van left, the Streekline pulled out, engine purring like a mouse as it easily paced the landscapers at a safe distance. Doc himself had "souped up" the already powerful Daynota engine with some spare rocket parts and other fast stuff.

From the driver's seat, sharp Marvan eyes watched the truck's progress. "If it turns, turn the same way it turns," offered his alien neighbor.

Doc, of course, pretty much new this from following other things, beginning with small animals when he was a child, so he could study their ways and make friends with them. He even followed Betty when they first met, though that had led to a bit of difficulty, initially. Oftentimes, Kro-Bar's advice seemed rather obvious but Doc let it go, reminding himself that the Marvan still had not been on Earth for very long, still thought of them as relatively "backwards" people. Which, in many ways, they were, thought Doc. Even 3-D was in its infancy.

The truck moved casually through the suburban streets, seemingly unaware they had a "tail" on them, as City Brad might say, using his special police force department professional lingo. They appeared to be moving out of Blendview, and Doc hoped they'd be returning to their base, be it Cottisill Landscaping and Loan down in the warehouse district or... somewhere else.

They had not gone half a mile when Doc suddenly got thrown for a loop. Fortunately, the scientist had been mistaken for a loop before, and tossed, hard, so he was not unready. As soon as the van made a sudden sharp turn and sped up, the Streekline was right on its tail, formidable Daynota engine humming like a birdbath.

Kro-Bar was thrown to the side as Doc whipped around a corner and kicked into gear, easily pacing the white panel truck. The alien was grateful for the Streekline's windows, another of Doc's special inventions. While all atoms intermingled on a subatomic level, paddiglass was of such a nature that its atoms blended on a higher level, but only momentarily, to the extent that its innate flexibility was brought into play. And in that moment that it was "cushioning" a person or object, they became as one: glass and person. By the same token, any objects coming from the outside, including projectiles such as bullets, were slowed down and bounced back accordingly. It was just the kind of vehicle you'd want to drive in if you were doing dangerous things and being attacked by stuff.

The van continued its mad pace down street after street, now entering the shopping area. Doc had been keeping up easily, until a sudden turn brought them right up against a car pulling out of a parking lot. The Streekline screeched to a halt and let the car clear, its angry driver shaking a fist, though they couldn't tell which one. Science was used to shaken fists; it came with the territory. By the time the car passed them, the white van was gone.

Doc revved the Streekline to the end of the street and pulled to a stop. There was no sign of their quarry. There were only two ways the truck could have gone: left to a residential section, or right to a more commercial area. As Doc wondered where to go next, the alien reached over and nudged his arm. He had learned nudging since coming to Earth, and found he rather liked it, though Lattis felt he enjoyed it a bit too much.

Doc's eyes followed his and saw what his friend from the stars was looking at: a sign that read STA-MOR-DOWN RUG COMPANY.

The veteran housewife from Earth and the rookie housewife from Marva were nervous. Betty had been through a lot with her intrepid rock-hunting husband, and it had gotten her somewhat used to danger and theories and long formulas and what she referred to as "sleeping lectures." But it had not really completely conditioned her to the scientist's eternal bedfellow: the unknown.

And Lattis might be Clackie Pottadew now, and she might have numerous planets and creatures under her space belt—one of which served as pet for a while, a decision the Marvan woman still questioned—but there were more than enough strange things on this little blue planet with green dressing to keep her considerably on edge at times. Like the deadly art of sewing and those smiling television commercial people.

Now, as they moved through their familiar, but no longer quaint and safe-feeling, environs, they could not help but notice how green everything was, seemingly more than usual: an overpowering miasma of encroaching vegetation, seriously dominated by the proliferation of perfectly round hedges. And sounds. Even the animals sounded different, at least to Betty. Though, if she thought about it, she wasn't really sure she could distinguish a squirrel chitter or bark or squeak or whatever they did, from the sound made by a mole or a garden snake.

Now, however, the air was filled with noises beyond her ken, even if a limited suburban ken. A steady pulsing rhythm of tweets and titters and ticks seemed to flow between the houses like a steady stream. It went with the heavier air which hung over the neighborhood like a damp shawl, like that one Betty's aunt kept for years. And, within that greenness, lurked something they had not sensed before: an unknown presence that seemed to watch their every move, even now as they continued their special canvassing mission.

They were being followed.

At first it was occasional twig snaps, easily explained away as a hopping bird or clumsy insect. Then it was a rustling of leaves far too substantial to be excused by the simple rudeness of a too proud vole shouldering its way through the underbrush.

Then the eyes. Not actual eyes, but the feeling of eyes. That eye feeling when you can't see eyes, but you know eyes are looking because they're looking at you, and you can feel the eyes you can't see looking at you.

Lattis felt it too. It was what she referred to as an "arm hair stander." It made the hair on her arm stand up. Just one. But that was enough. The other was immune for some reason.

It made them glad they were almost done with their survey: only four houses left. They had gone through almost all of Blendview and there were, as best they could tell without further proof, at least forty-two people missing. This was no longer just coincidence, thought Betty, no "vacation special" that everyone was taking advantage of.

The two women were about to round the front corner of the next house and froze. Something was scuffling on the porch. Betty looked at Lattis, who looked back at her looking at her. Without a single spoken word, but with an instant understanding that reminded Betty of those pale silent clowns that were becoming so popular, the duo began moving away from the house. Unable to see who or what was on that porch, yet feeling in their gut that it was not someone they knew, they continued, slowly at first, then speeding up, finally bolting through the trees and brush and shrubs of a neighborhood no longer familiar, shooting back glances like veteran cattle rustlers.

Foremost on Betty's mind, though loath to admit it, even to herself: the macaroon-headed phantom, whose lurking of late helped infuse Blendview with an undercurrent of unreality. Now, that briefly-glimpsed head loomed before her like a giant lollipop of unease, accelerating her flight. Surely the cookie-headed man was the poster child for the neighborhood's mounting dread.

Another sound crowded their escape, a rough pushing aside of branches by a third party somewhere behind them, yet unseen. Unseen, since a glance back might prove too costly.

But this housewife was made of sterner stuff. With an instinct born of years beside a rock-hunting fool, if fools can be heroes, Betty took a sudden turn between a house and garage, cutting through and hoping her companion would do likewise.

She needn't have worried. Her best alien friend was on her like a monkey on library paste and, together, the women threaded a needle of suburban alleys that took them to their own street, in the time it takes a process server to serve a process.

Yet, as Betty took the turn to her house, she caught a glimpse of dark roundness in the shadowy tunnel behind them, as if an ominous balloon were closing fast. With a final gritty determination that no cookie-headed fiend shall ever take them, the housewife poured it on, and clutched at Lattis's sleeve to urge likewise, while still retaining the wherewithal to not tear her friend's new blouse that she had so admired earlier.

As though sucked up by a friendly vacuum cleaner, the pair were whipped into the relative safety of the Armstrong house, the door quickly shut and locked behind them.

The ladies stood against the barrier, panting and winded, feeling as though they'd escaped an unknown fate they'd prefer to keep unknown. A sound rose above their breath-catching: footsteps on the porch.

Betty and Lattis kept still, holding in their breath in case some of it was noisy. The walking around that they heard seemed casual enough, and for a moment Betty wondered if it were her husband and Kro-Bar, returned at last. But, as she listened, it became obvious the steps were uncertain. Not like Paul's. Paul always came right up to the door of his house and then came right in. He knew it very well: both his house, and walking up to it.

Then the steps paused, and the women exchanged a tense glance. For a minute there was no sound but for their twin heartbeats, like steady road repair by dedicated crews, only inside their chest cavities and with no union breaks.

The scratching at the door was so quiet, at first they didn't hear it. In fact, Betty incorrectly surmised that it was Lattis scratching her fingers on the door behind her in some kind of eccentric Marvan fear custom. But she wasn't.

Something else was.

Chapter 12

OUR RUGS STAY MORE DOWN

Doc Armstrong and Kro-Bar had parked the car on a side street out of the way and now stood before the rather surprisingly large structure that bore the STA-MOR-DOWN RUG COMPANY sign. As a scientist and trained observer, Doc was surprised he had never noticed the building before. The front was quite imposing, if somewhat plain, but the sides were even longer, as it stretched way back like a massive hangar. To the right were more warehouses, but on the left was a wide scrubby field leading to some trees and, eventually, Blendview.

"I estimate they have forty-seven million rugs inside there," remarked Kro-Bar, casually.

"Well, of course it depends on the size of the carpets and whether they're at capacity, but let's not worry about that right now," said the practical scientist as they approached.

At the front door, they were able to read the company's slogan on a plaque beneath its name: "Our Rugs Stay More Down." This helped to explain the initially confusing "Sta-Mor-Down" which Doc now saw, and appreciated, as a clever play on words that comprised its snazzy truncated name, giving proof that only the highest level of modern marketing had come into play here. So appreciative, in fact, that he didn't even mind taking the next five minutes to explain it to poor Kro-Bar, whose normally quite advanced race had given up slogans eons ago. He finally grasped it, however, with a typical non-committal Marvan grunt. With both men now "getting" the slogan, Doc felt it safe to venture inside.

The reason he wanted to make quite sure that the Marvan knew all this was because, rather than stumble in without a plan (Doc still cursed himself for the Cottisill Conundrum, as he now dubbed it in his mind, where things were dubbed on a daily basis), the two would pretend to be buyers for a major carpet concern. They would wield these clever undercover identities like twin clubs aimed at the exposed noggin of this rapidly burgeoning conspiracy. Though the scientist's chief focus was the study of rocks, and every other science, he made it a point to have at least a working knowledge of all things, including, happily, the lore and magic of carpets. He was, therefore, able to brief the sharp-minded alien before they went in, and, with characteristic intelligence, Kro-Bar did not disappoint. By the time they reached the end of Doc's mini-seminar, instructor was almost ready to purchase a rug from student! Fortunately, Doc remembered in time that they were only pretending, and no actual money changed hands.

The inside of the building was somewhat more inviting than Cottisill had been, but then one would rather expect it to be a darn sight nicer than a landscaping company, since they're diametrically opposed—the latter so concerned with *soil,* which is practically the opposite of *carpet,* or better be at least, if one wanted to keep a nice clean home, chuckled the scientist inside his head.

Upon entering, the two were immediately greeted by a smiling receptionist who bade them sit. After Doc briefly explained to her that they were buyers interested in doing some wholesale rug purchasing, the receptionist made a brief call and, within twenty seconds, the pair found themselves inside a very pleasant office.

They were warmly welcomed by a nondescript middle-aged man with a pleasantly round face, wearing suit and tie. He introduced himself as Clyme Drydekker, and also bade them sit. Though Doc and Kro-Bar had their suspicions about the place, which is why they were there, they had to admit to themselves that there was no lack of bading to be found at Sta-Mor-Down. Another good slogan, thought Doc.

Doc gave his name as Bark Bowle and, before he could come up with an equally appropriate one for his friend, Kro-Bar piped in with Loanna Mars, which found the scientist wincing just a bit. But, as with his arms earlier, he managed to hide the wince.

"Bark, Loanna, if you don't mind, I love to start out by asking: how the gosh darn mcjeepers did you hear about us?" chirped the almost ridiculously friendly Drydekker, in his somewhat high nasal voice.

"Well, we spoke to several housewives who were impressed with just how comfortable your rugs are," smiled Doc who, for a lab guy, could talk pretty good salesman.

"Really," said Drydekker, impressed. "Their husbands were *that* vocal about it."

Doc thought for a moment before answering. "Well, I assume they reached their own conclusions."

"Wow. That's wonderful! Good for them for trying them on themselves. Now *that's* a dedicated wife!

Doc and Kro-Bar snuck a glance at each other, neither exactly sure how this was going.

"How much stock are you interested in purchasing?"

"That depends," said Doc. "What's the standard square footage you deal in?"

Drydekker looked confused for a moment, but then passed right over it, chuckling, "You must have some clients with very large heads." His chuckle built into a laugh.

Doc stared at the laughing man, desperate to get on the same page. He grinned. "Ego *can* be a factor, of course. In any business. But I doubt it will impact rug sales that much."

Kro-Bar's lack of participation was making him squirm. He felt he should jump in somewhere and chose this moment. "Do you have any suggestion on the preferred method of keeping them clean? So much dirt seems to get in them, which of course is only natural on a planet *made of* dirt."

Both Doc and Drydekker stared at Kro-Bar a moment, the former trying very hard to keep his cool. Fortunately, Drydekker was unruffled. "As long as you keep our rugs in a safe clean place when they're not in use, I think you'll find they stay pretty darn clean." The man was so good-natured.

Now it was Doc's turn to stare at him. "You mean... you pick them up when everyone's done... walking around?"

Even Drydekker's cheery self-assuredness seemed to be struggling now. "Yes, well... naturally you put them away. Overnight." Then he added with a chuckle, "the old skull needs to breathe."

Drydekker's chuckle continued, even as the horror spread across Kro-Bar's Marvan face. Finally, he found words, and no longer seemed interested in censoring them. "Your rugs give life to the Lost Skeleton?"

Before Drydekker's jaw could drop, Doc jumped in. "Oh, um... sorry. Loanna's thinking of something else. Loanna... I don't think Mr. Drydekker's talking about *that* kind of skull."

Kro-Bar did not look assuaged. Drydekker was blank, plainly confused, which Doc was also, just a bit.

Nevertheless, the scientist managed to ask, "Uh, Mr. Drydekker, what skull were you referring to, if I may ask?"

"What? Oh, uh, just a figure of speech. Sorry. I meant to say: you have to take it off once in a while. The rug."

"So, okay, let me understand... Your rugs cannot be left out for any length of time? Isn't that a bit... awkward to maintain? I mean, taking it up, putting it down, taking it up, putting it down?"

"Not really. If you take good care of your rug it will last longer."

Doc looked at Kro-Bar then asked "They *can* be walked on, can't they?"

Drydekker looked shocked. "I'd… hardly advise it. Why in heaven's name would you want to do that?"

"Well, what if you have company over and want to show it off?" Doc asked, pretty much stymied.

Drydekker was able to chuckle again, "Well, that would be very brave, I'd say. Most people don't even like folks to know they *have* them."

"Excuse me, but why would you hide a rug?" queried Kro-Bar. "They're not against the law, are they?"

"Against the law? Of course not."

Doc was perturbed. "I'm sorry, but I don't quite understand why a company whose slogan is 'our rugs stay more down' wouldn't want their rugs to just stay down where they're supposed to be."

"Well, when you're out and about, of course," That's when it counts. Our rugs grip the head. They don't fly off."

Doc and Kro-Bar stared at Drydekker for what seemed like a long time. It came to an end when Doc finally realized the kind of rug Drydekker was talking about.

Another minute, and all three were laughing, with Kro-Bar doing his best impression of an Earth laugh. If it was a bit brittle, and slightly robotic, he was to be forgiven because of the effort.

Doc and Drydekker explained to Kro-Bar how "rug" also referred to men's toupees, usually a slang expression. Doc was surprised to hear that this was the first time anyone had made this mistake: thinking it was a carpet company.

When Drydekker apologized for the confusion and expressed disappointment that they would not be doing business, it was Doc's turn to surprise him, stating that, in fact, they would still like to purchase rugs wholesale for their customers, knowing only too well that ninety-eight per cent of them were balding.

Drydekker was delighted and immediately got out the paperwork. As he was preparing it, Doc casually asked him if they were, by any chance, affiliated with Cottisill Landscaping and Loan, since they were doing some work in his neighborhood and Doc could have sworn he saw one of their trucks pull into the Sta-Mor-Down plant.

Though the undercover wholesale toupee buyers were watching the man carefully, they could discern no difference in the rug company executive's demeanor. He merely continued to organize the order forms, tossing off that Doc surely must have been mistaken. Then, with an enthusiastic smile, he handed the papers to Doc to look over.

As the man calling himself Bark Bowle perused the form, he calmly stated, "Terrific, Mr. Drydekker. This all looks in order. Now, before proceeding, of course, with an order as large as this, we'd first like to meet the owner of the company, if that's alright. We plan on bringing him a lot of business. Just a formality—you understand."

This time there was a shift in Drydekker's demeanor. It was barely perceptible, but the heroic duo were watching for it, the way cats are very wary of musicians. Instantly, Doc wondered if he'd overplayed his hand, like in a card game, when you overplay your hand. The scientist was pretending to look over the papers, but he was furtively watching the toupee tallier, whose hand slowly slid behind the desk with the subtlety of a llama or some other very subtle animal. Doc and Kro-Bar had no time to react, but each knew that Drydekker had pressed the button to a silent alarm, or a really quiet one.

With startling speed, the door behind them, through which they'd entered just a short time ago, opened. And, like its unholy twin, another door, this one behind Drydekker, also opened.

Immediately, from both doors, men began filing into the room, silently, eerily. They were stoic men, stolid and torpid men, in identical dark suits with striped ties of wretchedly unremarkable color. Worst of all were their heads. For each bore a horror of a toupee, sitting way too high, higher than any toupee seemed right, with nary an attempt to make them look presentable, so unkempt and slovenly were they. Something about these lofty and awkward mats of artificial hair actually made Doc Armstrong a little queasy. Doc Armstrong, who had traveled the world again and back, who had tasted disgusting food, who was used to far worse headpieces than this. Something about these furry noggin-saddles reeked of the foul and unsavory. And still, the strange men poured in, slowly, like automatons, and the trained scientist wondered if they were, in fact, poor misbegotten souls now controlled by something contained in those tall and slovenly hairpieces.

Of course, all of this flashed through Doc's wiry mind in a billionth of a second (he later calculated).

Drydekker's nasal voice was no longer pleasant, but rather a sneering and grating whine, pitched an octave higher. "I had a funny feeling about you two. Tell me. How do you like my *rugmen?*"

The science hero did not answer. He had a feeling the question was rhetorical anyway. Any answer from Doc would have been negative or derogatory, and Drydekker knew that. All of this had been in another billionth of a second, making two billionths of a second that had now passed.

Doc Armstrong shifted like an abacas and, before a single clutching rugman could lay a hand on him, went into action, starting with his patented *simul-punch* in which each of his arms punched at the same time, crossing to exact opposite sides, instantly decking two of his dull-faced attackers. It was a punch that seldom failed him.

His alien friend was no slouch either. Kro-Bar had prepared himself for the rougher side of Earth life by developing what he called his *meteor punch*, which was really just a punch, but thrown by him. Having heard Doc's famous punching catchphrase "Say goodbye to your Aunt Consciousness," the methodical Marvan had come up with one of his own, "Hope you don't mind having a nice cooty-lana!" referring to the Marvan word for picnic, which didn't make much sense to anyone but Doc and Betty. By the same token, he mirrored Doc's "I'm about to open up a can of science on your posterior" with "I am destined to expurgate a tin of live croutons on your subconscious." Try as Doc might, he could not convince his friend that this really didn't mean anything, though he had to admit it sounded good.

And yet, as capable as the two battlers were as they waded in—fists flying—incredibly, the room continued to fill with rugmen. For every one the pair would drop, it seemed that two more took their place. The whole thing was shaping up into something like a melee or, worse, a brouhaha. Either way, it was a daunting challenge for the intrepid two.

Doc and Kro-Bar pummeled their powerful but slow-moving attackers like so much road work, even as that so-called "road work" continued to close in on them, which actual road work would *never* do. Under the severest of conditions.

In one fleeting moment, in the midst of all this, Doc had the wherewithal to notice that Drydekker was no longer there. He prided himself on his wherewithal, even under extreme pressure, often going away for long wherewithal weekends to hone that very rare and underappreciated skill.

The well-named rugmen continued to drop before the unforgiving balled-up hands of a duo determined to give them a good dusting. Still, the sluggish dullards poured into the room, like batter into a waffle iron. Thanks to the use of yet more wherewithal, Doc was able to note this losing battle, see the bigger picture (a portrait of them no longer there) and decide on a tactical retreat. Drydekker was the only one who could shed light on this perplexing puzzle of hedges and hair, and he was gone. It was plain, no wig-wearing brute in a suit was about to help them.

And so, with a signal to Kro-Bar—seven, actually, before he got it—Doc led a quick and deft thread through the throng of rugmen, until they once again found themselves in the company's lobby. Gone was the receptionist and any trace of it ever being an office.

Kro-Bar seemed dismayed as they headed back to the car. "I fear we did not acquire that which we came to acquire," he bemoaned. "We have learned nothing."

"Not quite nothing," said Doc as he held up a particularly hideous hairpiece he'd stashed in his pocket at the height of the battle.

Chapter 13

THE CURIOUS INCIDENT OF THE COW
IN THE NIGHT-TIME

The ladies had not heard the scratching at the door for an hour. Lattis thought she heard soft shuffling at one point, but felt it might have been one of the rabid bushtails (as she commonly referred to squirrels), or her left foot. But, since then, one could have heard an egg fry, it was that quiet.

Betty was perturbed, more so than her friend. "If I don't get to the kitchen and start dinner it may never get done in time," she whispered to Lattis with a wide-eyed desperation the latter thought bordered on insanity. It was clearly an anxiety the alien woman would never identify with, and was all the more grateful for it. She would be fine with never even looking at a child's crude sketch of a kitchen again.

As Betty entertained the idea of a mad dash for her favorite room, like a commando contemplating a raid on a bunker, a new sound interrupted the cook's conundrum: the sound of faint footsteps. She made eye contact with her Marvan best friend, and it was clear she had also heard.

"I wish I had the transmutatron," whispered Lattis, "I'd turn whatever it is into something that isn't scaring me right now."

Betty found no fault with her logic. They needed weapons. Like the trained housewife she was, Betty's eyes scanned the room with a precision usually reserved for spotting barely visible dust, faintly upturned carpet corners or imperceptible micro-stains. Like tired wandering orbs, her eyes rested on something. Not wanting to make a sound, she gave Lattis a quick signal that she'd be right back, having to repeat it seven times before the alien woman got it and nodded understanding.

The Armstrong woman returned mere seconds later with two candles, one of which she handed to Lattis who stared at it until her Earth friend started miming jabbing downthrusts with it, as one would a knife. Lattis nodded, though a tad uncertainly, as even an alien would question the stabbing value of a candle, even in the direst of circumstances.

The footsteps had reached the door, but it had become quite evident that this was not the shuffling of potentially inhuman feet, but rather the crisp clear steps of human shoes. Nevertheless, it seemed prudent to wait, and the ensuing minute dragged on for what seemed like sixty seconds, until it became unbearable, almost like that flat silence that precedes a spoonful of ice cream going into a human mouth.

"Betty? Betty, are you in there?"

At the sound of Doc's voice, Betty threw open the door like a stripper ripping away the last shred of garb, and the hug that followed threatened to crush a lesser man.

The tiny pieces of machinery gleamed under the magnifying glass like very wealthy insects. Doc had been studying the electronic underbelly of the pilfered toupee for the past hour, and had determined without a doubt that it represented the complex mechanical mind control he had so suspected. Just where Mr. Drydekker's army had come from was anybody's guess, but it was certain they were mindless automatons under the pitiless reign of these hairy little dictators. Was Drydekker controlling them? Or someone above him? And how were they tied to the mysterious round hedges? Or the cookie-headed intruder? The disappearing neighbors?

And so, once again, like a rented burro or a bent tricycle, Doc found himself coming back to that strange parchment, as though he sensed it lay at the center of all of these mysteries. What cryptic and ancient secrets might it hold?

As if on cue, the doorbell rang, and the dedicated scientist knew it must be none other than the one he had summoned about that very artifact: his old friend and mentor, Professor Willip Caystorm Atroppasmirki. *One* of his mentors actually, for Doc had seven of them all told: seven gifted experts in various fields that helped guide him, from a young scienceless rookie to an extremely scienced individual. His seven mentors (or baker's six, as Doc liked to refer to them) had been indispensable in helping shape his path.

He first met Atroppasmirki when, as a young man, he had stowed away aboard the three-island steamer *China Eclair,* bound for Oleo, by way of Mollaco. Even at an early age, Doc had a thirst for adventure, already having thoughts of "far off lands" and "exotic ports of call" and "learning about girls."

When he was discovered onboard, it was the ship's master, Captain M'Gugagong—a rough-and-tumble adventurer who would ironically become another of his seven mentors— that put him to work as a deckhand to earn his passage. The English Professor Atroppasmirki, one of the steamer's few passengers, was on a quest to decipher the legendary Oleo Sarcophagus. The young soon-to-be scientist was fascinated watching him work, and it was here that Doc discovered his love of old markings and hard-to-make-out things. He gradually learned that Atroppasmirki's specialized fields included paleography, bibliography and parchmentology, the latter being of particular relevance: the study of funny drawings people put on flat dried animals.

Doc found the elderly mustachioed gentleman regaling Betty, Kro-Bar and Lattis in the living room, and it reminded him of past regales. The man loved his regaling. As usual, Kro-Bar laughed too soon, and too stiffly, which often scared strangers, but the Professor seemed unfazed. Lattis just stared.

"Ah, my dear Paul, so good to see you. I was just telling them about something I think happened once at sometime or other."

"It was very entertaining," deadpanned Lattis. Doc warmly greeted his old friend and, after passing some pleasantries and other baked goods, all retired to the home lab for a look at that parchment.

"Remarkable," gasped the elderly scientist, eyes pressed up against the parchment like a kid in the window of a stationary store. "Simply remarkable. In all my born years in which I was born, I've never seen anything quite like it. It seems to be the work of a civilization that's been long forgotten, or at least misplaced for a bit."

The four neighbors all looked at each other, except for Kro-Bar and Lattis who were too awkwardly close to look at each other, without one taking a step back, which neither would, though they did try gamely. Doc had suspected as much, and now it was confirmed by an expert in the field as well as the lab. He had not yet mentioned his recent revelation that was like an epiphany that had been revealed when it came to him. He wanted to see what the elderly professor found, without the waters of his findings being muddied by the boots of Doc's tromping suspicions. Doc Armstrong was neat, if nothing else, and liked to "take his science boots off at the door," a habit Betty certainly appreciated.

"Most remarkable!" Atroppasmirki continued, eyes looking huge through the microfying glass, though they were just his regular eyes. "This is truly remarkable. A precursory glance, before any cursing, would seem to indicate that this material contains properties of both parchment and papyrus, along with a hint of rosemary. I would estimate the age to be in excess of five thousand years, making it very very old as far as age goes."

"Professor, are you saying, in effect, that this material is parchpyrus?" asked Doc, coining a new word like he did it every day, which he did.

"I am indeed," uttered the Professor as he shifted his angle, adjusted his headlamp and continued. "As to its curious markings: note the curve of the round parts and the gentle sweep of the sweepy parts, as well as the sharp angular pointy things on the parts that aren't round. There is a looseness of hand at work here, as though an ancient wine had come into play. I see you applied some coffee—good. Dark roast, no doubt. Do you have any, Betty? Pray, get me some, there's a good woman. And a cookie, I beg of you. A nice cookie or scone of some sort, if you please, there's a good lady."

As Betty quickly left the room to fetch some coffee, Doc asked if Professor Atroppasmirki had any idea as to the parchpyrus's meaning and possible origins, and the elderly scroll-scrounger got a strange and far-off look in his eye. For a minute he didn't speak and the others wondered if he might not have passed away while standing, or perhaps fallen under the control of some mysterious and arcane power imbued in the ancient artifact. But the faint release of gas and slight jump of his Adam's apple soon put them at ease.

"I have not yet had time to study it, of course, and I could really use that cookie. However, an uneducated guess, meaning a guess that has never gone to school or sat through an entire class, would seem to indicate some Mayonnasian influence, similar to the works of Aruserius or Manpan. Yet, there are also indications that might lead me to believe... No, it's too fantastic."

"What is it, Professor? Please go on, I implore you," implored Doc, who knew that the cookie would arrive soon and hog the man's attention for a bit.

But Professor Atroppasmirki was true to the scientist's most annoying science rule: proof. He went on to state that he would need to study it in detail before he could make any worthwhile determinations. Doc was aware of this, of course, and mentally cursed himself for falling into the trap of being like that kid at Christmas time who doesn't want to wait for the chimney to open. He would simply have to occupy himself with the other facets of the mystery (and, no doubt about it, this case was lousy with facets), while the venerable genius went about his work.

Doc offered to set his mentor up in his home lab, if he so liked, and Atroppasmirki was most agreeable, saying "yes" a whole bunch of times, finding his protégé's resources more than satisfactory.

Betty returned with a cookie and some coffee and, as
expected, the latter turned out to be for the Professor himself,
rather than the parchment. Soon, the dedicated elder statesman
of old statements was fully absorbed in the mysterious missive
and cookie, and the others quietly took their leave.

As the foursome reassembled in the living room,
though none of them had been taken apart, Betty remembered
dinner and rushed to the kitchen to get something out of the
oven. Lattis thought it seemed like there was always something
in the oven, and that it always had to come out of there.
Nevertheless, she followed, partly from that "Earth housewife
pressure" she was feeling, but also hoping against hope that
she might learn something this time.

It had grown dark outside, as days will do, except
indoors, and Doc started a fire in the fireplace, which he
famously referred to as "one of the few entirely acceptable
places for open flame in the house." As he poked and prodded
the logs and kindling like a trainer at a wood circus, he and
Kro-Bar began recapping their eventful trip and the bizarre
attacking rugmen and how they punched many of them. They
had just started pondering the role of the mysterious
Drydekker, when a cry cut through the night, like a knife
through living cheese. Doc knew that scream anywhere. It was
Professor Atroppasmirki.

In a flash, the two men burst into Doc's lab, prepared
for action. They were astonished to see that the room was
empty. The Professor had vanished.

Kro-Bar pointed to the open window like a man
who'd been doing it all his life. Doc shot a glance there and,
sure enough, the window was open. They reached it in time to
see the bottoms of two shoes moving through the grass:
Atroppasmirki was being dragged away.

With nary a thought, Doc vaulted through the window,
landing in the grass with the agile lightness of an indicted
congressman. His old friend was disappearing into the deep
shadows between two of those cursed globular hedges, though
it was too dark to see anything but a pair of soles. That was all
Doc needed. Without hesitation he leaped, landing in the grass

on his stomach, holding fast to the Professor's shoes to keep him from being dragged any farther.

Almost instantly, a startling sound filled the air: it was that queasy high-pitched gobbling Doc had heard before. As the younger scientist held on tight, a furious thrashing started in the hedges, and several pairs of glowing orbs popped on like tiny headlights: *the eyes of the gobbling hedge things.*

Whatever they were, they made a renewed effort to drag the unconscious Professor Atroppasmirki into whatever foul den the hellish hedges held. Doc matched the things, renewing his grip, which actually just meant he kept on gripping. But more eyes appeared as more gobblers joined in, and it was becoming a losing battle for the famed meteographer.

Suddenly, Kro-Bar was beside him. Like their pilgrim forefathers, they each took a leg and dug in. Though outnumbered by glow-eyed gobblers, the combination of earthling and Marvan proved more than a match. With a final squealing plaint, the unseen things released their elderly trophy and the bright orbs were no more.

Fortunately for all, the rest of the evening passed without further incident. The exhausted but unharmed Professor Atroppasmirki was put to bed in the Armstrong guest room, and Kro-Bar and Lattis went home shortly after, leaving Doc and Betty to relax on the sofa and enjoy the last of the fire. At one point, Betty noticed her husband staring into the glowing embers like naughty children he was unable to fathom. She was not surprised, as she too felt a lingering disturbance and unease at the night's strange events, particularly Doc's description of the noises the mysterious creatures made.

"Wait a second, Paul, don't turkeys gobble?" asked the housewife as she refilled her brandy.

"Yes Betty—something our pilgrim forefathers found out the hard way."

"Well, could it be that, inside those hedges, there's one of those turkey's baths we hear so much about?" puzzled the wife of a scientist.

"Oh no, that's Turkish bath, honey. That's an entirely different thing," said Doc, swirling his snifter as though it might make answers appear.

"You don't think they were turkeys at all, do you, Paul."

Her husband sipped brandy, then paused thoughtfully, the reflection of the embers seeming to dance like ideas on his smart face.

"Betty, you recall in the first *Adventure of the Lost Skeleton?* The curious incident of the cow in the night-time?"

Betty thought a moment. "But… that wasn't bossy."

"That was the curious incident," said Doc.

Though none heard it while they slept, that night there was a faint rumbling in Blendview.

Chapter 14

THE SQUARE ROOT OF PLANTS

The crisp sunlight of the following morning chased lingering shadows away like lost beatniks, and the day began with great promise. The Professor, invigorated by his sound sleep and close call with unknown creatures, attacked the parchpyrus with a vengeance usually reserved for Chinese food.

Doc seemed distracted as Betty buzzed around him with a blur of breakfast items, but this was par for the course when science was involved, which was every day.

The truth was, Doc was feeling like his handcuffs were tied, so to speak. Oh, he had the best man for the job with Professor Atroppasmirki studying the ancient markings, and that was fine. But Doc Armstrong himself needed to be active. He longed to be in the trenches, searching for clues, coming up with answers, making casual wisecracks about it, instead of sitting there having breakfast.

As if mind-reading his brain, Betty spoke up while replenishing his bacon and pouring him more coffee. "You know, darling, they say that breakfast is the most enjoyable meal of the day."

"What? Huh? Oh, I know, Betty, of course you're right. I just can't help but think I should be out doing something constantly, but, frankly, this case has me stumped. I don't know where to start beginning."

"Well, Dr. Paul Armstrong, wasn't it you who once told me: when in doubt, go to the *root* of the problem?" Betty looked at him with a twinkle in her eye that went straight to his brain with a ripe bouquet of 4th of July rocketworks.

"Betty, you astonishing little mink. You have done it again."

His wife just smiled as he guzzled coffee, kissed her and started for the door. "Root. The root. It's so simple it's obvious. I'll go and examine the roots of those mysterious round hedges."

Betty was wide-eyed. "Oh. I hadn't even thought of that."

But her brainy husband was already out the door.

Doc stood before the world that he once knew as his neighborhood. Was it possible? Hadn't he just seen it yesterday? How could he not have noticed how *overgrown* it had become? Could this have happened overnight?

The preeminent scientist who came before all the eminent ones slowly scanned the incredibly lush vegetation. If someone dumped a gigantic can of something called Super Plant Grow on Blendview it could not have had more astounding results. Trees were fuller, taller, grass as high as an aardvark's eye, bushes bursting with green, tangled lovingly in carefully matching vine. But it wasn't just that. The nature of the plant life was markedly different. There was an exotic flavor to the mix, as though some phantom importer had been busy all night.

And those hedges. Larger, even rounder, in their very round roundness, and more *of* them. There was a symmetry to their arrangement; a satisfying pattern that made one forget the unsavoriness that lay just beyond their physical perfection. This was no accident. This was planned. Only an aerial view could fully appreciate the extreme care that had been taken.

Doc pulled himself away from the almost hypnotic spell of the plant-ridden neighborhood and got to work. He began with the hedges from last night's attack, between which poor Professor Atroppasmirki was nearly engulfed. Like the others, they'd grown larger, and the effect was that they meshed even more, further corroborating Doc's fanciful image of some sort of natural gears.

Though he never had been before, Doc was now quite wary of things that gobble. But science was not for babies, so brashly into the hedges he went. As Doc crawled along, he noticed the sunlight seemed to have trouble getting down there, but then he remembered that everything makes shade. Sometimes the scientist's attention to detail can make them overlook the obvious.

If the creatures had come from underground, there was no evidence of it, no ground disturbed. Which begged the question: just where was Professor Atroppasmirki being dragged to? Doc observed the branches intertwining in an intricate manner that confirmed their machine-like nature, though they were clearly wood. Of course, reason told him that the only machines made out of wood were marionettes, and some very old cars.

And the roots. The roots had sharp angles, even forty-five degree angles. Squares and rectangles, where, for years, nature was content to go steady with the curve. The well-rounded scientist had never encountered nature this square.

Doc decided to take more samples. He had tested his previous samples early that morning by cleverly setting a plate of scones in the kitchen for Professor Atroppasmirki. The home lab wasn't big enough for the both of them. So far, he had discovered nothing unusual on a cellular level. Perhaps pieces of these square-hinged twigs would reveal something of interest.

The sample gathering came to a sudden halt when a faint rustling came to his attention. Doc's immediate thought was that the glow-eyed gobblers of the night were returning to drag him into whatever foul depths they had failed to drag the Professor. This time... he would be the *dragee*.

But Doc Armstrong was not about to sit there and find out. Like a wraith, only solid and alive and well-adjusted, the friendly neighborhood science man slipped quietly through the bushes towards the direction of the sound. Something was approaching, and he would meet it head-on, as opposed to waiting for it to meet *him* head-on. He would actually welcome it, as he welcomed all answers the unknown could provide. Perhaps even bring it a gift. The gift of confrontation.

He had not yet heard a single gobble, any hint that he might be in for a bowl of mock-turkey soup. The rustling was closer now and, though the hedges were taller, he still had to stoop somewhat to keep hidden.

Doc emerged into a gap at the center of four hedge balls, then slowly stood to get a look, finding himself face to face with Kro-Bar. His alien friend was haggard, staring, as though in a trance. A little ways behind him stood Lattis, also looking shell-shocked.

Betty brought a tray of tea and pebble blankets into the living room, setting it down before the still dazed alien couple. They had barely touched the ink-cakes and other snacks already sitting there, though Kro-Bar did have a cheese nelson in his hand. The considerate Betty remembered he was a sucker for those. The hot tea was a welcome stimulant for the pair, and soon Kro-Bar began to relate their eventful morning.

It had started like any other, with the Marvan couple, in their matching purple sweatpants and sweatshirts with shoulder fins, taking their daily stroll around the normally quaint streets of Blendview. They called it their *earthwalk,* and they found it worked as a daily reorientation of where they were and what they were doing, as well as a chance to "pat things on the head," as Lattis called it. They made it a point to greet everyone they saw, though Kro-Bar did this perhaps a bit too loudly. Lattis was always ready with compliments for their neighbors, and if she praised such unexpected and diverse things as ankles, rakes, earlobes, handkerchiefs, nostrils and cuffs, at least her intentions were good.

Up until now, the closest thing to an "incident" would have to have been the time they used the transmutatron to turn a barking dog (Pilfy, the Webson's purebred pintagel) into a large oyster, though they managed to turn it back before anyone was the wiser. Since then, Kro-Bar left the device at home, as Lattis had always advised.

But this day, the alien couple was greeted, as Paul had been, by the startling sight of an overabundance of green. At first they took it in stride, trying to recall if this was a typical Earth idiosyncrasy they had simply forgotten about, like skiing or gargling.

"Wait. Could this be that leap year we were warned of, my husband?" asked Lattis.

"I think not, My Lattis. As I recall, that was merely an extra day. It came with no additional plants."

As they strolled through the strangeness of the neighborhood, their usual vim and vigor seemed to drain. And the more they saw, the less they liked. Not only that, it was quiet. Too quiet. Too silently quiet.

After a couple of blocks they knew there was something seriously wrong. No dogs, no kids, no milkman or postman or pineappleman. Not a single person had left a single house, not a car gone by. Could the tally of missing neighbors, gathered only yesterday by Betty and Lattis, have gone up already? It was like Anky and everyone else who was left had vanished overnight. Up until now, they had only seen everyone vanish overnight on Jeldor, the fourth moon of Syppitus, but that ended up being a practical joke. There was nothing remotely funny about this, even by primitive Earth humor standards, though Kro-Bar *had* tried laughing and pointing at some of the wilder vegetation when they first started out; something that almost immediately annoyed his wife.

They began to knock on doors to see if everyone was simply in bed with a cold (an Earth pastime Kro-Bar had told Lattis about). But door after door after door remained unanswered. After their twenty-seventh doorbell, Kro-Bar turned calmly to Lattis and screamed in her face.

A bit of calming down was in order and Lattis used her usual chin hold, in which she calmly held her husband's chin between her thumb and forefinger and he immediate;y stopped. It never failed.

They resorted to peeking in windows, something they would normally never do, as it was universally abhorred by earthlings, except for Mr. Cusper who lived by himself. No sign of a single neighbor did they see. It was as if neighbors didn't exist and they had landed on a planet of no-neighbors where even the idea of neighbors didn't exist, or had not been invented yet. The rooms they could see showed no signs of foul play or distress of any kind, just like that ship they'd read about in Earth history, the Mary Celeste, which had been found empty with perfectly fine dinners wasted—a fact that stuck in Lattis's craw, knowing full well the hellish trouble someone had gone to.

They were peeping in what must have been their seventh house, when Kro-Bar noticed a large round shape in a doorway, backlit by the bright sunny kitchen beyond. "I do not recall the Mebblesons having a hanging doorway disk," he commented.

Lattis left the window she'd been staring through and joined Kro-Bar at his. "What is a hanging doorway disk, my husband?"

"Obviously, it's a very inconveniently conceived decorative piece, hung in a doorway so one can admire it even as they constantly bump their head walking by it," countered her Marvan mate.

"That does not sound anything like a thing that *is,* Kro-Bar," scoffed his wife as she tried to see what he was looking at.

"Then how in the third planet do you explain that, my love? That right there?" he added snippily.

Both now observed the large round silhouetted shape, about the size of a two foot doorknob. Just as Lattis was about to attempt to explain it, the shape moved. In fact it turned and faced them. With eyes. That looked right at them.

Kro-Bar and Lattis jumped back as though poleaxed by a very soft poleax that did not split them open and smash their brains, but certainly pushed them back.

Instantly recognizing it as the biscuit-noggined phantom, the alien couple bolted down the street as soon its eyes rested on them. As always, when unexpectedly alarmed, they ran in the Marvan manner of both arms straight up in the air, palms forward; a habit that seemed the aerodynamic antithesis of a certain desired speed, though even Marvans admitted it was more instinctual than practical.

But on this morning there was no one around to witness their strange run, let alone laugh and point, as the pair ran blindly down streets they no longer recognized. The sight of the apparition in shadow, with its head of macaroon, had been the nightmarish capper to a less than relaxing constitutional.

They did not look back as they ran, but the abnormal stillness that had fallen upon Blendview made every sound louder, and they could hear the steady shoes of the cookie man in pursuit: a pair of Klelbins, and well kept, if Lattis was to be any judge. One thing the Marvan woman *had* taken to was shopping, like a chimp to expressionism.

By the time they approached the Armstrong house they no longer heard the steady clickety-clack of Klelbins. There was once again no sound at all in the deathly still neighborhood.

Doc and Betty took in the story like a couple purchasing their first lawnmower. In other words, they were speechless. Then Doc spoke, no longer speechless. "You've obviously had a very trying ordeal, both of you. I want you to know that Earth isn't always like this. Lost Skeletons, gobbling hedges and cookie men: that's just not normal. I guess what I'm saying is, I don't want you to let these recent horrors color your opinion and give you the wrong impression." He smiled, that ingratiating half-smile. "We're really a fine race, once you get to know us. And Blendview is usually a very safe community."

Doc paused for a sip of tea. Kro-Bar and Lattis looked only slightly convinced.

Their science friend went on. "I don't have answers at this point. I usually do have answers at this point, but I... just don't have them right now at this point. But I want you to know, I hope to have answers at this point, very very soon. Just bear with me, if you will." He smiled again. "Sometimes it does seem like science, good old science, moves slower than a batter full of egg pillows. Has to, of course, or we'd all run willy-nilly into the future." Doc paused wisely. "We have to have those checks and balances, those strict conditions, those tests and results and conclusions that make everything we do really really correct. So correct, there's little room for uncorrectness."

Betty, eyes gleaming with pride for the man she loved, wasn't even aware of the steady parade of pebble blankets passing her lips. Kro-Bar and Lattis looked somewhat renewed. They were about to dive into the snacks when Doc spoke again, chipperly.

"Speaking of which, what say we all check in with Professor Atroppasmirki and see what he's come up with?"

And so, at the reasonable suggestion, the foursome made their way to Doc's home lab, but not before the Marvans grabbed a couple of cheese nelsons. They found the venerable but amiable but likable scientist hunkered over the parchpyrus like a water buffalo at a candy counter. He perked up when he heard them.

"Ah, come in, come in, please, I suggest of you. Your timing is quite perspicacious, quite perspicacious indeed."

Doc grinned. "I'm going to take a wild guess that you've discovered some things heretofore unknown, Professor Atroppasmirki." he hinted, in a manner that sounded more than intelligent.

"Oh, I have, I have indeed, dear boy," enthused the aging parch-hound. "Here, please, gather round, watch, witness, wonder—"

"Wait, what?" sputtered Lattis at what proved to be too much to do at once, even for a Marvan.

Doc, Betty, Kro-Bar and Lattis surrounded the scientist, and his dried flat subject, like wagons circling a corpse just before the kill. It was plain he'd made some headway, and excitement filled the air like a veritable cloud of the popcorn of hope.

"Now, see here. Heed. This—you see?"

"Professor Atroppasmirki, please, we know you're excited, but please, try to remain calm. There's enough for everybody to learn about, I'm sure," offered Betty, in that same soothing, practical way she'd used on many a car salesman.

"Yes. There's too much sputtering," added Lattis.

As the Professor spoke, his audience began to see the parchpyrus take on a whole new look, almost as if the very understanding of it caused shapes to move and interconnect. Of course, it was all in the mind. Someone ancient had really known what he was doing. For once.

"This, my friends, and newfound acquaintances, is a schematic. A very old one, grant you. Ancient, wrinkled, faded, in terrible shape, but a schematic none the less. What we have here are plans for a great and terrible mechanism. A mechanism that may still exist, in the present day, which is now."

Betty, Kro-Bar and Lattis gasped audibly and looked at each other, each taking turns so that everyone had a chance to look at the other.

"The mechanism not only exists, Professor," uttered Doc. "The mechanism is Blendview."

Chapter 15

THE HIGH-RISE OF GULLER MOBIAN

Doc's words dropped like walruses onto the necks of his listeners. Betty, Kro-Bar, Lattis and the Professor gasped audibly and looked at each other, each taking turns so that everyone had a chance to look at the other. It all sounded fantastic. And yet here it was, whatever it was, right in front of them, something anyway. Each of the large round hedges was indicated in the drawing: the wheels or gears of a vast machine of nature, multiplied, carefully groomed, rounded off for optimum efficiency, exactly as indicated on the ancient and mysterious diagram they now soaked up, because of some spilt tea.

"Professor, you have no idea how relieved I am," continued Doc. "With your specialized knowledge you have backed up and confirmed my very suspicions which I had conjectured in my own head, but dared not say without the further proof I needed to be able to say, with utter certainty, what you just got through saying, and I capped off."

The Professor took off his tiny spectacles, both sets, and looked at his protege with the weary eyes of a long distance operator. "You… knew this the whole time?"

"I was pretty sure," beamed Doc.

"You might have said something."

"I couldn't be positive."

Still, I might have known what to look for—"

"You needed to be impartial. You were my control."

"I'm an old man, you know—"

"I knew you could do it," praised Doc, slapping his mentor on the back as he was putting his specs back on, sending them flying. "My friends, there is something serious going on in Blendview. Something 'history book' serious, in that dull and important manner of all truly important things. Our little community has shouldered this burden long enough. I think it's high time we brought the authorities in on this."

No sooner had the action-scientist said "high time" and "authorities," and no sooner had Kro-Bar and Lattis started wondering what those things were, than, like a gift from a football team owner, the doorbell rang.

Leaving the weary Professor to a much-earned lie-down in the guest room, the two couples were elated to see City Brad and two of his uniformed police officers, Jaxhart and Michaelskin, standing in the doorway. Kro-Bar and Lattis looked less elated, but that was only because they'd had a trying morning and still had a ways to go before reaching elation.

It turned out City Brad had not been idle either, except for breakfast. He had done some further checking on the Sta-Mor-Down Rug Company and found out an interesting bit of tid. Turned out the company was owned by none other than that notorious and reclusive millionaire, Guller Mobian. This elicited yet more gasps from the listeners, except Kro-Bar's, which was more of a breathy hoot. It was a morning for gasping.

What was more, missing persons reports were now prevalent enough that they warranted some serious investigating, plus two more guys, Jaxhart and Michaelskin, which City Brad thought was neat.

It was immediately decided that Doc and City Brad would drive to Mobian Towers, try to get an audience with the rich recluse and find out what he knows. Meantime, Jaxhart and Michaelskin would poke around the neighborhood, with a special eye out for anything cookie-headed or gobbling. Kro-Bar and Lattis were particularly intrigued by their "special eyes," but thought they'd wait till they knew the officers better before asking to see them. City Brad also told his men to confront any landscaping trucks, but to exercise extreme caution as "these were no ordinary landscapers."

Doc asked Betty, Kro-Bar and Lattis to stay at the Armstrong house and keep an eye on the Professor, whose further work on the parchpyrus at this point was vital. Turned out they didn't need any coaxing to stay put, given all that was happening, and all three made jokes about "taking strolls" and "playing in the yard" and "merrily gathering blueberries" with a definite eye on Sister Irony. They followed that up by explaining that absolutely none of them intended to do anything *even remotely* like what they were suggesting, which tended to undercut the effect of the previous irony. At any rate, they were more than happy to stay inside with the doors locked. There was little comfort these days in taking a stroll through an enormous hedge mechanism.

Between the Blendview neighborhood and downtown Viewton was a modest commercial district, mostly the smaller shops. Doc and City Brad had only just entered this area when Mobian Towers came into view. Not surprising, since, at twelve stories, it was easily the highest building in the little city, made even taller by the high radio antenna on its roof. There was actually only one tower, one single high-rise, such as it was. Reportedly, Mobian thought the plural sounded better without the added expense of actually building a second one. Over eighty percent of those once polled by the Mobian Corporation believed they had seen a second tower, giving rise to the phrase "the tower of suggestion."

City Brad found parking on the building's own block, and he and Doc walked towards the relatively impressive structure. City had wanted to blast the siren on the way down, saying it was something "you just have to hear," but Doc cautioned against, favoring the "low key" element instead, to which his police friend begrudgingly agreed.

In truth, they had no idea to what extent Mobian or his company were involved, if at all. They might simply be unwitting dupes, which were the worst kind of dupes. If the millionaire was part of it, there was little doubt he would make a formidable enemy, given his almost infinite resources. But at this point it was hard to fathom how a reclusive millionaire could be tied in with an ancient Earth-mechanism of apparently natural origin.

Doc and City Brad entered the crisp clean office building and proceeded right to the guard at the security desk. Usually there were people coming and going, recalled Doc, but now the lobby was empty. Hardly what you'd expect of Viewton's largest, and only, skyscraper. City Brad flashed his badge like a man proud of the shiny things in life. The guard picked up the phone and spoke briefly, telling someone that the police where here to see Mr. Mobian, as well as some scientist. He hung up and directed the pair towards one of two elevators, instructing them to please go straight to the penthouse.

Doc and City Brad entered one of the elevators, the doors closed, and they were soon speeding to the top, like two men in a box on the way to the sky. Doc marveled at the smoothness and speed of the machine, appreciating how far Old Man Technology had come in just the few short years since the invention of what he liked to call the "vertical raising chamber." As they neared the top, Doc thought: just think, there was a time this would have taken two days.

The elevator came to a stop and the doors opened, revealing a pristine but rather cold antechamber. No one was at the reception desk.

As Doc and City Brad warily approached, an office door opened up and, to the scientist's surprise, in walked Mr. Clyme Drydekker. The toupee company manager smiled.

"Well, if it isn't Mr. Bark Bowle, or should I say, *Dr. Paul Armstrong?* How's your friend Loanna Mars doing?"

Doc could not have been more shocked if you'd bowled him over with a tree surgeon. "Drydekker. You've got a nerve showing your face, or any part of you. I'm here with a friend of mine, City Brad, an actual police detective friend of mine with an actual badge."

"I suppose you're going to try and tell us you were attacked by mentally-controlled rugmen at my toupee company." Drydekker's laugh was both abrasive and cutting.

"If that didn't happen how did you know he was going to say that?" asked City Brad, immediately showing why he was a member of the police force.

The triumph on Drydekker's face faded at the grim realization, until it became an ugly scowl. "So. You *are* a police detective aren't, Mr. Deductive Reasoning? Well, it will do you no good. It's his word, and his friend's, against mine and forty mind-controlled rugmen. Just what is it you want here anyway?"

Doc had never heard such acid bitterness in Drydekker's voice, even though he'd known the man for a day. "We're here to see Mr. Guller Mobian. And while I might be just a civilian, though a particularly resourceful one, City Brad is with the police and can easily go get a warrant if he so desires."

"Well, actually—" City Brad began uncertainly.

"Unless you don't want Mr. Mobian to know what's been going on at his hairpiece concern," added the intrepid scientist coyly.

"Alright. You can see him. I warn you, Mr. Mobian is not in the best of health." And with that, the newly unpleasant Drydekker went back through the door he came in. And with that, Doc and City Brad followed through that same door.

The spacious inner office was just as chilly looking as the outer one. Rather than a desk of some sort or a liquor cabinet as one would expect, the single dominant feature was a large bed surrounded by an opaque curtain. Sliding glass doors provided much light and led to a wraparound penthouse balcony. Drydekker turned to them, attempting to summon some of the charm he oozed earlier, though not in a disgusting way.

"You will have to forgive Mr. Mobian. He has been bedridden for quite some time now, in his bed. He must also avoid an excess of light and too much air, thus the thick and powerful bed curtain." And with that, the rugmen wrangler lifted a microphone by the side of the bed and spoke into it. "Mr. Mobian. Mr. Mobian, sir, I am sorry to disturb you but there are two gentlemen here to see you, including one I've met before who may say some bad things about me that are lies."

"Hey, you cut that out," protested Doc, restrained by his police friend. The scientist calmed somewhat and addressed the bed. "Mr. Mobian, we're sorry to disturb you in your time of being in bed but this is important. Your company, Sta-Mor-Down, and its subsidiary, Cottisill Landscaping and Loan, are mixed up in some disturbing business that has to do with a lot of strange occurrences in the Blendview neighborhood I call home. I can tell you for a fact that your man Drydekker here is in it right up to his hairy toupee."

Doc waited a moment, wondering if his words were even making it through.

"I assure you, gentlemen," assured Drydekker, "he can hear you. It takes a moment for him to respond using the special bed loudspeaker he had installed for just such a purpose."

Sure enough, true to Drydekker's unpleasantly delivered words, a voice emerged from the bed curtain. A voice seemingly aided by electronic amplification, possibly to compensate for the invalid's general lethargy. The effect was unnerving, giving the poor man a tinny and unreal sound, like the mechanical clown that takes one's money at a carnival, though the similarity was probably not intentional.

"What you are saying... Dr. Armstrong... is certainly news to me... I assure you I know of no such unusual activity taking place at any of my various successful companies. And if I did, I would certainly not allow it to go on. In fact, I would stop anything like that right in its tracks. If it was walking. Even if it wasn't walking. And had no tracks. In which case, I don't know how it would get around. But I have long been against bad things of any kind, particularly really bad things. Those are the worst. I hate those. Anyway... Oh yes, well I want to thank you from the bottom of my probably very weak heart—you'll forgive me, I do ail so—for bringing this terrible inconvenience to my attention. As a compensation, though I know nothing can really take away the hurt—people can be so cruel—I would like very much to invite you and your lovely wife on a little trip, all expenses paid, to some far-off attractive vacation spot where you've always wanted to go. You name it. Don't be shy. And please don't think I'm trying to buy you off, or get you out of the way, because that is not the case at all, no siree, Bob, and don't think I'm calling you "Bob" cause I'm not. It's just an expression, and where *that* one came from is *anybody's* guess, funny old world. I know you're Dr. Paul Armstrong and not at all Bob, or anyone like Bob, whoever *that* troublesome person is. Anyway. I hope that I've been able to answer even some of the many questions you good people must have, and I so appreciate you're taking time from your busy science day to stop by and tell me all this. I know it couldn't have been easy—thank heavens for elevators though. These blamed twelfth floors, eh? Anyway, it's been delightful. Thanks again, and I hope you'll come back soon. Don't forget to take a complimentary toupee of your choice on the way out, compliments of me, and make sure you specify your size and roundness. Thanks again and take care. So tired, think I'll nap."

And with that the verbose and tinny millionaire began some metallic snoring. Doc and City Brad exchanged a mystified glance.

"Well, he's friendlier than I thought he'd be," offered City.

Drydekker stepped towards the door, ready to usher them out. "Now, gentlemen, if you are quite satisfied, I fear Mr. Mobian is quite tired from his long speech to you, wasn't that wonderful, and if you would be on your way, perhaps he can acquire some much needed rest. And let's get that vacation set up for you."

But Doc had his suspicions. Before Drydekker could stop him, with the boldness of a Viking picking up a pillaged waitress, the man of science stormed the bed and ripped aside the curtain.

There, where there should have been a sleeping person, was a mechanism of some sort, complete with speaker and tape recorder. Though there was a horrible toupee on top of it, this lame attempt was not fooling anybody.

"Guller Mobian... is a machine!" cried City Brad, aghast.

"I don't think so, City Brad. *There* is Guller Mobian." Doc pointed dramatically to the person in the room who wasn't City Brad: Clyme Drydekker. Startled, the man started backing away.

"How did you guess?" hissed the backing away man.

"You had not introduced us, yet the tinny voice behind the bed curtain knew I was Dr. Paul Armstrong, which meant that you had anticipated my visit and recorded the recording accordingly. Plus the tinny part I mentioned."

City Brad stepped forward, quickly producing a pair of handcuffs, probably from some spare parts he had. "Mr. Mobian, you are under arrest."

"On what charges?" sneered the under arrest man.

"Faking a recording and pretending it's a real person is a felony," said the policeman as he slapped a cuff on Guller Mobian's nearest wrist. "And if that's not true, I'll find some other charges. We can be very creative. Come along with you."

What happened next was so hard to believe that for a long time afterwards both men swore they didn't believe it, even though they did. As City Brad started to walk off, tugging his prisoner's wrist, a door opened up in Drydekker's suit, just about the torso area, and a small man stepped out and onto the bed. And the head formerly known as Drydekker detached with it. In fact, Mobian's head was the only thing that had been real about the man. Of course, that normal-sized head now looked abnormally large on a body that was about the size of a spider monkey. The small, wiry torso was dressed in casual shirt and slacks that might have been doll clothes. Without a word, the little large-headed fellow sprinted lightly to a wall switch as though weightless.

"How is that possible, what we're now seeing?! Assuming you are also!" blurted a surprised and uncomfortable City Brad.

"That suited dummy is *lousy* with mechanisms," observed Doc, referring to the abandoned Drydekker body that just stood there. "A walking automaton of some sort that this little fellow jockeys around in."

The miniature man with the big head was furious, and he expressed it in no uncertain terms, not to mention a voice that was shriller, more nasal, than his Drydekker voice. "No one has seen the real Guller Mobian and lived! I will need a little assist from some friends of yours, Dr. Armstrong." Mobian reached for the switch beside him and pulled it. Two doors opened up, and a steady flow of slow moving, all-too-familiar rugmen began to file in.

"Those are no friends of mine, Mobian, but why do I have a feeling you knew that and were rubbing it in sarcastically?" spat Doc as he and his pal backed away. The relentless stream of dark suits and tasteless toupees circled them, and Doc and City exchanged a glance, nodding in silent agreement. This signaled a ploy they'd used once before: a deceptive move, based partly on pat-a-cake, partly on hopscotch. The very childish nature of these elements added a surprise factor that tended to put adversaries off their guard. Unfortunately, in mere seconds, each realized they could not exactly remember the moves so, with more silent agreement, they simply started punching.

City Brad, remembering he was still handcuffed to Mobian's empty automaton body, made the most of it by swinging it into their attackers left and right.

Doc, on the other hand, was using what he liked to call his *science punch*. Whenever colleagues asked him about it he always shrugged and gave the same answer: "It's just a punch with no obvious solution. In other words, it's really hard." Some chuckled, getting it right away, while others looked askance. Still others simply rolled their eyes or other things that were handy.

But none questioned it. Who were they to say how one should or shouldn't go about slugging the unknown? And any in doubt about *that* little bombshell could just look up Glantzenburk's First Principal of Myopia.

But Doc had no time to ponder this right now. Readying two pipe-like arms, fists clenched like rocky rabbits, he waded into the mass of mindless rug-bearing toughs.

"Say goodbye to your Aunt Consciousness," came the familiar stinging barb as another two toupee-toppers toppled.

City Brad managed to unlock his cuffs in a fleeting moment of non-punching, and now he and Doc were back to back, slugging rugmen as fast as they came.

"Go ahead. Continue your constant slugging," bleated Guller Mobian, standing atop the bed, directing his minions. "I have an almost endless supply of my rugman army as I like to call them. You will wear out long before they do, I assure you!"

If there was one thing Doc hated it was being assured. Nevertheless, the noted wrangler of radioactive rocks persevered, coming up with science punch variations even *he* didn't know he had. It was evident before that the rugmen were not skilled pugilistically, instead depending on the broad sweep of a heavy arm, or your general clutching and grabbing that could really get annoying.

And yet, despite renewed efforts on the part of the two punchermen, the endless tide of striped tie-bearing onslaughters just kept on coming, adding sheer numbers to their list of "things to be proud of." Soon Doc and City Brad found themselves side by side, being backed towards the open doors of the balcony.

Fearing the heroes might actually get away, Guller piped over the fray, "Give yourselves up and I promise to let you in on all my plans!"

"You'll never let me in, Mobian!" returned a defiant Doc, though City Brad was weighing the benefits of such an offer. They were now outside on the balcony.

"Which way?" yelled City Brad above the din of punching people.

"Right!" Doc returned with a sharp holler.

"Yours or mine?" barked the slowly backing policeman.

"We're on the same side!" yelled his scientist friend.

Realizing his spatial error, City Brad bolted with Doc, and the two made a mad dash towards one of the corners of the high-rise balcony.

The hairpiece army moved slowly, and the heroes quickly put space between them. "Now to find another way down," said Doc as they neared the corner. City Brad tried a window, then another, finding them tightly locked.

"Let's try the other side," urged Doc Armstrong with the confidence of a man who'd gone around corners before. They were about to do just that when from around the bend lurched another gaggle of follicly-challenged goons. They were a ghastly sight against a darkening, lowering sky: matted toupees untouched by human comb, eyes glazed, ties horribly striped, living only to come at things slowly.

Surrounded on either side of the balcony, City Brad looked over at the twelve story drop below. "It's a long way down, Doc. Too long to jump," acknowledged the detective.

"When you can't go down..." said the scientist, looking up at the roof. City Brad waited a moment for his friend to finish the sentence, then realized he wasn't going to because he almost didn't need to. He quickly gave Doc a boost, and the crackerjack scientist was able to grab hold of a corbel or cornice or one of those parts of a roof that one can grab. He reached down and hoisted City Brad up, just as the two tides of rugmen slammed together in the middle of the balcony.

The duo found themselves on a flat roof with radio tower, stair or elevator housing and the usual fans and ducts that make tall building rooftops beloved of millions. They immediately ran across to the other side and looked down.

City Brad grinned. "No bad hair in sight."

"Not even a cowlick," returned Doc with a smirk. They had a bit of a chuckle, but both realized they could just as easily have a chuckle reminiscing later, when stopping and chuckling wouldn't endanger their lives.

"Shall we?" asked Doc, knowing full well he needn't have. Both men jumped down to the balcony below. As fortune would have it there was a sliding door right there.

Finding it unlocked, Doc started to slide it open, but it proved to be sticking. As he worked on it, a particularly large rugman, possibly a stray, stumbled up and grabbed City Brad from behind. The policeman barked protest, just as Doc managed to slide the door another inch, wondering where the bark had come from.

Struggling to get loose, City Brad slammed his attacker back against the balustrade. The rugman now tried to drag the policeman over the side, and Doc left the stuck door to help his friend. Before he could get there, City Brad pushed off of his attacker, freeing him from his grip. The rugman stumbled backwards over the balustrade, dropping with an eerie silence into the chasm of the street below.

Doc helped City Brad up and the two looked over the side at the regrettable, yet unavoidable, fate of the Mobian minion, each wondering where the miniature millionaire recruited his pathetically-pieced army.

Hearing the shuffle of others approaching, the two finished opening the stuck door together, ducked inside and slid it shut. Finding themselves in what appeared to be an empty office, it was little effort to find the hallway and, from there, the hallway's bosom buddy, the emergency stairs. Knowing full well they were only to be used in the case of an emergency, Detective City Brad made it official by declaring it an emergency, and the pair soon clattered down the stairs pursued only by the echo of their own clattering down the stairs.

Once outside, Doc and City Brad made a beeline for the car and then followed it. Sure enough it led right to the car.

The dutiful detective was quickly on his radio, calling for help. But after several attempts it became chillingly evident there was none to be found: police headquarters was not answering. Scientist and cop exchanged a grim look. It was then they became aware of the streets around them. For the heart of downtown Viewton was quiet as dark clouds continued to roll in. In fact it was downright desolate.

Before they could exchange more grim glances, City Brad's radio squawked. It was Officer Jaxhart. His voice was broken up, like something was interfering with the transmission, or maybe it was something he had eaten.

"— tective—... read me? This is—"

"Jaxhart? Is that you? I read you, over."

"Officer Michaelskin... gone ... took him. Don't—"

"Jaxhart?... Jaxhart?" City Brad, still holding the mic, turned to Doc Armstrong. "Do you know any of those police numbers? I haven't had a chance to learn those."

"I know ten-four," said Doc.

"Ten-four! Ten-four!... Oh, it's no use. No one's answering at headquarters and I'm fearing the worst, which I hate. Doc... I think we're on our own."

"That's not necessarily true," spoke the science man evenly, as the wheels in his brain turned like mindwheels.

Chapter 16

GENERAL SCOTTMANSON HAS A SNOOTFUL

The general was covered in fruit salad. Literally. Oh, he was well decorated, no doubt about that, and deservedly so; those medals were hard-earned. But lunch at his desk, lunch that had once seemed like such a good idea, had not worked out. Not on this particular day. And certainly not with that rather unwieldy bowl of rather delicious fruit salad. The one he now wore, and attempted to dab in vain off his nice general's tunic with a handkerchief. Not exactly the kind of thing he needed to be doing after receiving an urgent call from his friend Dr. Paul Armstrong, the eminent scientist.

General Scottmanson had grown fond of Doc and his wife Betty since the high-ranking military officer had sent government agent Reet Pappin to flush the scientist out from the depths of the Amazon, resulting in the tragic death of the latter by way of jungle monster—a terrible and unforeseen mishap for sure, and only the fourth such in the Scottmanson's career. The General's role had been vital in the ensuing series of events collectively referred to in military annals as The Living Skeleton Incident. Since then, his friendship with the

Armstrongs had grown steadily and included his wife Murtha, an amateur beekeeper.

The call from his friend came when the General was buried knee deep in concerns over the arms race. He had to admit the term "arms race" was no little cause for amusement for the much-honored officer. No matter what the circumstance, no matter where he was, including high level briefings, that term was destined to send him into gales of uncontrollable laughter. He couldn't help it. It always conjured the same picture: two disembodied arms, complete with sleeves and cuffs, crawling desperately towards a finish line. Maybe that's good for us, he thought. An image like that to point up the absurdity of man's shameless propensity for self-destruction.

Certainly preferable to the sight of those huge ugly bombs that could wipe out all living things, the technology of which grew increasingly more terrifying each day. The latest, the fureon bomb, was capable of wiping out all life on Earth so neatly and precisely that it cleaned all the rooms and buildings afterwards, swept the streets and actually put away dishes. He and Doc Armstrong shared a profoundly mixed sentiment about the birthing of such annihilative fruit from a mother they both loved and respected: Mother Science. It was part of the reason Armstrong had started developing his anti-bomb bomb, though the General made a note to himself to try and convince Doc to come up with a less adorable name.

At any rate, the many-starred officer was not the least apologetic about falling into paroxysms of laughter at the sound of the term "arms race," sometimes up to two hours, until his secretary or the president had to shake him. If ever the world needed a laugh…

Doc had sounded serious on the phone, getting that grave tone in his voice like when he talked about mastodons. The General knew it was not like him to call so urgently if he wasn't sure of all his facts, or at least a whole lot of them. This Blendview neighborhood had certainly had more than its share of troubles, he thought, thinking again back to the Living Skeleton Incident. And the shorthand of facts the scientist had rattled off for him on the phone, even without going into detail, had sounded strange and mysterious and serious enough to act upon without hesitation, except for that little bit of hesitation that was expected of all top brass.

But General Scottmanson was never a man to lollygag, even in military school when some of the other guys were lollygagging. When it came down to action or lollygagging he always opted for the action part. Leave the lollygagging to Congress. And maybe himself, just a little, after all the hard work was done and recreational lollygagging became more acceptable.

So, without further lollygagging, he was just about to assign one of his best men to head to Blendview and look into the mystery when, oddly enough, his secretary buzzed to tell him that General Roostus Krayper was there to see him. Scottmanson smiled. He knew Roostus well—the two men went way back together, almost tripping at one point.

Krayper entered with his usual cheerful bluster and gung-ho swagger. Barely forty-three, the man was one of the younger generals, and it showed in his brisk youthful persona, plus the aforementioned bluster and swagger. It was even rumored he still played tag. It seemed a natural to call him "Rooster" or "the Rooster." But no one ever did.

"How are you, you old warhouse?" he barked, after the prerequisite salute just for old times' sake.

"Fine, Roostus, just fine," beamed Scottmanson, shaking his hand, though it hadn't been offered. "Let's see, how long has it been?"

"I think it was that charity dinner for the Reet Pappin Victims of Monsters Fund wasn't it?"

"Last week—you're right. You look great. The days have been kind to you." General Scottmanson waved his visitor to a seat and poured drinks and the two got down to brass tacks.

"I'm willing to wager I just read your mind, Scotty," grinned Krayper slyly as he downed his schnapps.

"Wouldn't be the last time," chuckled Scottmanson. "What's on your mind? Or should I say, what's on *my* mind?"

Roostus watched his glass being refilled, smiling coyly like he was waiting to drop a bombshell, but not the bad kind. "Little place called Blendview, if you want to know."

Scottmanson perked up. "How in Hannibal's crushing Alps did you know about that? I only just got a phone call myself."

Roostus Krayper threw back his head and laughed, long and hard, until Scottmanson feared for his sanity.

"Let's just say I've had my suspicions for a little while," uttered the visitor, lightly touching the tip of his nose twice for effect—a move Scottmanson had never understood. "Thanks to something that some folks have accused me of lacking on occasion: military intelligence."

Now it was General Scottmanson's turn to chuckle heartily. "You, Roostus? Never. In fact, I'd say when it comes to generaling you're almost as smart as me. But tell me, why do you have operatives in Blendview?"

"I don't. And you'll forgive me for being a bit… covert, if I may. Not *in* Blendview per se, but my operatives know a little something of what's happening there through sources, the very existence of which, I would have to immediately disavow if I ever even avowed them. Scotty, there are certain things going on right now that I'm not at liberty to divulge. Even to you, old friend."

"But… I have clearance. Really impressive high-up clearance." Scottmanson looked hurt, like a kid in a pickup game picked on for not being picked. In fact, it was because of those games he *became* a general.

"Now now, all will be explained, Scotty. You know it's always for the better when nobody knows anything. I *still* don't know about that whole *bay* thing."

General Scottmanson had never been fond of compartmentalization, or that bay thing. It was stuff like that that led to CIA guys drugging each other's water coolers.

"I take it you want my greedy little hands off of this one, eh, Roost?" he said, refilling Krayper's schnapps a sixth time.

"For the time being. You know how it is," grinned the younger man as he downed another glass.

"You do realize that I outrank you?" offhanded the proud owner of one extra star.

"No, I think I outrank you, actually," said Roostus Krayper extending his glass for more, like a sideshow barker reaching for a fresh chicken.

"Have you counted the stars lately?" asked Scottmanson as he poured.

"Only at night. They don't just go by that now, buddy boy. I have higher clearance because of some stuff that I did."

"I don't think you do," said Scotty, his dander now up a bit. This went on for fifteen more minutes until the bottle drained. Scottmanson finally let it go, realizing it just wasn't worth it. He knew his own value, and he wasn't about to ruin a longtime friendship over whose swagger stick was bigger. Besides, Krayper was a capable officer. Blendview was in good hands.

"Look, I'll keep you posted, Scotty, how's that? I know you have good friends there. And I know you've always enjoyed being kept posted on stuff. You know, when I keep you posted?"

"I love being kept posted. Always been fond of that. It's almost a hobby sometimes," admitted Scottmanson lightly.

With that, the two men rose and shook hands, saluted and shook hands again, and General Roostus Krayper was out the door, one empty schnapps bottle later. At which point General Scottmanson took a nap.

Chapter 17

THE KRO-BAR HOME SECURITY SYSTEM

As soon as Dr. Paul Armstrong and Detective City Brad had left to check out Guller Mobian's involvement, and police officers Jaxhart and Michaelskin went out to scout the neighborhood, Kro-Bar had taken charge of protecting the Armstrong household. This now consisted of Betty, Lattis, Professor Atroppasmirki and himself. He was not elected, or even suggested. It was simply understood. By him. Something he took upon himself, given his natural inclination for organization or at least his own firm belief therein. He seemed right at home.

Kro-Bar was never more "space alien" than when he took on an important task. His demeanor at times like this toyed with the boundaries of overbearing, but never quite tipped over into arrogance because his confidence was so darn charming somehow. If he wasn't certain about something he proceeded to look even more confident, thus instilling others with a confidence they never realized might be lacking in the man himself. Eventually, their confidence in his confidence would inspire him to a solution. For Kro-Bar, leadership was seventy-three percent appearance.

Not that he didn't know what he was doing. He trusted the instincts natural to an advanced race. Marvans were battening down the hatches eons before Earth people hammered their first cave door.

He began by having all the windows closed, something Betty felt was fairly obvious but didn't say anything. He then had them locked; something she also probably would have done on her own. From there, however, everything diverted, at least from what Betty might have dreamed up.

Weapons were not just fire pokers or kitchen cutlery. Every pen and pencil they could lay their hands on was stuck into a pocket or belt. Kro-Bar explained to a mystified Betty that these may be handy to jab small things, if any small things attacked in great number, as had happened to Lattis and him on one of Neptune's moons, the name of which escaped him at present. This was what Kro-Bar referred to as "an annoying weapon," or "annoyer," as opposed to a killing or maiming one. The repeated little digs were enough to discomfit even the most relentless attacker to distraction, not unlike a more mobile version of Chinese water torture. Lattis concurred that "repeated little digs" were something her husband knew about all too well—a remark that didn't even merit a look askance from the intensely focused Kro-Bar.

Next, he had the ladies remove pictures from the wall. These were what he called mini-shields: shields that could be moved quickly up to protect face or elsewhere, much faster than something large or cumbersome. Betty found this part agonizingly painful, constantly changing her mind as to which pictures or frames were acceptable for destroying. Kro-Bar gently reminded her that this would make little difference if the unknown were hurtling toward her face; a logic the professional housewife could not easily deny.

When it came to pots and pans on the head however, the ladies flatly refused, and nothing Kro-Bar could say would scare them into changing their minds.

"If I'm going to die today," uttered Betty, "it will be without the indignity of wearing my own cooking tools."

Kro-Bar acquiesced, and Betty and Lattis felt at least one smug and prideful victory.

Comfortably ensconced in Doc's home lab, lost in the parchpyrus from a distant past, Professor Atroppasmirki had been happily ignorant of the flutter of preparations around him. The windows in the lab were securely locked, and the door left open to periodic checks.

And periodic checks were the rule of the day, once Kro-Bar had assigned Betty and Lattis to their separate "lookout windows." As he explained, a lookout window was a window carefully selected for its optimum viewing potential, offering the widest possible vantage. Betty was stationed at a living room corner, giving her a view of both the front and one side of the house, while Lattis was at a dining room window that afforded her observation of the other side and a bit of the back. They also were able to see each other, through the front hall, thus offering a sort of failsafe or "visual vacancy valve" should one of them be incapacitated by the unknown threat from outside. As for Kro-Bar, he posted himself in the kitchen, where he was able to keep an eye on the backyard and a corner of the same side Betty was watching.

However, he also went from post to post on the aforementioned periodic checks. These proved to be a somewhat aggravating three minutes apart. He felt it was important, and did it in a rapid enough time that anyone or anything approaching via backyard would not have the opportunity to reach the house before his return to the kitchen.

As Lattis said to Betty from across the hall, "He does this all the time on the spaceship. When we're in space."

Among his making-the-rounds duties, he also appointed himself Official Snackbringer, or *vandoloto,* which Lattis explained was Marvan for "bringer of snacks" or "replenisher of the pleasure food." At first it seemed thoughtful, but even after a short while they began to accumulate, until Betty wondered just what she'd do with the bag of flour or canned pumpkin.

Nevertheless, despite the eccentricity of the Marvan's security arrangements, the Earth housewife felt somewhat better just for the structure alone. This formal shape to their watchfulness made things seem manageable and under control: important qualities when dealing with the unknown. It made whatever was out there seem less terrible, even if the scientist's wife had absolutely no idea what it was, which might be really terrible.

The procedure went well and without incident for the first hour or so. Kro-Bar showed neither signs of tiring nor a depletion of his imagination as far as snacks were concerned. The only time he switched stations with Betty was to allow her to make some of her highly regarded coffee: something the Marvan inhaled with the proficiency of a caffein-addicted bull elephant.

It was shortly after this that things began to happen.

Betty had found herself getting antsy and decided to fight the creeping boredom by taking the opportunity to study the neighborhood flora's recent growth spurt. At first she was content to tell herself comforting things using her mind's "extra soft voice." Things like "Oh yes. This is what is known as *false spring*" and "That bush is particularly lovely." But the more she studied the enlarged hedges, shaggy grass and bursting trees, the more absurd it all seemed, like something from *The Mr. Greenlawn Show*. This was definitely not normal.

She also noticed that the interlocking hedges appeared to form some sort of a maze. This put her in mind of the old legend she once heard about the hero who went into a vast maze looking for the "minute tour," but finding a monster instead. Even in the warm weather she felt a chill just thinking about what might lurk in all that unexpected fertility. As much as the child in her liked the idea of a maze, she decided then and there that she would never be tricked into taking that "minute tour."

The stillness began to lull her, and her mind continued to wander. Now Betty thought of the old fairy tale about the tinker, the young girl and the giant lily pads. Or was that a joke Paul told? She wasn't sure now, her mind growing fuzzy and lint-ridden before this oppressive world of green. She was unusually drowsy, so drowsy she feared she might actually nod off. She needed to stop nodding and stop nodding now.

Betty thought about turning on the TV, knowing somehow that it was time for reruns of *I Married a Robot* and *Pronto, the Dog That Comes Right Away*. But when she called to the kitchen and suggested it to Kro-Bar he sternly lectured her on the negative impact of television entertainment while fighting for one's life. She admitted she hadn't felt like she was fighting for her life. Maybe it was time she did think she was fighting for her life, thought the first class homemaker. Maybe it would keep her mind clear and awake in this wearying vigil.

The sleepy Betty was numbing over like lips on an igloo, when a sudden rustling in one of the hedges jolted her awake. Despite the closed window she heard it clearly: a strange trait of some of the louder rustling. She was about to call out, then realized there was no need to since Kro-Bar was due to stop by on his regular house rounds. Thank heaven for regular rounds.

Sure enough, after checking on Lattis, the well-organized Marvan came her way, expecting a full report on the preceding three minutes. She quickly blurted out about the rustling, helpfully pointing out the offending hedge cluster. Kro-Bar stared out the window with the heightened concentration of a vice principal. But no further rustling was forthcoming. "It appears to be 'rustled out' as one might say," suggested the alien. "And yet I suppose I should go out there and see what it was."

"Probably a rabid bush tail," called Lattis from the other room, never letting go of her deep-seated squirrel mistrust.

Betty was concerned. "Just the same, perhaps we should all stay indoors where we think it's safe."

"We would all always like to *stay indoors,* Betty," smiled Kro-Bar understandingly. "But often in life, both Earthen and Marvan, we have to venture out of doors, out where the other things lie, lest we spend our life ignorant of all the other things, the other things that out there lie."

As the wife of Dr. Paul Armstrong, Betty could not agree more, though it often scared her. It was almost as if Kro-Bar had uttered a sentence engraved on the skull of her scientist husband, though she would never want Paul to actually have anything like that done. The determined Marvan called Lattis in to keep Betty company and bid them check on the Professor every couple of minutes, should he be gone that long. Kro-Bar explained that it might just be a trick to get him outside, but when Lattis questioned him on why they would do that, and how they would even know he was in there, he had no clear answers. And so, though it held certain security risks, the brave Kro-Bar stepped out.

Betty and Lattis were on the window like glue, only the kind that washes off. They watched with trepidation because it was all they had.

Kro-Bar approached the bushes cautiously, his mind racing back to times on his home planet when he had approached bushes. For when anything moved in the bushes on Marva it was considered a wise thing to be cautious about them. Yet, by the same token, nothing was prized higher than the acquiring of knowledge. Therefore, in such an instance, there was never any turning back from bushes.

As he drew closer Kro-Bar felt a bit of apprehension, to the point of even considering a nervous gulp. But the Marvan gulp was known to be surprisingly loud for some reason, and common Marvan sense overcame any potentially reckless Marvan gulp impulse. The alien knew and valued the importance of sneaking up on things quietly, and only a fool would sneak up on something noisily.

Arriving at the cluster of hedges, Kro-Bar looked back at the house for guidance from the watching women of the window. Betty gestured, trying to indicate the specific bush that was the rustling offender and possible host-hedge for something unknown. Each time Kro-Bar moved to a spot, Betty gestured again, trying to get him to the right one.

Possibly trying to help, Lattis also started gesturing, without really knowing what she was gesturing to, or why she was doing it. Her husband just looked like he really needed some gesturing, and she was not one to let her husband down.

Kro-Bar became frustrated with the wildly semaphoring pair in the windows, and he was about to give up when a sound froze his thoughts like bananas left in the snow.

It was a gobble, a high-pitched gobble.

Betty and Lattis didn't hear the gobble because of the glass in the windows and also because of their wild gesticulating, though it wasn't noisy gesticulating. But when they saw Kro-Bar freeze, both women froze also, as though with sympathetic freezing.

Kro-Bar stared at the round hedge that seemed to emit the sound, but it was far too dense to reveal anything, least of all anything gobbling. Before he had a chance to act, another gobble came. Then another. And another. But they were spread out, seemingly from different hedges, leading Kro-Bar to a hasty but not unjustified *multiple gobbler theory:* a conclusion Doc would have been proud of.

Being outnumbered by something that remained unseen and gobbled in a pitch higher than a turkey proved too much even for the representative of an advanced race. As much as Kro-Bar hated not understanding things, hated it with a passion even he couldn't understand (and so hated that too), he also remembered his promise to himself to protect the house and its occupants. Like a state official he began slowly backing up, in careful Marvan micro-steps—steps almost invisible to the naked eye.

The ladies could do naught but watch helplessly from the window, unless they went outside. With her husband in imminent danger, Lattis, ever the tower of Marvan strength, managed to remain composed except for a subconscious release of unintelligible m words.

Now it seemed that every inch of foliage in the newly lush yard was alive with gobbling things, and the effect was like an eerie electronic blend of some sort, like the night songs of frogs on a distant planet except it was day.

When Kro-Bar felt he was far enough that his almost imperceptible Marvan micro-steps were no longer needed, he turned and ran for the house.

Betty began to urge him on, instinctively resorting, as she always did in times of great stress, to her high school cheer. It was an odd one, having to do with emory boards, cole slaw, and tiny shoes, and when Lattis joined in—doing her best to pick up the words—it added an almost subliminal confusion for the running Marvan man, wafting over him like a soft billowing sheet of discord.

Betty stopped cheering, opened the door for the barreling Kro-Bar, then locked it after him. The three then pressed against the windows and saw that they might not have been quite so frantic, for nothing whatsoever appeared to be in pursuit, nor had anything emerged from the bushes. Nevertheless, this did little to deter Kro-Bar from often referring to the "Thousand Gobblers of Blendview," with a shudder in his voice even an alien couldn't hide.

The high school cheer made it difficult to determine exactly when the infernal noises had ceased, but deathly quiet returned to the neighborhood like an aggressive pie salesman: a grim reminder of the current dearth of population.

Kro-Bar ordered everyone back to their posts. He had just checked on Professor Atroppasmirki (who was unaware of any excitement beyond his own exploration of the parchpyrus), when movement outside caught his eye. At one corner of the yard, a partially obscured figure seemed to be struggling. A glimpse of a dark sleeve indicated it might be one of the police officers. Suddenly, it was engulfed in green, as though swallowed by the ominous hedges.

The stunned Marvan was about to alert the others when Betty called out from her living room window post to say that one of the policemen was coming up the walk.

Kro-Bar quickly joined her at the window and, sure enough, there was Officer Michaelskin, walking slowly and calmly towards the house. Betty started for the front door to let him in, but Kro-Bar spoke sharply.

"Wait, Betty. The Earth policing man is not in any immediate danger that we can see. Let us wait a minute."

"Wait a minute," blurted the Armstrong woman. "Wait until he *is* in immediate danger? Why wait for immediate danger when we can completely skirt immediate danger?"

"Betty. There's a an old Marvan proverb… Open a door for danger, close a door to safety."

"I beg of the differing, my husband," interjected Lattis. "I believe it goes… open the door for a false friend you think you know, let in a threat that may surprisingly harm you because you do not know them after all really."

"Mine is clearer," said Kro-Bar.

"Mine is explanatory," defended Lattis.

Betty found herself momentarily confused by the wise sayings, until it finally dawned on her that her friends were essentially saying the same thing. She realized this just as Officer Michaelskin's steady and deliberate footsteps came to a stop on the front porch.

Though they were expected, the three loud knocks jolted Betty, Kro-Bar and Lattis—something about that resounding fleshy-bone-on-wood finality that made some knocks more important than others.

Betty, now sharing the Marvan couple's suspicions, played her part well. "Who is it?" she cooed in her pleasant singsong nothing-is-wrong voice.

At first it seemed like there would be no response, and the three exchanged the confused glances of soccer players swapping shirts. Then came a voice, dull and measured.

"Why. It is I. Officer Michaelskin. Surely you remember me from before when we met in common cause."

It seemed to be the policeman's voice, and yet something about the flat unnatural tone set their teeth on edge and gave them queasy thoughts, particularly Lattis who seemed easily affected by human inconsistency.

"Officer Michaelskin? This is Kro-Bar, the Marvan."

Lattis shot her husband a look and he quickly realized he'd misspoken. "Correction. Officer Michaelskin? This is Hildon Pottadew, the Earthman." Fortunately, the alien's second reading had lost none of the deceptive naturalism he hoped to employ in relaxed conversation with the alleged patrolman in order to glean information that would confirm the man's identity.

"Yes… Of course, Mr. Pottadew… I remember you well," said the stiff voice through the door in a manner unlikely to convince a lower mammal.

"Yes," said Kro-Bar, tiny keen-edged mind-wheels fluttering like sparrows. "Perhaps you recall our talk about chairs and how they are delightful." The alien's nostrils flared with the expectation of trap now baited, as he allowed himself to enjoy the thrill of the hunt. There followed an awkward silence, like that moment just before one's library book is stamped. Then…

"I do… I do, Mr. Pottadew… I remember how we talked about how chairs can be delightful… so delightful…" the oddly lethargic voice wandered like a false prophet.

Kro-Bar turned to the others with an excited barely-audible-but-exaggerated mouthing of "We never talked about that!" How the Marvan loved a well-earned victory.

"Are you going to let me in now… Mr. Pottadew?… I really should come inside…. don't you think? Sir?"

Betty was about to suggest something, and Kro-Bar frantically waved her quiet. He knew this was no longer a man, at least, as we know them. Neither human nor Marvan, this *thing* was something else. Just what, at this point, they could not say.

"Actually, I think it might be better if you continue to look about the neighborhood as Detective City Brad, your superior, assigned."

The silence that followed reeked of things displeased, of things "put off just a little bit" by entities good and wholesome, entities who weren't afraid to "put off" any and all spawn of foul and unknown origin. Even through the door they felt the vexed troubling that only the unspeakable and corrupt can experience when the flashlight of truth cuts through their alley of lies. Who knew the alternate channel such pent-up frustration and fury would now select, being that its unclean ruse was up?

Of course it was possible they were reading too much into the silence, but it certainly didn't seem your typical fake-policeman-on-the-other-side-of-the-door type of pause.

Then a new sound: a soft patter of things quickly disassembling, followed by a soft dull plop, like someone dropping a hen in the rain. Kro-Bar was quickly at the window, craning to see. But all he could spy was a pile of empty clothing; the dark uniform of a police officer.

"What do you see?" asked Betty.

"Please tell us, my husband, unless it's too disgusting." added Lattis.

Kro-Bar remained calm as he turned from the window. "I think it's Earth laundry." Of course, he really didn't think that was all it was, but he felt no need to alarm the women any more than they were already alarmed. This was a trait he'd learned on his new home planet: don't tell wives things that might upset them. He actually wondered why they'd never tried it on Marva.

It was quiet again outside and, while the current inhabitants of the Armstrong house were glad, Betty did ask if she could make some cookies to help calm her nerves before resuming her window post. Lattis explained to a confused Kro-Bar that it was nothing in the actual cookies that would calm the Earth housewife, no narcotic per se, but rather the very act of making them that would help put her in a more relaxed state, much like when he himself went out with a water jug on a sunny day to make (what he felt were much-needed) puddles.

While Betty made cookies, Kro-Bar made the rounds, but without the housewife at her post it simply meant checking on Lattis again and again, which the latter found both annoying and unnecessary.

Fortunately, the repetitious ritual was soon broken by one of Betty's typically grand cookie entrances: smile beaming, strawberry-golden perfect hair gently bouncing, outstretched arms in an open and giving manner as she presented the shiny inviting platter of piping hot baked goodness in the form of pleasingly precise circles of sweet macaroon delight. Lattis rolled her eyes. Even as she admired it.

"Macaroons. Come and get them," came the familiar cry as Betty placed the offering on the coffee table in the living room. Kro-Bar, covering her front window post, felt it permissible to leave it momentarily; even his advanced intellect had come to appreciate the benefits of a good cookie break. Lattis came in from the dining room, and the three partook of coffee and cookie, grateful for this crunching and sipping respite from the dead silence.

Till a noise from the kitchen froze them.

Kro-Bar quickly stood, but before he could even think about investigating, their attention was diverted from the kitchen to the front porch. Once again, it was the unmistakeable sound of footsteps, but this time they were more deliberate, less halting. They came right up to the front door and, after a brief pause, there followed a knock.

"Betty? It's me, your husband, Dr. Paul Armstrong."

With a sigh of relief and other things, Betty rushed to the door, but before she could unlock it, Kro-Bar stayed her hand.

"Beware of false friends bearing—" The Marvan searched for the words. "Beware of gifts that... If people who say they're... Let's make sure it's him."

Betty grasped the reference to their recent false police officer visit and cautiously put her face up against the door. "Paul?"

"Betty, is that you? Is everything alright?" came the familiar voice that sounded familiar but might just be trying to sound familiar.

"Yes, darling. Yes, I think it is." Betty looked to Kro-Bar for encouragement, and the alien nodded.

"Well, do you... think you could let us in?" came the voice that still insisted on sounding like her husband.

"Us?" asked the award-winning housewife timidly.

"Yes. City Brad and me, who else?" came the voice that sounded confused but might just be pretending to sound confused, and still sounded just like her husband.

Kro-Bar made several silent signals to Betty which she didn't understand at all, so she simply went on as she felt best. "Paul, you know how sometimes someone isn't who they say they are, because they're pretending to be someone, but they're not?"

"You mean, like when Kro-Bar and Lattis first came to Earth and pretended to be Bammon and Tergasso Taylor?"

"Well, yes. Only not as nice as that." Betty struggled for the right words to describe a hostile possession.

"Oh, a more sinister application. Like some sort of evil takeover," suggested the Paul voice.

"Yes," said Betty, excited that he understood. "That's exactly what I'm talking about, Paul."

After a brief pause, the Paul voice continued coyly. "Betty... remember on our wedding night when I—?"

"Oh, Paul!" Betty quickly unlocked the door and threw it open, greeting her husband with wide open arms.

Kro-Bar, however, looked alarmed and uncomprehending. "But, Betty, how did you know—?"

Betty turned to him from her tight embrace. "Silly. Who else would know about our wedding night?" And with that, the contented housewife buried her face back in the warm hug. It was only interrupted by the return of the sound from the kitchen: a faint shuffling they had all but forgotten about in this front porch excitement.

As Doc, Betty, Kro-Bar, Lattis and City Brad turned in that direction, a voice came. But not from the kitchen.

The voice came from one of the cookies on the tray.

Chapter 18

SURELY MORE COOKIE THAN MAN

It took the group a moment to register on the actual words being spoken. Because, it was coming from a cookie. Obviously a reflection on mankind's continued lack of acceptance of the concept of sentient baked goods: a primal and hereditary fear left over from a time when early man was prey to some sort of predatory scone or sticky bun (obviously of much larger prehistoric proportions, and possibly sabre-toothed or woolly)? An ancestral memory that kicked in whenever someone bit into a turnover and imagined it complaining (as we all have)? Or did the five simply believe it a product of their own vivid imaginations: the same imaginations that gave birth to ventriloquist dummies that would, by all accounts, appear to speak—or those strange characters that invite people to come and eat their cereal?

Whatever the reason, the minds of the people standing there had to play catch-up in order to even begin to grasp the content of what the cookie was actually saying.

"Hear me, for I can speak to you only through this object you think of as a delightful snack. I am not familiar with your world and I have no idea how I got here or, in truth, from whence I came. My appearance is as shocking to you as mine is to yours, believe me. You look worse actually."

"I—I doubt that," managed Betty. "You're a cookie."

"Hear me, lady of your world, for I am not this cookie, as you call it, not this one. The baked disk is merely a vehicle through which I am able to transmit my thoughts in such a manner that converts them to human speech so that you may receive them. I don't even know what 'words' are if you want to know the truth."

Doc turned to his wife. "Betty, did you make macaroons? Are they macaroons?"

It was all bewildering to Betty, who was bewildered. "What? Macaroons? Cookies? Voice? What? I—"

Doc shook her gently, as he often did. "Please, Betty. Think. This could be important."

"Yes. Yes, I made almond macaroons. I'm sure of it now."

Lattis nodded. "She knows I like the almond ones—"

Doc turned towards the kitchen like a man determined to turn towards a kitchen, as though no power on Earth would stop that particular turning.

"You can come out," he uttered. "We can face the sight of you. You'll find we Earth people are made of sterner stuff." Kro-Bar cleared his throat, and Doc hastily added, "And Marvans, also," to which Kro-Bar nodded approval.

They stood like people waiting for a bus in the rain, except they were dry and waiting for the source of a cookie voice. A source Doc already knew…

For out of the kitchen stepped the macaroon-headed man, the fleeting phantom that had so alarmed Blendview with its mysterious appearances and unappearances. Now, at last, they finally had a clear look at this strange visitor who could only communicate through a macaroon: the very cookie the odd visitor so resembled.

That was just the head of course. The rest of the body seemed of rather normal appearance, whatever "normal" may be—at least by human being standards, which were often low. He was dressed in a rather plain suit and tie, nothing really remarkable. His head, however, was three times larger than a human's, and—like his hands—was the exact color and surface and texture of a typical macaroon, not unlike the batch Betty had just made. In fact, if she had set out to make a *tribute batch* she could not have been more accurate, though that was not usually something she would do. Upon closer scrutiny, however, one was able to get past the macaroon and discern the vaguest suggestion of facial features. Nose and mouth were fairly negligible, battling for attention with numerous crevices that would no doubt be more pleasing in one of the smaller edibles. But the beady gleaming black eyes, once spotted, had an almost mesmerizing quality in their restless and highly un-macaroon-like animation.

This creature was out of place, even to beings as wide-rocketed as Kro-Bar and Lattis. All stared at him with a fixation usually reserved for floor-waxing demonstrations.

Betty was the first to speak. "He must be from outer space. Or at least another country."

Sensing the strange visitor's awkwardness, with instincts honed by years of petting small animals, Doc made the universal gesture for sitting in something comfy. Though the cookie man was likely not of a sofa-based society, the strange creature nevertheless grasped the concept and took a seat accordingly, even before Kro-Bar could bark a "fold yourself" command.

Betty, about to offer their guest a macaroon, realized it might be in poor taste and simply sat with the others.

"Can you hear and understand us, and can you hear us?" asked Doc with careful halting words like in a Western.

"Yes," said the cookie who talked like a man. "Yes to both. I have been running around confused, not knowing where I am. I searched some of your domiciles for baked goods of just the right frequency through which I could communicate, but alas—whatever that means—I could find none."

"You must be the one who ransacked several houses," piped in City Brad, ever the clue-clutching copper.

"Yes. I sacked and ran. But, until this particular batch, I was unable to transmit, which is the way my kind communicates, as I said already."

"My wife's the best cook," beamed a proud Dr. Paul Armstrong, putting an arm around her.

"I'm so glad I baked macaroons," bleated Betty with the enthusiasm of one who seldom gets to perform science experiments.

"Please. Tell us everything you know," requested Doc. "And leave out nothing, I beg of you. What is trivial and unimportant to you might be really neat to me."

And so the apparently egg white, sugar and possibly ground almond- or coconut-based life form began his extraordinary tale. His voice was deliberate and quavering, with an oddly metallic ring to it, but fairly distinct considering it was coming through a small piece of dessert. It was even a tad musical. As he (or his spokes-cookie) addressed them, he remained fairly still. Only his little black eyes darted about, making him oddly reminiscent of the hapless foil in a silent comedy. The fascinated fivesome listened raptly, especially Doc who, typical of his profession, was extra-rapt by nature.

"As best I can recall I first found myself in your place several of your days ago, if days are things of time, each containing one light piece and one dark."

"Night and day!" exclaimed Betty before Doc could put a quieting hand on her shoulder.

The round-headed being continued. "I was simply here, and I know not why or how. I had been engaged in blowing Os into my sky for inner-lining berries, but you cannot understand that, any more than you can understand the invisible strings we must constantly rearrange ahead of the sliding tent to continue our existence. But enough of my special world. Once here, I wandered about, trying to communicate but sadly unable to. Finding a suit of what you seem to call clothes hanging on a rope for all the world to see,

I took the liberty of seizing them that I might shuffle them over my form and move among you undetected."

"Well… " began Doc but thought better of it.

"Despite my hasty mastery of the Windsor knot, my appearance seemed to bring alarm, even fear, and I clung to the shadows like a drottorontidger, ever wary of direct contact until I could find out more. I managed to learn that, except for constant warfare, you are a peaceful race. So I waited for my chance. That chance finally came in the form of delightful baked goods, and for that I am eternally grateful to the well-practiced housewoman."

Betty grinned fondly, "You know I was almost going to make—"

"Do you have a name?" asked Doc. "Just so we don't keep calling you macaroon-headed man," smiled the ever-thoughtful scientist.

"I do, but it is impossible for you to pronounce in this present existence. I will tell you anyway and see if you can grasp it. My name is Macaroon-headed Man."

Doc and the others exchanged glances. "Either we *can* understand it after all, or by some trick of that cookie lying there—or the filter we know as our reality—the words are actually coming out in a form that we can comprehend. Whatever the case, we shall refer to you as Macaroon-headed Man and hope that no disrespect is inferred."

"How about Mac for short?" suggested a delighted Betty.

If cookies could smile, the slight and brief upturn of a baked-in crevice might be interpreted as such, though it was gone before it really had a chance to register. Doc put his arm around his wife. This was why he loved her.

"Mr. Macaroon-headed Man—?" began Lattis awkwardly.

"Mac, please," corrected their strange guest.

"Mac," she went on, "do you have any idea about the other strange things in this neighborhood, such as the inordinate increase in foliage?"

The Macaroon-headed Man turned his large round head towards the Marvan woman much the way a giant spoon turns. "That depends," came the cryptic reply. Then he fell silent.

Kro-Bar turned to his wife, speaking quietly. "You've broken him, my woman."

Before Doc could probe further, the helpful man-cookie added, "For I do not know what a neighborhood or foliage are. Any more than I know what all of you are. How do you even have facial features? They are so pronounced and despairingly clear. And what is shaving about?"

Doc Armstrong could tell that there was a sharp division of reality here. Yet he pressed on. "The vegetation, the living green matter expanding so rapidly around this place. Is it a product of your existence?"

The Macaroon-headed Man thought a moment, finally comprehending. "There is no green where I come from. The only colors range from yellow to blue. And plants do not exist, for they are not crumbly. We do have wrenches."

As he feared, Doc realized the strange visitor knew no more about what was going on than he and the others knew any more about what was going on. "I wish there was a way to find out where you are from. Another planet? Another dimension?"

"I was going to say the same thing about you," said the cookie that talked like a man, except in a quavering metallic voice sent through a dessert item.

Following the fascinating conversation with Mac, Kro-Bar filled City Brad in on his two patrolmen and the rather ambiguous events witnessed through door and window. The detective mentioned that the empty uniform found on the porch might come in handy if they ran into a police dog, though it seemed unlikely one would show up just then.

Fearing the worst, which was never good, City Brad headed out to see if he could find them. Meantime, with Doc back, Kro-Bar felt it was a good opportunity to go home and fetch the transmutatron which might come in handy. Doc went to see what the Professor had learned, while the others, somewhat more at ease, partook of coffee and macaroons, save one that Mac held onto for communication purposes. He did not try one of the cookies himself, indeed finding them a little too close to home, though he admitted they looked tempting.

Doc found Professor Atroppasmirki as he had left him. In fact, the elderly scientist had fallen asleep with his eye against a microscope, which is never a comfortable thing. Nevertheless, upon waking, after some elderly befuddled sputtering, he revealed that his studies indicated some rather fantastic possibilities, but that he first needed certain vital information to "put the cork in the mushroom," as he liked to say. Doc had no idea what that meant, but he listened listenfully to the Professor's precise needs, nodding wherever he felt there was an appropriate place to nod. Doc Armstrong always generously held that nodding was "the fuel that allowed the other person's talking to continue," a typically selfless notion indeed from the veteran stone studier.

Doc rejoined the others just as Kro-Bar returned with the transmutatron and a grim City Brad who had found no trace of the missing patrolmen. He also reported his car radio not working: something Doc believed was caused by whatever was afflicting Blendview. The concerned detective then tried the Armstrong's telephone, hoping to contact headquarters and let them know what was happening. But it too was "deader than the nail of a door," as he liked to say, referring to one of most notoriously dead things on Earth.

Concerned now, Betty turned on the television, watching as its small central glowing light slowly bloomed into a black and white beacon of hope for the housewife. "At least the TV's working," she sighed. "Look, *Dance Shower's* on."

"Not surprised, Betty," offered Doc. "Televisions are made to keep working, even in the event of nuclear attack. Even in the event our very extinction."

Betty grew wistful. "Well, at least there'll be some record of how funny we were," mused the housewife.

It looked like City Brad had no choice but to drive to the Viewton Police Station, hoping to find out some information and bring back some help.

Doc asked if he could ride along with him. Without going to detail, he indicated there was certain information that he needed to obtain from the outside in order to confirm Professor Atroppasmirki's developing theories on the mysterious parchpyrus. Though his wife wanted to go with him, Doc suggested she and the others huddle at the Armstrong house, including Mac, who, at this point, was glued to *Dance Shower*. Having heard about Kro-Bar's prowess at security, the scientist asked him to once again take charge, and Betty was sure she heard a peevish grunt of some kind from Lattis.

Doc and City Brad stepped outside and halted. The vegetation had grown another foot.

Chapter 19

THE PARAMETERS OF THE PERIMETER

It was an eerie feeling as the lone car drove slowly through the wildly overgrown suburb. It reminded Doc of that first time walking through an abandoned carnival sideshow after midnight, or being inappropriately dressed in a library full of elderly people.

Neither man had spoken a word for several minutes, at least not until the first one spoke. It was Doc who broke the silence by saying a sentence.

"In all my years of doing science put together I have never seen a single thing like this single thing that I'm seeing."

Despite the strangeness, Doc somehow managed to take notes as they drove, scribbling them on a street map of Viewton. He had asked City Brad to skirt the Blendview area, not with a dress of any kind but in a geographic sense. The latter did not ask him why, knowing it was probably something really scientific, more than likely at Atroppasmirki's request.

The car drifted slowly through street after street with a feeling of unreality that was downright sickly. The roads had not yet been encroached, nor houses buried, yet it seemed only a matter of time before the filthy green miasma engulfed it all. Doc had never before thought of vegetation as unclean—it seemed anathema, which was one of his favorite words. And yet here it sat heavily like a pestilent sickness poured from an unknown tap, unmoving and unmovable, laying claim to the suburb like an unspeakable sprawling ogre of leaf and vine and twisted twig. Even the air seemed to hang stagnant, as though no longer granted movement by this vile clutching jailor.

The men lost track of time and streets, flowing slowly through the verdant nightmare, this bushy tunnel outside of reality. Blendview seemed to stretch on and on, normal laws of physics no longer applying.

And in all of this forlorn foliage not a single person stirred, neither dog nor squirrel, nor gobbler even—where were they? Those hedgy gobbling dwellers? For the newest residents of the new neighborhood remained invisible. Not the slightest shrub stirred or bent from their movement.

Doc spoke again. He had nothing to say, but it seemed important to put words into the air, to both send and receive human speech, and to rejoice in even its humblest impact upon the unhealthy quiet that lingered.

"I'll be glad when we leave this place, City Brad. But I worry for the others."

City Brad glanced at him but said nothing, even thought his silence agreed (sometimes his silence preferred to say nothing). They were now but two streets away from the Viewton Police Station.

The noise was so unexpected it did not register as real, at least right away. A jeep. An army jeep, rounding a curve, heading straight towards them. City Brad pulled up abruptly.

Two helmeted men were seated in the open vehicle which pulled to a stop right beside them. Doc and City Brad were so startled neither spoke a word. Both soldiers wore gas masks.

The one in the passenger seat, a corporal, stood and addressed them, but they couldn't understand a word he said.

"Excuse me?" said Doc.

The corporal pulled his gas mask away from his face a tiny bit and tried again. "Dr. Armstrong?"

"Oh. I'm Dr. Paul Armstrong," came the reply.

The corporal continued. "Glad to find you, sir. If you gentlemen will follow me we'll escort you to General Krayper."

City Brad chimed in. "Detective City Brad, Viewton Police. I'd like to stop and check the police station on the way, if you don't mind."

"I'm sorry, sir," came the reply. "There's not a soul left there."

City Brad slumped in his seat, and Doc was glad he didn't criticize his friend's posture as they exchanged a concerned glance. The jeep pulled a quick three-point turn and started on its way. City Brad shifted into gear and followed.

The soldiers led them through downtown Viewton, now a ghost town, though much less choked by vegetation than Blendview. Store after store looked empty and abandoned, while a newspaper or two blew through the streets. Doc wondered why newspapers were always left in the streets in times of abandoned crises. It just seemed wasteful to him. There was no one there to read them. Why not keep them indoors for later? As always, Doc the optimist was looking forward to the populace's return.

Now the jeep passed a checkpoint with several soldiers on guard, also in gas masks. They waved them on, and jeep and car moved through clusters of military vehicles and personnel.

Doc and City Brad both expressed relief. "Looks like martial law," said Doc.

"I don't know any of them by name," said the policeman, "but I'd say this is definitely a military operation."

"Good old Scotty. I knew he wouldn't let me down." The two felt a sense of elation. No longer were they fighting a private war. They now had the full-on support of the United States Army behind them, and apparently in front of them.

The jeep pulled in beside some tents alongside factory buildings at the far end of downtown Viewton. One tent bore a sign: BATTALION HQ. The soldiers here wore no gas masks, evidently considering this area beyond the danger zone.

As Doc and City Brad got out of the car, the corporal approached. "If you gentlemen will step this way."

"Thank you, Corporal," said the scientist, showing that he knew all about different ranks.

As they entered the HQ tent, General Krayper was just finishing a call on a field telephone. "… and I want that area sewn up tight. That's all."

Krayper hung up, saw the newcomers and his face brightened. He extended a hand. "I'm guessing you're Doc Armstrong? Scotty's told me a lot about you. I'm General Roostus Krayper."

Doc happily shook the man's hand, using one of his own. "Is he here? Or is he letting you have all the fun?"

Krayper laughed. "Just me and a battalion. Of course, it needs to be a much bigger emergency to warrant Scotty's *personal* attention." Both men laughed.

"Of course, he's a great guy, and we're both kidding, which is so much fun to do" said Doc. "Oh, General, this is Detective City Brad, Viewton Police."

"Glad to know you, Detective."

"General," Doc went on, "I have some important information I need to get back to Professor Atroppasmirki, who's working on this very problem. It might hold the key to the whole mystery."

"Fine, Doc, fine. Why don't you give it to me, and I'll see that he gets it."

"Unfortunately, it won't make sense without my interpretation. Sorry, sir."

General Krayper clipped a cigar and lit it, looking Doc in the eye. "Doc, I can't let you go back in there. Until we know for sure what's happening in Blendview that entire area's off-limits except to essential personnel."

"But, I was just in there. I came from there. If there's any… contagion of any sort that you're worried about… well, I'm afraid I've already got it."

"Where are my manners? You boys like some coffee?"

Doc and City Brad exchanged a glance, not sure the military man was getting the gravity of the situation.

"General, I don't want to be the poke-in-the-back-duck, but my wife and friends are in there and a man that you'd swear was a cookie. The sooner I get this information back—"

Krayper put a hand on his shoulder. "I know how you feel, son. Like I said, I'll have someone run that right to your house. Besides, I need you here working with me. From what Scotty told me, you're essential to any successful operation here. Let me get you fellows to a tent where you can get refreshed, then we'll talk more later."

Before the two men knew it, they were being escorted by another soldier to a nearby tent. Doc had recalled the "pick your battles" tactic Betty used when she wanted new clothing, often yelling that the house was on fire, hoping that her husband would be so happy when he found out that it wasn't that he'd buy her a new dress. He decided he'd renew the discussion with General Krayper in a little while, possibly after yelling that the tent was on fire. Meanwhile, not wishing to appear rude, Doc and City Brad partook of coffee and sandwiches.

Through a mouthful of ham, cheese and tomato. City Brad managed to say, "Did you happen to notice those soldiers outside?"

"Yes, it's a battalion," quipped Doc, guzzling some coffee.

City Brad chuckled good-naturedly. "Oh, I know that. That's not what I meant. You notice, except for that corporal, none of them spoke? And they all have a funny kind of look in their eye."

Though City Brad had only been on the force a short time, Doc admired his policeman instincts. "It might well be that these boys have never come up against the unknown before. Remember when we first saw the magraclop?"

"It's not that, Doc, it's something other than that."

Doc saw the concerned look on his friend's face, making him sorry he'd awakened Old Man Levity at a dire time like this.

He was about to say some better words when a soldier entered. As they watched, the man quietly removed the tray of food, turned and left without a word.

Doc went to the tent opening and peered out. Several soldiers walked by in a similar state. There was no question: the policeman's keen eyes had caught an unmistakeable glazed quality in the soldiers' faces. The scientist's tone was quite a bit different when he returned to City Brad. "It's possible they've been exposed to something that's induced an almost… narcotic state."

"But we haven't been affected by anything like that. And we've been here longer. A whole lot longer." reasoned City Brad.

"Maybe that's why. Maybe Blendview residents are immune. We have to see General Krayper. At least he's not affected. It's time we convinced him of the urgency of getting back to Blendview. I'd like him to get a firsthand look. Maybe we can get him to accompany us."

"Mention the macaroons. Couldn't hurt."

Doc nodded, though he wasn't certain how much of an incentive a snack would be just now.

The determined pair headed outside the tent, and immediately found themselves obstructed by two soldiers. "We have to see the General on a matter of the utmost importance, in fact it couldn't be more utmost."

The soldiers did not move. Their glazed eyes observed them with the dull indifference of a lounge piano player. "We're civilians," said City Brad as he and Doc abruptly pushed through the soldiers. Instantly, four more were there and the two heroes braced for a struggle.

"I didn't plan on fighting the U.S. Army," said City Brad.

"I didn't plan on fighting *any* army," observed Doc, "except maybe some gobbling things, if they even have an army."

Doc and City Brad struggled to break free of the enclosing ring of soldiers.

"Hey, what's going on here?" It was the Corporal who'd brought them there.

"Corporal, are we glad to see you. Don't answer that. Of course we are. We need to see General Krayper on business that is, as I stated just minutes ago, very utmost."

Moments later, Doc and City Brad were again entering the General's tent. Krayper turned to them and smiled. "What's all the fussing out there? Somebody lose their favorite crackers?"

"Look, General," began Doc, "with all due respect, and even a little extra thrown in, we need to get back into Blendview so I can help Professor Atroppasmirki get to the bottom of this phenomenon. This is one time science could win over might."

The General relit his cigar and tossed the match. A corner of the tent caught fire, but Krayper quickly stamped it out. "Seems to me the two are often the same these days, science and might, wouldn't you say, Dr. Armstrong?" Something about the smile in Krayper's eyes made Doc think of a grocer who'd taken leave of his senses. Or anyone who'd taken leave—didn't have to be a grocer.

"We're civilians. You can't keep us here," restated City Brad, obviously proud that he knew that.

"This is martial law, Detective."

"Can you at least put me through to General Scottmanson?" asked Doc. "Just to say hi?"

"Now look, Doc—can I call you Doc?—Scotty's fully aware of procedure. Fellers, I don't want to fight you *and* a phenomenon. That's three whole things. Why don't you leave it to me a bit, we'll compare notes later, then laugh over the whole silly business as we look back on it fondly. My priority right now is to contain the area. Hey, it's almost dinner time. Go to your tent and I'll have some mess brought in."

"Expecting us to clean up for you only adds insult to injury," complained an affronted City Brad.

After they were back in their tent, and Doc had explained what "mess" was, they noticed that guards had been posted outside. They no longer felt like guests.

The General's actions were mystifying, nothing at all like the way the situation would have handled by Scottmanson: a shrewd and seasoned military man who understood the importance of cooperation, with more than a healthy respect for the uses, and abuses, of science. "A man's reach should extend all the way from his holster to his test tube" he used to say, and "Before you split an atom, you better crack a book" and "An army doesn't march on its stomach, it marches on its fulcrum." After a while it could actually get a little annoying.

Doc and City Brad decided there was no way in funhouse they were going to sit still and stagnate in that tent, no matter how roomy it was. Doc's plan was to slip out of there somehow and try to contact General Scottmanson, let him know his fellow officer was on the wrong track. Then Doc could get back to Blendview pronto and provide the Professor with the information he needed to crack the parchpyrus.

While Doc stood watch, City Brad took a peek through a slit in the back of the tent, reporting that there was only one guard standing there, with his back to them. Doc was pleased. The best possible types of guard, when a person's escaping, were the ones with their backs turned. If luck was with them, he'd also be the silent type that made no noise when struck.

They were about to act on Doc's plan, when a soldier entered holding a tray a food. The man ignored them, moving slowly to a table where he placed the tray down. Then he paused a moment and stiffly turned to leave.

On a sudden impulse, Doc stood before him. "Excuse me, do you have a light?" asked the scientist who didn't smoke. The soldier made an effort to turn his head slightly, as though uncertain what Doc had asked for. City Brad came around and stood beside him, so that both were blocking the entrance. Without answering, the soldier started to go around them, and Doc suddenly pretended to slip, stumbling into the man.

"Oh, excuse me very much," apologized Doc as the soldier stumbled back and his helmet tipped forward over his face. Doc helped a bit by yanking it off. He and City Brad stared at the now bare-headed guard. Atop the man's head was an awkward thatch of hair: the unnervingly fake hair of a rather tall and abominable toupee.

"Rugmen!" exclaimed Doc with hushed excitement.

Alarmed, the soldier made a clumsy swipe at Doc who gave him a quick jab, knocking the man unconscious.

"No wonder they're all quiet and slow-moving and don't look or act smart or anything," said City Brad with equally hushed excitement.

"This entire battalion, except for that corporal, are under the control of Guller Mobian."

"But General Krayper—" began City Brad.

"I can't explain why, but I'm afraid the man is either insane or out of his mind. Or he's taken an enormous amount of money from our Mr. Mobian."

"I hope he's never *our Mr. Mobian*, cause that sounds awful, like a terrible show I would never watch," said City Brad. "But I can't believe a high-ranking military officer could be that corrupt."

"Every bunch has one rotten apple and it's usually the one with the worm," observed Doc. "The worm that stares back at you when you try to take a bite, and then laughs and says things. But for every one like him, there are thousands of good apples like General Scottmanson: the kind of worm-free man we can depend on to do the right stuff."

But interesting discussions could wait. It was time for escape.

The unconscious rugman soldier's uniform was closer to City Brad's size than Doc's, so the scrappy policeman donned it like a clothes contest winner. The plan was to bluff their way past the other rugmen, counting on their slowness and robotic lack of reason to convince them that Soldier Brad was taking Doc somewhere under orders. They hoped to not encounter the corporal who appeared to be the only other non-rugman in the battalion besides Krayper.

It was late afternoon when the two ventured out. They grew confident as the other soldiers barely gave them a passing glance, some not even passing. The duo headed towards a jeep, hoping that the keys were in the ignition.

They reach the vehicle, and suddenly the corporal was there, looking surprised. "Hey—" was all he managed to get out before City Brad dropped him with a punch. Doc jumped into the jeep and to his dismay found there was no key.

"We'll have to hoof it!" yelled Doc, "Or should I say, *foot it* since that's more appropriate?!"

Rugmen soldiers were slowly turning to them now, starting to wander over.

"Not we! You!" said City Brad breathlessly. Before Doc could question him, he went on. "Both of us can't make it. It's obvious that if anything's going to save us, it's science. Your science. I'm leading them in the opposite direction."

"No dice, copper," Doc snapped back. "I'm not letting you play the escapegoat."

"Don't be a fool! You've got to make it!"

The rugmen in uniform were converging.

"Alright, City Brad. But I want you to know we'll never forget what you—"

"Run!" yelled the valiant policeman as he ran in the opposite direction.

Which is just what Doc did: in the *other* opposite direction. City Brad's path skirted the oncoming line of false-soldiers, so that he managed to draw them like metal fibers to a horseshoe. Doc had one final glimpse of them trailing after him before he had to turn and look where he was running.

Viewton was a small city, and Doc knew he wouldn't have all that far to go before he reached Blendview. A glance back revealed that City Brad had succeeded in his noble task, for not a single rugman chased the scientist, who was now able to slow to a jog. It would be wise to pace himself.

He rounded the last corner before his home neighborhood and suddenly stopped. So stunned was the scientist that he stood there for what seemed like minutes.

Before him lay his home turf. But Blendview was now entirely covered in greenery. Not a single rooftop protruded from that veil of vile vegetation.

Chapter 20

THE SUBURBAN JUNGLE

It took a lot to stop Doc in his tracks, what with his thoughts on Betty and getting the Professor vital information that might save the world. It also took a lot to start walking again. For no formerly recognizable street lay before him. The suburban dream had finally become so choked by weeds that it was no longer recognizable, the once happy houses within now subject to eternal dusk.

Doc's progress was slow, to say the least. With street signs draped in mossy clumps and no visible houses, his only method was trial and error. He would push his way through thick brush to identify a house he knew and try to proceed from there: a laborious and painstaking process. He might as well have been back in Menaleusia, back in the Amazon, the Valley of the Monsters, for all the sense of direction he had. The memory caused him to suddenly want a drink, and for a fleeting instant he longed to be "the man in the corner" again, that pathetic jungle wretch awash in bitterness and self-pity— the easy way out.

But then he saw Betty's face, and it chased away the demons. Betty, reminding him that science was only as good as the people who use it, though she'd say it in a more confusing way.

He was well into the thick of it now, this underbrush he once called home, whose proud hedges he'd once trimmed and whose lawns he'd once mown in satisfying, and only slightly overlapping, grid patterns he'd worked out in the lab. The weary scientist wondered if the suburbs had brought it upon themselves with their carefully manicured obsession. Can nature truly be tamed? Or was it only a matter of time before it fought back, like a small boy tearing off the Fauntleroy imposed by his maiden aunt?

Doc's pontificating was cut short by a sound that pierced the dull dead air. It was a whistle. An industrial whistle perhaps, but unlike any Doc had heard. It was shrill and ominous, the kind of whistle that wouldn't take no for an answer, if you were arguing with a whistle. Heaven only knew the depths of the hellish lunch to which this beckoned.

Hoping to get some idea of its source, Doc sought higher vantage. He had been pushing his way through a yard and now managed to find the railing of a porch, upon which he hopped. Reaching for the gutter, the scientist, who kept in shape for such a climb, pulled himself up onto the roof, and from there made his way to the very top. Though it was draped in twisting vegetation like the others, Doc managed to stand atop the mess and survey the great green mantle before him.

It was quite a sight, this eerie emerald sea, with each swell representing a house. The covering actually heightened suburban uniformity; rampant vegetation was the ultimate equalizer.

Everybody was now the Joneses.

The whistle blasted again. It seemed to have regular intervals. And Doc could see the source. He somehow just knew that the whistle was coming from the large facility that housed the Sta-Mor-Down Rug Company. It looked squatter, grimmer, than it had on their visit. It appeared to dominate the horizon, second only to Guller Mobian's high-rise.

The whistle went again, but this time it held: one long extended blast. As it did, Doc felt a rumbling beneath him.

And then another sound: a vast soft clicking that seemed to come from everywhere, as of myriad things grinding together. It had a strange, almost rustling quality to it.

Doc quickly climbed down, jumping from the porch roof to the yard. Then he stared in astonishment. The clicking was the slow turning of every round hedge in sight, twigs and leaves scratching as they interlocked like the gears of a vast machine of nature. It was a sight as otherworldly as any the scientist had beheld.

And as the whistle continued above the rumbling and the clicking of the hedges, another sound emerged, something very different: odd bleeps and sputters and chirps unlike any Doc had heard. And the gobbling. That infernal gobbling, pitched higher than turkey.

Dr. Paul Armstrong needed to hear no more. It was time to move and move quickly. He had to find his house.

The determined meteographer shoved his way through the brush, specifically avoiding the large round turning hedges. Each house he was able to identify became a new landmark as he fairly groped his way along.

Roads were still the best best, though grasping tendrils clung to them like life rafts. Doc was on one when the whistle finally stopped—much to his ears' relief—and, with it, the rumbling and the grinding of round hedges. As he made his way, he wondered what possible purpose it all had served.

Doc rounded a corner and froze. At first he believed his eyes were playing tricks on him, like out-of-control jugglers at a children's birthday party. But as he watched, partly hidden by house, he saw what appeared to be two lizards of enormous proportions engaged in mortal combat. Forty feet long, if a foot, they hissed and clawed at each other, finally locking their mouths together, at which point they began to roll and thrash in a savage life-or-death struggle. Doc wondered what madness this could be. If it was real, where could such monsters have come from?

Initially overwhelmed at the size of the beasts, he now became aware, in his methodically observant way, of rather odd secondary traits. The lizards appeared almost colorless, in shades of gray, as though having evolved in a desaturated environment. There was also a kind of flatness to them which made them appear "not really there" in some way, and the scientist wondered if he were witnessing a projection of some sort. Yet it seemed too vivid, too solid.

Doc realized he was letting the man of science in him waste valuable time and he cursed the inner scientist, making threats of privilege removal, before realizing it was essentially him. As fascinating as the endless giant lizard struggle was, he needed to move on. Cautiously, he skirted the titanic duel until, finally past them, he was able to continue on at speed.

He emerged onto another road and, after careful scrutiny, determined he was mere blocks from his house. The knowledge refreshed him, made him forget how torn his clothes and body were by rapid progress through unfriendly bramble.

The renewal gave him an idea: shortcut.

Doc stood before what was once a vacant lot but was now dense forbidding jungle. His shortcut looked pretty daunting. The lot had grown wildly, ridiculously, more so than even the backyards. And though the gobbling had subsided, this seemed the perfect place for its return. But if he could just make it through it would save him much time, putting him within a single block of his home. It was worth the risk.

The lot called for special measures.

Throughout history, man had sought refuge in a simple disguise born of nature herself: the common leaf. When used in abundance it had the singular gift of causing great confusion among one's fellows, hopefully one's enemies, by interrupting the regular visual pattern of a human being, allowing them to fall away into the obscurity of any adjacent greenery. Doc only wished there was a name for it.

With this in mind, the scientist afforded valuable minutes to attach clusters of leaves tied with vine, in the hope that whatever might lurk in the dense brush, whatever might gobble and drag people off, would not try it with him.

The late afternoon was already filling with dark clouds as he started in, and the leaf and vine canopy pushed it even further, to a near dusk experience. Despite exhaustion, despite the danger, despite the obstacle course of nature gone mad, Doc moved with the lithe grace and panther-like agility of a trained mathematician, bobbing and weaving in a manner that was careful, yet still retained his pace.

Even with that caution, the sounds of some muffled rustling and crunching were unavoidable. But then, off to the side, came a thrashing not of Doc's making. He paused, senses on fire, like a watchmaker caught in headlights. The foreign rustling continued, then multiplied, as several things tracked through nearby hedges.

Doc knew it was not animals, not squirrel, cat or chipmunk, nothing native to the neighborhood. Not anymore. They were gone the way of the neighbor, which was not nearly as romantic as it sounded. The scientist had no time to ponder as he moved again, eyes darting like waiters at a gangland brunch. The rustling seemed to pace him, moving adjacently. In fact, the entire wall of green on one side was now alive with murky movement.

The gobbling returned. And there were a lot of them.

He thought of Professor Atroppasmirki, almost dragged into the night. There would be no help for Doc as he and Kro-Bar had helped the Professor.

Doc's sponge-like eyes spotted a hefty fallen branch, and he swiped it up without skipping a stealthy step. He had a weapon. In a way, for all of man's progress, the stick was still probably the most dependable, not counting rocks.

Ahead of him, the way thickened with tangled growth. He had no choice but to continue. It would bring him out right on his own street. Going around at this point could cost valuable minutes. Passing through could cost more. He pressed on.

The tight tunnel of jungle was akin to night. Branches tore at him like shoppers in a bargain basement, only drawing less blood. All Doc could hear now was his own breathing, bouncing off the suffocating leaves, and the slithering scrape of his own progress. A gobble from one side made him squeeze the stick like a child's hand in a whiteout as he instinctively turned towards it. But it was from the other side that the thing came.

Some instinct, some seventh or eighth sense, made Doc turn. No amount of unhindered creative speculation on the scientist's part could have prepared him for the thing that bobbed into view far closer than comfort afforded. Early in his training, Doc was taught that there would not always be time to study a thing in detail, particularly an unknown with little point of reference. So much of his development as a man of science involved rigorous exercising of observational skills, often forcing himself to read technical manual pages taped to the blades of an electric fan on high. So the unique and robust eyebrain muscles in him, that determine and understand and interpret, were always on alert. This was no exception. It took precisely one tenth of a second for Doc Armstrong's brain to register the following...

The moment he turned, the face of the thing jutted from the brush and loomed mere inches from his. The large bulbous head was the first impression: a cranium that appeared disgustingly pliant, its very repulsiveness discouraging further scrutiny, so crossed with throbbing lumps and veins was it. The face, if it could be called such, inhabited the lowest portion of the head. Its eyes were not immediately apparent because they blinked stupidly from either side and might have been deemed fish-like were they not so large, and were their pupils less hideously human in appearance. Below the lack of nose, several small mouths worked independently, as though carrying on multiple conversations, the end result being those ghastly gobbles now familiar to Blendview. Its body was way too small for that large head: a skinny and spidery afterthought that looked like it would never carry such weight. The limbs reminded of a scrawny, lizard-textured monkey, its long-fingered claws clutching branches in a manner that suggested disconcertingly speedy dispatch through the trees. All of this, in a dank gray-green with unpleasant red highlights.

Doc's tenth of a second was over, and the scientist whipped the heavy stick up in front of his face just in time to catch a wiry claw that sliced towards him. The madly gobbling thing grabbed the stick with both claws, and, after a brief tug-of-war, Doc cracked it sharply against that bulging head. Surprisingly, the little monster shot back into the blackness, like a funhouse dummy whose work was done.

Doc immediately turned and was not at all surprised that a similar horror was scrambling at him from the other side, yanking branches to self-propel. His stick met the thing before it got close, and it too whipped away into the leafy void. Then Doc himself flew, onward, towards the beckoning openness of the street.

The cacophony of angered gobbles behind him was startling in its evocation of nightmarish electronic feedback, but he dared not look behind him. Instead, Doc tore through the dense mass until the slightly brighter tones of the street began to filter through. He became aware of little scratchings and hookings and knew those filthy claws were grasping at him from the horrid horde that tracked him. He also knew that if he stopped to fight it would be for the last time.

Multiple claws found purchase, tearing at clothing and flesh and the last of that leafy subterfuge that had not fooled them, as Doc surged those final few feet. He burst forth into the relatively open street, hurtling through the air and landing with a roll, shaking off small assassins with a fury fueled by a potent mixture of survival and revulsion.

Doc grabbed up the stick that had fallen beside him and whipped around like a cyclonic one-man version of the Blendview Nine at pepper practice. The bulb-headed furies flew about as though weightless, and their gobbles rose beyond shriek level. Clearly getting more then they bargained for, the loathsome mites skittered back into the underbrush in a single wave, like drops into a sponge—suggesting the possible dominance of a hive mind. Doc swayed a bit, dropped the stick and collapsed to one knee. Though he wasn't sure which.

Chapter 21

THE SIEGE OF BLENDVIEW

When Doc and City Brad left the Armstrong residence, the remaining folks (or Armstrong Home Defense Team as Kro-Bar referred to them) did not return to their previous posts. With the foliage considerably higher it was now necessary to assign someone the upstairs. Kro-Bar designated Betty for this post, placing her at the front window so she could continue to cover the same area, only higher up, thus affording increased view of the street and neighboring houses.

The addition of Mac the macaroon-headed man was a a mixed bag. He was another body, he was willing to keep watch, but he had very little understanding of what that entailed or what was required of him in an "alarm" situation, something the managing Marvan felt was crucial. The best they could hope for was Mac's cookie (the single remaining macaroon) speaking loudly if he saw anyone or anything approaching from his kitchen vantage.

Kro-Bar felt satisfied with the arrangements and congratulated himself with an empty tobacco pipe and a good half-hour's pose in a chair.

Betty planted herself in a chair by the window, overlooking the street. She was at least comfortable in the main bedroom. The only other upstairs rooms were the guest bedroom, bathroom and small attic area, all presently unoccupied. After a short time, though, she realized she might be a bit too comfortable. For staring out at that oh so jade and chartreuse neighborhood was once again having a lulling effect on the Blendview housewife. This made her angry. "Oh, why does everything have to have a lulling effect on me?" she mused with that pouty downturned mouth that Doc loved. Even *thinking* about lulling proved to be lulling, as her mind drifted back to that first encounter with atmosphereum, the rock, and former meteor, discovered by her husband. She was always proud of his discovery, but that whole lulling thing was just so annoying.

Betty became less aware of time passing. Time no longer meant anything. No cars moved, no people, no pets. Reality was now unreality. Betty's head was floating and its eyes were two windows out of which she was watching everything. There was not a sound to be found. So much so, that she gradually began to hear white noise akin to an ocean though they were nowhere near a beach. The sense of that sound seemed to dominate everything as she peered at her expansive green world.

Suddenly, it was clear. She realized that every leaf, every plant, every tree, were part of a great sea and that sea was rising. Too imperceptible to point out, too slow to swear to, but a thing inevitable, like changing seasons or bedtime. Surely it must be the bedtime of the world, she thought, as Earth drew up its vast verdant comforter for one final slumber.

Betty shook her head, trying to keep herself alert. But the reality of unreality returned like a mysterious night cat that waited for one's stillness before approaching, to do, heaven knows what. It troubled her, this night cat of a sea, and she wasn't sure why. She decided to focus on something, anything, rather than this terrifying *awareness* that was too hard for her to cope with just yet. Maybe later. Yes, later.

She focused on a leaf, one single innocent leaf at the head of a vine train that would soon arrive at the station house roof directly across the street. She could understand that one leaf. She could pity it or love it, at her discretion. Even trim it if she had to. It was just a leaf.

It was the worst thing she could have done.

Not for the general good, but for her own sense of ease, her own comfort. For now she saw that it was moving: leaf, vine train, all leaves, all vines, when watched in juxtaposition with a background of roof and board. With that clear frame of reference, she could now see movements imperceptible. She wished she could go back.

Betty could no longer escape into the big picture or the little day-to-day details. Neither brought comfort. She had nowhere to go but downstairs to warn the others. This was happening and it was real, at a rate more alarming than any realized. Betty had the high vantage. It was up to her to maintain that in every respect.

She rushed downstairs.

What she found was Lattis in a non-responsive daze, staring out the dining room window. Kro-Bar was in his chair, pipe clenched, peering across the room at nothing she could discern. Mac, their cookie-headed ally, was in the kitchen, and while it was harder to tell with him, he too seemed in a trance, or half-sleep.

The plucky housewife leapt into action. Whatever soothing effect this hothouse world imposed, she would fight it the only way she knew how. She would make coffee. Lots of it.

Within a short time Betty was delivering cups of java around the house, like Florden Tremopher, the famous Coffee Girl of WWI—forcing comrades to snap out of it, making them hold the cup, making them sip—in the nurturing manner her husband and friends had come to love.

It was not easy, but within a half hour the feisty Armstrong gal had them drinking coffee, talking, aware of what had happened to them. Kro-Bar was the most distressed. Betty could tell he felt responsible, having prided himself on his strict security measures. But this was an unknown, and, like a disturbed sock puppeteer, he had not seen the enemy within:

the turgid stupor that was a side effect of their newly engulfed Blendview.

Soon he was up, redoubling his efforts, which meant four efforts total. After sincerely thanking Betty, the first thing he did was survey the outside and, of course, the look on his face was similar to Betty's except for makeup. The combination of approaching dusk and the infinite and grasping horticultural horror was seriously limiting visibility at the downstairs windows.

They had barely noted this claustrophobic discomfort when a sensation gripped them: the shrill whistle from the Sta-Mor-Down plant—at the same time Doc was hearing it—quickly followed by the massive rumbling and grinding hedge gears. Lattis joined them at the window where the threesome wondered what could possibly happen next.

Betty didn't say it (she usually didn't), but she feared for her husband and City Brad, out she knew not where, doing she knew not what, returning she knew not when. The combined sounds only increased her fear for them. They stood there listening for minutes—how many they could not say.

When the whistle, having sustained its last long blast, finally subsided, and with it the rumbling and the grinding, the silence that followed was somehow deader than before: miserable and hollow, as though everything was sealed in a vacuum.

Not knowing what might be coming in the wake of the sounds, Kro-Bar advised more coffee, and Betty went to do that and look in on Mac in the kitchen. The Marvan then double-checked his transmutatron and his wife returned to her dining room post.

Betty found the cookie man unchanged, and it was really hard to tell how he was doing. The kitchen windows were disconcertingly dark, and she doubted they could keep lookout in these conditions.

She was returning to the living room, passing the foot of the stairs, when she heard a noise. Little more than a creak, it only gave her pause because it came from upstairs. There was no one upstairs.

She immediately told Kro-Bar and he started to investigate but the hardy housewife insisted. "Kro-Bar, you're needed down here, especially with your telling everyone stuff and pointing to things the way you do, and that's important. And there's no need for both of us to go, because if something happened then that would be—"

"Two."

"Two of us lost. There's an old Earth saying," offered Betty. "Better one of us lost, than two of us lost."

Kro-Bar doubted that was an Earth saying, or at least he hoped it wasn't. But he conceded that what she said was right and, though he had trepidation, he let her go.

Betty ventured upstairs with the calm of a bowler heading down a blind alley. She turned lights on as she went, but they seemed less effective than before, as though unable to provide as much illumination. She wondered how much longer they'd have electricity.

The sound had seemed to come from the area of the guest bedroom, and Betty rounded the landing and paused before its closed door. With a bravery born of daily exposure to a toaster, the champion pan-wrangler grasped the knob and slowly turned, listening for the faintest sound.

Immediately she flicked the wall switch, throwing not nearly enough light into the small room. Everything looked as it should: bedspread too tight for humans, tables dusted, reading chair by the window with carefully placed volumes chosen for their houseguest appeal: *The Adventures of Carm Charmer, Great Buttons, In the Wake of Kittens* and other such light reading.

Betty listened. There was nary a sound. Was it possible that it was merely the house settling, as Paul had said so many times, enough so that they should be at the center of the Earth by now? Her eyes trailed slowly around the room, eyes capable of spotting a speck of dust in a wind tunnel, as she liked to say.

Then her eyes stopped and shot back to the window. It was open. Not a lot. But enough.

Had they forgotten to lock this one? Had it slipped by them? Betty had a sinking feeling deep down in her gut, like the time she made cakes and realized she'd used her husband's collection of dried beetle elytra instead of almond slices. She knew what she had to do. She had to look on the other side of the chair. The chair that was right by that open window.

With an instinct born of years of picnics, Betty slowly reached for the most effective "smacking" weapon within grasp. It proved to be one of the carefully splayed magazines on the nightstand, specifically the latest copy of *Fount and Finial.* As Betty moved closer, never taking her eyes from the chair, her hand seemed to act independently as it curled the magazine into a tight tube of insect fear: from delightful read to deadly weapon within seconds. Deadly if one knew how.

She was almost at the chair, almost able to peer over that far arm—that plush comfortable shield for whatever might lurk below. The housewife hadn't moved this slowly since last summer's egg carrying contest at the county fair—a competition so deliberate, no one stayed for the end.

She was at the chair now and began craning her head, squeezing the magazine enough to draw ink. She could almost see the floor…

The thing jumped out from behind the bed.

Betty teetered back. She had been blind to the option of anything off to her side, and the upset was startling to say the least. And no small part of that was the appearance of the thing. Though gobblers might appear different to other gobblers, the horror observed at that very moment by her husband in the vacant lot, was identical in every way, with its bulbous, veined, pulsing head, tiny moving mouths and eyes popping on the side, above that scrawny and unwholesome spidery body.

She had no time to lapse into shock, planning to do that later, and fell back on the other side of the bed, as the monstrosity clutched the covers and dragged itself towards her.

Summoning pure moxie, Betty slapped the rolled up magazine hard, again and again, and the lightweight thing danced away safely each time. It appeared so weightless as to defy gravity, all of this accompanied by that wretched gobbling, stretched even shriller by the beast's excitement. Its goggly eyes seemed ineffective on their side perches, yet it saw her strikes and slipped away, repeatedly, like a really good ballet person.

The housewife saw that wasn't working and stopped swatting. As soon as she did, the thing flew at her. As soon as it did, Betty brought the rolled up magazine before her face, end straight out, and jammed it lengthwise into the creature's array of hideous mouths. Its force, combined with hers, was a terrible thing, and the monster appeared to instantly choke and fall back.

Betty slammed the door hard, meeting Kro-Bar on the stairs. He had started rushing up when the commotion began; the entire fray lasting mere seconds.

Lattis's yell gave them no time to confer, and the pair ran downstairs to find gobbling horrors scratching and breaking windows all over the house.

Kro-Bar hurtled the last few steps, arriving at the foot of the stairs in time to level his transmutatron and unleash an bolt of energy in the direction of three gobblers that had just busted through a living room window. The force of the beam stopped them and turned them into delightful tea cozies.

"You made them tea cozies," blurted a surprised Betty.

"Well. We're in your house, Betty. I always thought you were a bit short on them. Whenever you have company—"

But there was no time for discourse on hosting etiquette. Three more creatures whipped through the shattered window.

Kro-Bar had the transmutatron up in no time, and three more cozies wafted to the floor.

"Really, six is plenty," sniffed Betty.

"I don't have time to reset it now! Live with the cozies!" And Kro-Bar was right, because a crash came from the kitchen.

The Marvan man was there in a flash, aiming at a fresh flurry of gobbling intruders. As Mac watched helplessly, seated at the kitchen table, the beam smacked the attackers before they could assault the cookie man. Despite the adrenaline of the moment, Kro-Bar couldn't help but notice that the tea cozies landed on the table almost perfectly.

"Did you see—?" he began, halting when he saw the Macaroon-headed Man's blank expression.

In the living room, Lattis was ambushed by several small fiends dancing towards her. She abruptly turned to them, and they never knew what hit them. The Marvan woman employed what was known as *the yap*, which actually stood for "Sonic Mouth Punch." Somehow. An ability possessed of all Marvan women, the sharp yell lasted no more than a half-second, yet could shatter glass or push objects back with formidable force. It was a power to be used wisely. She had only used it on Kro-Bar several times.

The stunned gobblers were slammed into a wall and slid down, apparently unconscious, if such a thing applied to them.

Across the room, Betty was backed into a corner by five of the little devils, and the best she could do was swing her rolled magazine non-stop as their circle tried to close. She did her best to conjure the image of mosquitos, and that sense-memory proved effective in two ways: it made the monsters slightly less frightening, and it reminded her how much she hated those darn mosquitos. Unfortunately, she was only one woman, wielding one magazine, and the five were beginning to claw at her weapon most effectively.

With a sudden idea, she let the clutching things have the magazine and remembered Kro-Bar's "annoyers." Reaching into her belt and pockets, she began pulling out knives, forks and pencils and jabbing the maracas out of the nasty things. Kro-Bar's defense, once seeming so silly, had saved her life.

She grew weary though, and fortunately Lattis chose this time to open her yap, and so precisely that the offending five were knocked back with no residual harm to Betty whatsoever. "You're going to have to show me how you do that," chuckled the unflappable Armstrong woman.

It would have to be later. Another window crashed. And another.

Betty and Lattis spread out to meet them. The former spotted the fireplace tools and rushed to them. She was about to grab a poker when two of the creatures shot down the chimney and out the fireplace. Betty screamed, unable to grab the poker as they tore at her dress. Just then, a ray of light and energy waved through the air, hitting right in front of her, and the collection of tea cozies grew by two. Kro-Bar had appeared in the nick of time, and there was nothing closer than a nick.

"I do have to say, the patterns are nice," remarked Betty as she watched them gently fall. She then snatched up the poker and turned to face the onslaught with a fierceness usually reserved for exclusive offers.

Hearing commotion from the kitchen, Kro-Bar ran back that way once again.

Meantime, Lattis had been backed into the dining room by gobblers, even as more climbed in the windows. She reared back and yapped, knocking down a whole row in front of her. In order for her yaps to be effective, there were valuable seconds needed between them—costly seconds given the sheer number and ferocity of the attacking force. Again she yapped, slamming several back out of the windows. Lattis spun to face another small onslaught, and they too were almost upon her, when, at the last second, she was able to yap them back.

In the kitchen, Kro-Bar found a cluster of gobblers surrounding their cookie-headed friend at the table. Mac had apparently not moved and sat with an absolute stillness that indeed seemed to fascinate the small attackers. As they would later learn, stillness—actual stillness—was an important thing to the Macaroon-headed Man and his kind: a thing to aspire to.

That did not stop Kro-Bar from transmuting some tea cozies. Mac clearly had his way, though it was not something that would aid the rest of them just now.

Lattis grew tired, shooting off her big yap, as Kro-Bar referred to it. The sheer energy expended had taken its toll.

In somewhat less elegant fighting, Betty swung the poker in an arc, keeping the loathsome things at bay. One slipped through and clawed at her leg, and she screamed.

As if in answer, the front door banged open, revealing a haggard and torn Dr. Paul Armstrong with a number of the fiends clinging to him. The scientist did not look happy.

"Paul!" yelled Betty with a mixture of horror and relief.

"Betty!" returned the scientist with a similar tone, colored by exhaustion from his trek. But, with renewed vigor at the sight of his wife, the battered lab jockey threw off his attackers and plowed through the door.

Just then, a gobbling thing jumped on Betty, knocking her to the floor. Before Doc could reach her, a bunch of the little horrors dragged her off towards an open dining room window. Doc struggled to make his way, stumbling over tea cozies and spindly creatures. A fresh assault hit him from the side, slowing his progress. The last thing Doc Armstrong saw, before a fresh clutch of gobblers bowled into him and knocked him unconscious, was Betty being dragged outside.

Chapter 22

TALES FROM THE MEEGAW VALLEY

Doc opened his eyes. His first thought was that he was awakening from a nightmare: some ghastly gardening fever dream in which mankind was reduced to minuscule size amidst a mile high jungle that was no longer controllable, stalked by predators with no natural predators.

A life out of balance.

As his mind cleared, he realized the truth lay, like the second triplet, somewhere in the middle.

Lattis handed him a glass of water and he drank like a thirsty man. Then he remembered Betty and sat up. Lattis and Kro-Bar had to restrain him as the latter explained.

"Paul, Betty was not taken by gobbling clutching bigheads, but by men in a vehicle. Human men in a human vehicle. Not a living vehicle—I mean, one made for humans."

Dire as that fate was it was clearly preferable. His wife was prisoner, not victim. He spoke what first came to mind. "Mobian. Guller Mobian's taken her, probably to use against me, as hostage."

As Doc sipped water and ruminated, Kro-Bar caught him up on the trials at the Armstrong house, right up to the curious coda: the factory whistle blowing again and the creatures immediately leaving as one, or at least one that was made up of many—further indication of hive mentality. Besides some scratches, Kro-Bar, Lattis and Mac were unharmed, though the latter's cookie had been smashed, rendering communication with him temporarily impossible. Amazingly enough, Professor Atroppasmirki had slept through it all and remained completely unmolested by the devils.

At the mention of the Professor's name, Doc jumped up, heading for the lab, which was just as well since Kro-Bar and Lattis had begun arguing over her ability to make a fresh batch of communication macaroons—an event Kro-Bar likened to a flood or similar natural disaster.

Turned out the unruffled Professor had survived the attack by simply surrounding himself with a ring of very powerful acid, thus shielding him. Though the acid had now evaporated, the lab floor definitely needed some work.

Doc wasted no time in providing the coordinates his elderly mentor requested, with margin for error duly noted. It also took little time for the figures to confirm the man's findings, and he now felt confident enough to provide a dissertation, which Doc headed off at the pass.

"Professor, please understand that Betty has been kidnapped and time is of the essence. I do need to understand the nature of the dark machinery in play here and, for that, I await your revelations. But please, if you can, be as brief as possible, I beg of you."

"Of course, my boy, of course. I quite understand," assured the older man. He cleared his throat. "The history of the parchpyrus is as important as the parchpyrus itself—"

Doc rolled his eyes.

"We are fortunate that everything that has befallen this artifact has been inscribed along its edges, in these teeny itty bitty words right here, you see? You can barely see them, and I had to go over them with a fine comb tooth, literally. For, over the years, each successive owner has managed to decipher the ancient language and master it, thus the fascinating account that lies before us. First of all, the parchpyrus is very old. Very very old. Ancient in fact, in its oldness, which is old, believe me. It first appeared in modern times when it fell into the hands of a one-eyed pelican trader named Hermabob Lapse. And to the question I know rests on the very tip of your lips, as to whether it was the trader or his wares that were one-eyed, that information, I fear, is lost to time."

"That's not the only thing," muttered Doc under his breath.

"From there it next turned up in a small curio museum in East Annapa where, we are told, it was admired by none less than then President Weslin Thompson himself. It was then bought by a collector of historical oddities named Sir Chemsy Wockslitt, though she was neither a knight nor a man. For a while nothing was heard of the piece, until it next turned up on the wall of a popular restaurant, the Right Angled Swan, where it was to gather dust and neglect for some forty years. Are there snacks?"

Doc paused for a frustrated moment before rushing off to the kitchen. He quickly returning with a variety of nibbling objects, of which the Professor partook with the precision of a switchboard operator before continuing his tale.

"Upon the demise of the restaurant owner, him having no kin and dying intestate, which can be very painful, it went into storage for another ten years, until the lot was purchased by an antique dealer from New Cawspindale. When, some two years later, his life was saved by a kindly forest ranger during a surprise bear attack on a routine hunting trip, so grateful was the dealer that he gave the ranger the parchpyrus out of gratitude, and because the latter had commented that it looked 'neat.' That history should bring us up to date."

"Now, Professor—" began Doc.

"Ah, but the really interesting part—"

Doc rolled his eyes.

"The parchpyrus is, as I have stated, quite ancient— from at least 3000 BC, the Hyperhernian Age to be precise. It originated near a natural formation in the Meegaw Valley known as the Soot Soot Mound. The people that settled there were the Arradash, an irritable people by all accounts, but a proud and fluffy race—their headgear you know, very plumey. It was there that they founded the fabled city of Odarr."

"Of course!" interjected Doc. "I read about it when I was looking for the fabled city of Lopeel. It was—"

"Exactly, my boy," continued the Professor. "The Arradash were widely believed to possess mystical powers and their chief at that time, Mearkinbeeto, was rumored to be a god or at least a demigod or partial half demigod, it isn't clear. They worshipped the god Struthiomimmom plus two sticks named Filberk. They were a strange race, and their history was marked with contradiction: essentially a happy sad people who liked and hated dancing, but were partial to a very singular seafood sauce that had a very tangy kick to it, though none survives to be tested. Now, into the thick of it as they say. Struthiomimmites believed in the existence of many worlds adjoining our own."

Doc perked up. "Interesting. A belief that possibly looked forward to quantum physics' multiple universe theory."

"Precisely. As you may recall from your ancient agricultural studies, the Meegaw Valley was incredibly dry and non-fertile, having few sources of irrigation. It was in this environment, and with this problem in mind, that the Arradash sought to transform it into a lush fertile paradise. They began experimenting with rituals that might align numerous alternate realities, rich in greenery, with their own arid valley. These would take place in areas high in magnetic anomaly, employing high-pitched chanting and the use of certain shapes, specifically—"

Like a boy scout before a tiger pit, Doc jumped in. "Hedges carefully trimmed to perfect roundness, whose interlocking 'gears,' so to speak, would provide the mechanism to unlock the doorways to other worlds."

"Bravo, my boy! Head of the class. The Arradash had the round hedges imported and replanted from greener climes," chimed the elder proudly.

"I've witnessed it, Professor. It's happening right here. For some fiendish reason known only to Guller Mobian, he is merging our world with another, possibly more than one."

"But why? What possible motive?" mused the Professor.

"Which also begs the question *how?* How, if we have the parchpyrus right here, is he able to do all this?"

Professor Atroppasmirki thought a moment then his glasses popped off. "Of course! I forgot to mention, Sir Chemsy had a copy made, likely for display, and as a historical record should any harm come to the original."

"That's it!" cried Doc. "He doesn't want to steal ours. He wants to destroy it so he'll have the only copy."

At that moment, Kro-Bar rushed in, looking as excited as a Marvan man could possibly look.

"There's a note pinned to the front door!"

Chapter 23

YOUR MIND, AND OURS

Betty opened her eyes. Then she opened them again. Then again and again and again and again.

She was still there.

The last thing she remembered was being dragged by those foul gibbering—no, gobbling—monstrosities, then being pulled from their nasty grasp by a pair of thuggish landscapers. Before she could thank them and ask their rates, she was tossed into a vehicle where she hit her head, which was the last thing she remembered. She realized she must have been knocked out, or conked—that's what they said on television, "conked on the head." Every TV hero she knew of was conked on the head at regular intervals, but it never seemed to hurt them in the long run. Else how could it keep happening again and again? Surely the writers of television shows must have researched conking.

She opened her eyes again, this time accepting her fate—its reality, if not finality. Betty was suspended, arms and legs splayed wide, in what had to be, as far as she could tell, the most complex and impossible apparatus for holding a person prisoner that anyone could possibly devise. Thick webbing, steel cable, clamps and claws, tubes, dials, levers... All in what appeared to be a very large warehouse or hangar of some sort.

"It was made for foes far more powerful than yourself, pretty lady," came the nasal and querulous tones from below. As Betty craned, the tiny man with the normal-sized head moved into her periphery. It was her first look at Mr. Guller Mobian.

Betty's scream reverberated through the cavernous facility like a cage full of monkey-bats in a hurricane.

"Come, come, my dear," purred Guller. "Surely my appearance doesn't startle you that much."

"Even you have to admit it's something of a shock," came a deeper, more resonant voice as an army general stepped into view.

"Very amusing, Roostus." Mobian's whiny voice carried a tinge of annoyance. "You know I was not always like what you see before you."

"Here we go," quipped General Krayper. "I already know your story, Guller."

"But she doesn't."

Betty's eyes were riveted on the tiny terror as he related a saga he'd obviously told before.

"I was doing science. I was always doing science, though, untrained as I was, it was more of a hobby really. A talented amateur. I believed it might be possible to cross into alternate realities, and I started getting results almost immediately, using mirrors and lights and things—it was exciting. Beginner's luck, I suppose. I made my trips quickly, for my greatest fear was not being able to return. One day, while crossing back from a particularly pesky dimension, I suddenly found myself stuck between that world and our own. My head had returned, while the rest of my body remained in that other reality. It was a world made up of people much like ourselves, only tiny and doll-like. I feared the worst: doomed forever to be 'a man of two worlds.' I would simply be a head moving around in our existence, while those doll people would see a small body like their own, walking about, only with no head. Imagine the embarrassment. And what about driving? At the last moment, just as the link to that world was closing, I managed to extricate myself. Alas, as I pulled free, to my horror I saw that my body had remained tiny, like the people of that dimension, whilst my head remained normal-sized."

"It doesn't look normal-sized," said General Krayper.

"Well, it is. It's normal-sized."

"It looks really big, to tell you the truth. Way too big."

"Well, it's not. That's only by comparison."

"I dunno, I think even then it's way too big. Probably too big to start with."

"Shut up. Shut up, Krayper."

Krayper laughed, the harsh and brittle laugh of a man having fun with a coworker.

"Excuse me, but aren't you an army man?" asked the bound housewife. "Why don't you stop him? And rescue me? Is there any way you could do that?"

Guller Mobian laughed, a more sneering one than his confederate. "Tell her, Roostus. Tell her what an army man you are."

"Don't deride me, Mobian. I still am an army man. A darn good one. And doing what I happen to believe is right, Mrs. Armstrong. You'll understand when you know more. Who knows? You may want to join us."

"I—I don't understand. What could be good that involves too many plants and things that gobble?"

"Well, tell her, Guller. You're dying to tell someone."

"I'd rather wait till her husband is here," demurred the tiny wealthy normal-headed man.

"Oh, go ahead. Consider it a dry run."

"I don't want to have to explain it all twice. It will lose something in the second telling—I know it will. And I'm already well rehearsed, thank you. My speech is highly detailed and all worked out." Mobian was growing defensive.

"Well, you can tell me *some* of it." Betty pouted. She seemed crushed.

"No. Besides, who are you anyway? Except something to barter?"

"Here now, Guller, that's uncalled for," cut in the General.

"Whatever it is you're doing, my husband will put a stop to it just as he did the Lost Skeleton of Cadavra," declared the defiant Armstrong woman.

"Well, that's just spite now," hissed Mobian. "We'll know soon enough. When he arrives with the parchpyrus."

"Mrs. Armstrong," began General Krayper, "I don't have a speech—"

"Why would you?" gibed Guller.

"But I'm happy to tell you what I'm up to."

"Thank heavens somebody will," said Betty.

Krayper grew solemn. "Soon everyone will see what I'm up to. See it… and know that I'm right."

Betty looked almost pitying. "Oh, General. So so many have said that in history, from… someone to… someone or other…"

"But it's history that will prove me right, Mrs. Armstrong," uttered Krayper with a coy grin. "As it did Fluvonius before me, and Casper Timber and Avonocles… Lipa Wren… Colonel Cake… You see, unlike many higher-ups in today's military, what I'm doing will save this planet, not destroy it.

Betty looked at him aghast, not even sure what the word meant, but knowing somehow that it was the thing to look just then.

"Don't look so aghast, Mrs. Armstrong," said the General. "It's too late to turn back now. Even your husband, and the entire U.S. army under General Scottmanson can't stop us."

Just then, a soldier—obviously a rugman—entered a door of the huge facility and slowly began walking across to them. He was carrying a field telephone.

"Ah," smiled the General, "It's just one of my obedient soldiers, courtesy of Guller Mobian.

"He means one of my rugmen, Mrs. Armstrong," added the tiny millionaire.

"He's—he's made out of rugs?!" Betty was horrified.

"Never mind," said Krayper. "Needless to say, they are under our command, ready to carry out any orders necessary. There weren't enough actual renegade soldiers in my command —well, one actually, a corporal, nice guy—so Guller here built them up from an army of criminals and lowlifes. Most obedient soldiers I've ever commanded."

The rugman was still approaching.

"They're just a little slow—hurry up, will you?" snapped the high-ranking officer.

Betty was about to nod off, when the rugman soldier arrived at General Krayper and handed him the field phone, which the latter barked into. "This is General Krayper."

Far away, in the nation's capital, an impatient General Scottmanson was on the other end of the line. "Roostus, what the devil's going on there? I've been sitting on the other end of this line till I'm tired of sitting on the other end of this line."

"Oh. Hello, Scotty. Sorry about that."

"And don't any of your men talk over there? Where are your talking men?"

"We, uh… Security, you know. Don't want to take any chances."

"No, I don't know. What's going on down there? Why haven't you checked in?"

"I wanted to confirm my suspicions first, Scotty. I'll have a full report soon. Rest assured, everything's under control."

"Don't believe him, General Scottmanson, he's lying!" yelled Betty. "And he's up to no good! Don't trust him!"

Guller Mobian quickly cranked a lever and a mild electric shock passed through the courageous Blendview housewife; just enough to make her pass out. "Should have done that first," muttered the little man.

"What's that commotion?" exclaimed Scottmanson. "That sounded like Betty Armstrong!"

"Oh no, Scotty." Krayper remained cool and collected. "Nothing to worry about. That was an excited woman down the street. In downtown Viewton. I think it's a… supermarket opening." Krayper shrugged at Mobian. "They're giving away free yam puzzles, I think."

"Yam puzzles?" repeated Scottmanson.

"In cans, of course. Puzzles of canned yams, they're quite charming actually."

Scottmanson puzzled. "And this is why a woman at the supermarket opening doesn't trust you? The canned yam puzzles?"

Krayper thought fast. He chuckled. "You know me, Scotty. I shot my mouth off that this store, Hammafins… would be out of business within two weeks. Because of all the canned yam puzzles—I mean, they're just *giving* them away. *Free.* Are they crazy?" Krayper chuckled again in his robustly good-natured way. Guller gave him the high sign common to clever conspirators who don't want to speak out loud, but want to let the other know they're doing really well.

"Why are you at a supermarket opening?" General Scottmanson was thorough if nothing else.

Krayper covered the field telephone mouthpiece, looking helplessly at Mobian, who thought a moment, then whispered to him. General Krayper spoke back into the phone. "We heard they might be selling radioactive kale. It was a false alarm, as per usual." He covered the mouthpiece again and both men started laughing silently, but trying not to.

"Well. Alright," said Scottmanson. "As long as everything is going alright."

"Oh, it is, Scotty, it is."

"Tell that loud woman you have every right to concern over that store's longevity due to the possibly unnecessary overhead of canned yam puzzles."

"I will, Scotty, I will. And thank you, as always, for your support, old friend."

"Sure thing… But you know, I have to tell you, Roostus, we're getting some very strange reports from down there."

"Oh. Well, I know what that is. There've been a lot of publicity stunts lately for that new jungle picture that's opening, *Loota and the Tradebearers.*" Krayper looked to Guller who gave him another high sign.

"Oh yes," said Scottmanson. "Supposed to be good. My wife loves those Loota movies. Well, sounds like you have everything under control. Just get me that full report soon will ya? You know, so I can… tell those other guys." He chuckled, as did Krayper on the other end. And with that, General Scottmanson hung up the phone.

As soon as he did, his smile faded and grave concern shadowed his features.

He'd known Roostus Krayper for a long time. There were no canned yam puzzles. Not free ones, anyway.

Chapter 24

THE ROAD TO ODARR

The group looked small in green-world.

It wasn't that Blendview had gotten larger. But in the day's strange light, in the vegetation plague that lay like devil's cloak over house and street and car, this daunting mass, more frightful than fertile, could dwarf by sheer abundance anything not contained. Including these weary but determined four, so out of place in their ungreen contrast as they plodded, no mean feat, down tangled street.

Doc was the lead. On his back, among other things, was a tube with something vital. In his hand he still clutched the note, as though letting go of it was letting go of his poor wife's hand. Pinned to the door, it demanded the Parchpyrus of Odarr in exchange for the woman he loved.

Behind him came brave Lattis, then Mac—incommunicado, courtesy of a smashed cookie—and finally Kro-Bar, sturdy Kro-Bar, bringing up the rear with faithful transmutatron, extra power packs strapped to his back. Professor Atroppasmirki stayed behind, not up to such a journey, but manning base camp Armstrong, as it were.

The difference between the previous evening and the present morning was like night and day. The caterwauling, gobbling, screeching, window-smashing nightmare in darkness, replaced by that dull and plodding stillness they'd come to know so well, in so short a time. It begged the venturing wayfarer to be that much quieter: nervous whisperers in an overgrown museum, not yet clear on the rules of a new world whose cross-dimensional horrors had yet to share their habits. What may lurk, and how, and where, and when? And, while none admitted it, there was an unacknowledged reverence for this great unknown. Just to be in its presence.

Plus no one felt like talking. Not before unfinished business. That being Betty's return and the reverse-engineering of the Blendview-Viewton growth spurt, and any affected environs under the ever-expanding spell of Guller Mobian.

At that very moment, the small genius himself stood before a detachment of rugmen dressed as soldiers at his large facility. Off to the side, General Krayper chewed a cigar as he surveyed them. "Question is, can they handle commands as complex as that? Just how much have you field-tested these brain-dead recruits?"

"Now, now, General, no reason to hurt their feelings," soothed the tiny man with the normal-sized head.

The rugmen didn't show much, but several did seem to have a helpless look in their glazed eyes.

"All they have to do," Guller went on, "is meet up with Doc Armstrong and his party and escort them through New Odarr, safely back to us."

"Why do you care if they arrive safely?"

"Because I want to see the Parchpyrus of Odarr destroyed with my own eyes."

"You have... some kind of eye beams?" gasped the General.

"Idiot. No, I mean I want to make absolutely certain the thing is destroyed, or in my hands. And then destroyed. Or in your hands, then mine and then destroyed. Or in my hands, then your hands and then destroyed, if I decide to let you—"

"Alright, yes, yes, I understand," grunted Krayper impatiently. "Then you'll have the only remaining copy. And there's only one way to make absolutely certain of that. I'm going with them."

"Why would you do that? Why would you not take advantage of having minions? That's practically the whole idea of minions. You're a general, for goodness sake, surely you understand that."

"Let me tell you something, Guller. Just because I'm a renegade doesn't mean I'm afraid to get my hands dirty. These rugmen know that I never let my rugmen do anything that I wouldn't do myself."

"No they don't. How would they know that? They don't know anything."

"Okay, maybe not them, but other soldiers and stuff— they know that. If they were... actually here."

"Very well, very well. I guess I'm just too much of a mastermind to grasp that, but very well. But I warn you, Krayper, take care. Even *I* don't know what things are lurking out there right now. Not until I'm able to initiate the dimensional clean-up phase."

"Don't worry, I'll take care of any annoying little critters running around out there," assured the officer brusquely with a pat on the .45 automatic at his hip. Hey, how about those two landscaper thugs of yours coming along? I could use someone to talk to."

"Landscapial engineers," corrected the touchy genius. "Very well. Their electrical trimming is completed anyway." Mobian's eyes darted to a clock on the wall, and a smile came over his normal-sized face.

"Ah. Time for the next mobian wave."

The foursome stood listening to the shrill blast that cut so rudely through the pervasive pall. It seemed wrong in a place so still.

The grinding of the round hedges and the rumbling began. They had experienced this in the house, but this was the first time outside. The earth seemed to swim beneath them which of course was not possible. It wavered, and parts drifted, as though not really there. The effect was sometimes of a person seeing double, as though the world itself were trying to focus. Doc and his party glanced at each other, but none spoke. They could only remain planted, hoping that they were planted, as they waited it out. Thirty seconds later all sounds ceased, and stuffy silence refilled the stagnant air.

Doc Armstrong took inventory.

It had grown again. Rooftops vanished beneath the green, making houses even more a part of that voluptuous vegetation sea. The spaces between them dropped off even less now, filled in by choking weeds, like a great green blanket lain across a child's train set village. It meant more twisting mazes, dark and mysterious overgrown tunnels. Vine masses, some a ghastly bright red (a new color for the neighborhood) strung from telephone pole to house to parked car like overripe laundry.

Only streets allowed reasonable access, but only on foot. The vehicle that transported the kidnapped Betty was the last to make any such excursion. Roads were simply too cluttered, and parked cars tendriled prisoners. Thus, the questing band forced to trudge those mean green streets.

Doc had been noting the diverse nature of the flora. It was like an explosion at a travel agency. Deciduous and coniferous contrasted with tropical and exotic flavors, some not seen in millions of years. Some never on this planet.

The group had not resumed. Lattis and Kro-Bar looked to Doc to make the call, and the experienced scientist seemed fixed on the dense underbrush, eyes squinting like the gunports on a frigate, only without those little doors.

It was subtle. Unless you knew what to look for. A wave of air, like heat, like a mirage, hung above the landscape, making everything shimmer ever so slightly. Then, something else.

A soft confusion of odd noises slowly insinuated itself into their awareness, with the cautious deliberation of an orchestra tuning up. Natural sounds, only not to this place. Doc had heard something similar on his trek home, in that vacant lot. Only this was amplified tenfold. Each reality shift brought new guests. The scientist reckoned it to a composer adding musicians, one instrument at a time.

Doc turned to his group with a warning to stay on the alert because anything could happen now. And "anything" was just too wide open to take for granted. And so, with wary eyes on everything they could possibly be on—but not at the same time—the adventurers soldiered on.

They were almost at the end of Blendview now: the beginning of the outskirts of downtown Viewton. Kro-Bar and Lattis looked from side to side as they went, leading one to the realization that Marva had things on the sides too, just like Earth—more proof that underneath we weren't really so different.

Mac just walked along. The cookie-noggined visitor was comprehending even less without his cookie, and simply wandered after them, hoping they knew best.

The commercial area of Viewton began with Joytey's five-and-dime, Lowdle's Drug Store, Gome's Barber Shop— the small businesses one might expect—now veiled in botanic splendor.

Doc halted so abruptly, hand in the air, that Lattis bumped into him, which she did so abruptly that Mac bumped into her. The group followed Doc's gaze straight ahead, down the overgrown main street.

A soft grunting announced it first. Then a loud clicking. A couple of blocks up ahead, a giant beetle came into view from a side street on the left. It was the size of a garbage truck, shining dark copper in the muted sunlight. As the group held its collective breath, the monster poked around a little in the tangled vines of the street, then continued on its way, disappearing down the corresponding side street to the right.

Doc held there, hand raised, like a man requesting a bathroom he did not need. He only *hoped* he'd need one again.

He hoped they'd *all* need bathrooms. Except Mac, whose physiology he could not conjecture. But he remembered the old saying: only the dead don't need bathrooms.

Deeming it safe, the scientist waved them on.

They had taken two steps when the giant beetle popped out again from the right, now one block closer. Again Doc paused, hand up, and again Lattis bumped into him, and Mac into her. The group stood very still.

The monster turned and saw them. It raised its beetle head defiantly, mandibles chittering rapidly, nauseatingly, because mandibles could be nauseating. The beast charged.

Beetles look extremely awkward when they charge and this giant one was no exception. That, however, did not lessen its threat.

Eyes locked on it, Doc waved Kro-Bar forward and the masterful Marvan stepped up, dropped to one knee and leveled the transmutatron. As the charging beetle let out a bleat, or some bleat-related sound, Kro-Bar fired. A bolt arced to the galloping titan, making it flinch, then stumble, but not transforming it. It plopped to the ground—not a long way to go for a beetle.

The four waited a moment, making sure it didn't move, then started walking towards it. "Looks like a member of the beetle family," commented Doc. As they walked, Kro-Bar worked on adjusting the transmutatron, as it so obviously needed.

Just in time too. They were far too close, when the giant beetle suddenly was on its feet, turning about, with intense rage, if anyone could determine rage in an insect.

Kro-Bar fired. This time the running monster was quickly turned into an immense tea cozy.

Knowing the harmlessness of even a giant cozy, Doc and company continued walking right past the enormous and pleasantly flower-patterned covering.

"Haven't you changed that setting yet?" asked an annoyed Lattis.

"I was a little depressed for time, as some Earth people say," replied her husband.

"*Pressed* for time," corrected his wife. "I'm depressed for time."

"Paul, it seems the transmutatron might need separate adjustments, depending on each new dimension an entity comes from," stated Kro-Bar. "I will endeavor to correct that."

"Don't just endeavor," said Lattis. "actually do it. It's bad enough, all these repulsive plants, my husband, without having to inconveniently step around giant tea cozies. Cannot you set it for, perhaps, a charming musical instrument?"

"Perfect, my woman. Perhaps we can stop at intervals to watch you perform with a band, as Earth people call it?"

"More practical than a tea cozy large enough to keep a garage warm," she snipped.

Kro-Bar's glare held on Lattis so hard, Doc feared the alien might be using some Marvan power he didn't know about. "Alright, let's stay alert. We can all have that lively tea cozy debate when the work is done."

They decided to stop and rest a minute, sitting on some tree trunks that had fallen across the road. Doc preferred the openness of the streets, sky above, away from the depths of that unfathomable underbrush with its continuing cacophony of strange life. Life they'd rather not learn about, just at the present.

The small company reached the heart of downtown. The buildings were larger—library, museum, city hall—too large to be entirely contained by the creeping growth. Because Viewton was a fairly old community, the structures had something of a stateliness to them, the result being that the crawling vines and inexorable foliation gave them the appearance of ancient tombs abandoned to time. The four companions walked shoulder to shoulder between the rows of these strange new ruins, in silent awe that it had come to this. Though none would admit it, they felt insignificant, like puny mortals before Olympus, or ticketless waifs before an usher. Except Mac, who knew blessed little of ushers.

They were continuing down Viewton's avenue of
tombs when a sound came from up ahead: a simple snapping
of a stick, but it sounded loud in this place. Doc waved them
to one side, and they took shelter among enormous leaves
between the post office and Vanton's Department Store.
Footfalls sounded, indicating a group, hopefully people.

Doc peered with the eyes of a reindeer. Sweat dripped
into them from the swelter of this hothouse world, stinging
them, but his mind bit that pain in half like a candy cane, and
his eyes resumed their nail-hard looking.

A group of men came into view, walking down the
center of the street. At first Doc thought they moved
cautiously, as did his group. Then he saw that they were
rugmen soldiers, and knew that was the best they could do.
They were led by General Krayper, Doc's new traitor
acquaintance that he didn't much care for. With him were the
two landscapers he had tussled with: Smash Nose Cliff Face
and Weasel No Chin, as he liked to call them.

Motioning the others to stay hidden, the crackerjack
scientist stepped out into the street. Krayper raised his hand
and the rugmen, after several stumbles, quite a few actually,
halted.

From hiding, a determined Kro-Bar aimed the
transmutatron, just in case. If these toupee-tomatons wanted
to become something entirely different they came to the right
place, he thought with a fair amount of grit for a Marvan.
Lattis leaned over and whispered softly, "No cozies."

As Doc stepped up to Krayper, the General grinned.
"Believe it or not, we're your escort, Dr. Armstrong."

Doc smirked. "I don't believe it."

"Guller Mobian wants to make sure you get through
all this, uh, unknown stuff intact. He doesn't like loose ends."

"I still don't believe it," came Doc's terse reply.

"Look, it's just me and these no-witted rugmen, and
two thugs with green thumbs. Your group could probably take
us if you wanted."

Doc's eyes gripped his like they were little more then baby cheetahs. "I *still* still don't believe it." He then decided it was nonproductive to just keep saying that over and over, particularly if he wanted to rescue Betty. "Very well, General, I'll play your little game. For now."

"Hate to disappoint you, but I don't have a little game. Wish I did have a little game. It would pass the time."

"For now," nodded the scientist, and he signaled for the others to come out of hiding.

"So, you had them in hiding," murmured an appreciative General Krayper. "Very clever, Doctor. I knew there was a reason I didn't see them. I like when an opponent shows the skills that make them a *worthy adversary*."

Doc smiled, but not amicably. More like smugly, like the way you smile at an enemy. He also appreciated, at least intellectually, a challenging game of cat-and-monkey. "A little trick I learned while playing with other kids. It's called hide-and-seek, General. You should try learning it sometime."

"Maybe I will," The General squinted at Doc like he was a mad alchemist for whom he now had more respect.

Krayper's eyes then fell on Mac, and after picking them up he looked to Doc for an explanation.

"Just a cookie-headed friend of ours," said the scientist cryptically. "That's all you need to know."

General Krayper addressed Docs group. "It's alright, folks. The Doctor and I have just formed an uneasy alliance."

"It's not really an uneasy alliance," corrected Doc. "We're still on opposite sides, just traveling together."

"Oh." The General looked disappointed. "Are you sure? This feels like an uneasy alliance to me."

"No. Then we'd have the same goal. Believe me, I know what an uneasy alliance is."

Krayper stared hard at the man, then let out a sinister chuckle. "Alright, Doctor. Have it your way. For now. But before we're done, we'll have an alliance. And mark my words, it'll be uneasy."

"No. It won't."

On they trekked, these two groups as one, past Mobian Towers, which was far too tall to be topped by any plant life, as of yet. They were nearing the wide steps of the courthouse when the sound of grinding stone made them halt, except for the rugmen who needed some prompting.

A large boulder came hurtling through the air, crashing onto the steps of the courthouse and rolling to the bottom.

Everyone whipped about, wondering where it came from. Doc's meticulously trained trajectory-vision had already calculated, however, that it came from the other side of the courthouse, and could only have been thrown over its very high roof: a feat of great strength indeed.

More scraping. Doc immediately knew another was about to be thrown.

"Run!" he yelled, and everyone scattered, although "scattered" was a strong word when it came to the rugmen. At any rate, they started moving.

Unfortunately for two of them, the boulder came hurtling down and landed on them with crushing force.

The impossibly deep and gurgling roar that followed could only make them wonder what was coming around that corner.

Chapter 25

AS THE WORMS TURN

Massive ground-shaking stomps preceded the thing's entrance. The giant was between twenty and twenty-five feet tall, with long scraggly hair and tattered clothing. The belt holding up its pants looked like string but was in fact thick rope, such was the monster's size. Its joints were knotty and gnarled, as were its facial features, of which the most remarkable was a single large round blinking orb.

"A bicycle!" yelled Kro-Bar.

"Cyclops!" corrected Doc as the giant pounded towards them.

"Fire!" barked General Krayper, and the rugmen started lifting their rifles slower than he had in mind. The landscaper thugs, Smash Nose Cliff Face and Weasel No Chin, pulled gats, because they were thugs. They started blasting.

The cyclops was almost upon the rugmen when they finally fired a volley. The monster roared and jerked back, stung by the bullets but not seriously wounded.

Kro-Bar fired his transmutatron, hitting the thing, but once again it had no effect.

"Adjust it, Kro-Bar! It isn't from this reality!" exclaimed Lattis.

"I guessed that, having never seen one in Blendview, Lattis!" shot the frustrated Marvan. "I really don't like inter-dimensional things," he complained, as Doc snagged his shoulder and hustled him out of there.

And just in time. The cyclops stomped into the spot he vacated and kept going. It plodded heavily, with a hard booming rhythm. Two of the rugmen were too slow and the monster swiped them up, one in each hand. Both unfortunates let out a yell, but the extent of a rugman yell was a very slight opening of the mouth, followed by a lazy sort of ahhh, like an actor walking through a part, wanting to save his voice and energy for the actual performance. The ahhhs did go well with their glazed-over eyes, however.

There were many half-hearted ahhhs now, as rugmen attempted to walk out of the giant's way. The monster tossed the two ahhhing unfortunates into the trees and continued to stalk down the street after the others.

General Krayper had unloaded his .45 automatic into the brute with little effect, and simply turned and ran.

Kro-Bar ducked into the brush to desperately adjust his device, and Lattis stood by him protectively. She picked up a stick but it was too small, so she threw it down, and then picked up another that was a little larger but still too small. She kept doing this, and the sticks got bigger, until she was satisfied with one she just could not lift.

"Hurry, my husband," she urged as the monster passed by, chasing the others.

"I am trying, my love. It is difficult to tune to the frequency of this bicycle!"

"Cyclops."

Running ahead of the monster with the others, Doc had not been idle, though he hadn't really done anything. What he had done was that invisible thing that looks like idleness but is really very important, or can be. Even though it looks lazy.

The man of science had been calculating—coordinates, distances, angles and percentages—with that precision mind he'd trained since childhood when he shared candy using mathematical formulae. All this, while running with General Krayper, the thugs and the two remaining rugmen.

Behind them, that steady pounding walk took on the aspects of a relentless machine. As usual, the two rugmen were most at risk, and the pair dropped back to be fair game for the one-eyed monster who grabbed them easily amidst a chorus of ahhhs.

It did have the effect of delaying the cyclops, allowing the others to stay ahead, as they rounded a corner onto another street. Their lead was short-lived, as those booming footsteps grew rapidly louder: the cyclops had hastened its stride.

Doc seemed to be looking for something and quickly turned down another street.

"Where are you heading?" barked General Krayper slapping another clip into his .45.

The giant was catching up, a mere twenty yards behind them.

Doc suddenly saw what he needed and waved Krayper and the two thugs on. "Keep going!"

"What?"

"Just go!" hollered Doc, and the renegade officer had no choice. General Krayper, Smash Nose Cliff Face and Weasel No Chin continued down the street. The resourceful meteographer ducked to the side, dragging out a long flagpole that had been toppled by the intrusive foliage.

He strained to lift it, using the extra muscles he'd encouraged through mental exercise, tendons cording like tendon-cords, until the flagpole would have been a fool to resist anymore. Doc turned as the cyclops began striding past and—in that microsecond—calculated everything he needed to, just as he had those jelly beans so many years before.

At the precise moment, like a horseless jousting knight, Doc rushed forward with a grunt and jammed the flagpole between those massive ambling legs as they were scissoring. The legs snagged, immediately jolting the cyclops's progress. Its knotty frame began to topple in what looked like slow-motion.

Doc held fast the pole with all his might, planting his feet like a senator on the witness stand. The monster finished its fall by cracking its head on some concrete steps.

The scientist dropped the heavy pole with a clank that reverberated in the empty streets. The strain of his exertion showed. Surprisingly, General Krayper was beside him, but not to see if he was alright. The renegade officer grabbed at the tube on Doc's back and, despite exhaustion, the latter grappled with him for control of the thing.

Their struggle took them away from the building, into an overgrown field that sloped off to a densely tangled ravine. Krayper was having more difficulty with the scientist than he bargained for, and he yelled for his two thuggish gardeners who had just come around the corner of the building.

"Get over here and help me get this thing!"

Doc and Krayper stumbled along the steep knoll at the edge of the ravine, hands locked on the tube between them. When Smash Nose Cliff Face and Weasel No Chin slammed into them, also grabbing for the tube, the momentum sent all four tumbling down the steep slope. Only the unusually tall grass through which they rolled prevented serious injury, and the broken-up clump of men came to a stop, scattered about the thick brush of the ravine.

Krayper stirred first, quickly getting to his feet. His immediate thought was the tube, and he whipped around, looking for it. Not an easy task, for this narrow cut was crazily overgrown with all manner of strange shrubbery. As the two thugs got to their feet, the General barked, "Find that tube. Now!"

Doc, at the limits of endurance—but not yet over the town line—became aware of the three men searching the brush as he slowly pushed himself off the ground.

Smash Nose Cliff Face, poking around a bit farther than his companions, paused before some bushes. Something that looked dark and shiny and tubular was partly visible underneath. He got down on all fours, reached in and grabbed hold. A strange bubbly roar jolted the thug back.

A shape pushed through the brush that could only emerge from therapy. The dark shiny tube was only one of many black legs dragging the pale fleshy abomination that followed: a large hulking grub-like thing about the size of a walrus. Its only indication of a face was the huge open mouth that now clamped onto Smash Nose's foot. The thug felt it was time to let out a long howl.

General Krayper was quickly over, firing his automatic into the thing which continued to roar as it dragged itself through the tall grass.

Doc was up now, looking to the sound of the commotion.

Krayper still fired into the brute, as it succeeded in drawing the entirety of the screaming Smash Nose Cliff Face into its expanding maw with a series of big heaving gulps.

Weasel No Chin was hurrying over to help when a silent shape rose up beside him in the high grass. The thug turned wide helpless eyes on the sallow mass next to him, a quivering translucent jelly, peppered with little squirming branches. Weasel barely had time to start a yell, when the creature effortlessly absorbed him. He could still be seen wavering inside for several moments, a look of horror on his face, before being lost to view.

Doc was heading for the other confrontation when he nearly ran into the jelly thing. He quickly snatched up a heavy stick and began beating it. It seemed to have little effect.

General Krayper, moving away from the grub-thing, had just shoved another clip into his automatic, when he spotted the parchpyrus tube sitting in the grass a few feet away. A grin split his features like a walnut and he darted towards the object of his mission. He had just stooped to pick it up, when a queasy sort of chittering arose. Snaking through the brush towards him, almost like liquid, came a long and enormous myriapod of some kind, its quivering fibrous legs in the hundreds, if not thousands. It reached him quickly and reared up its forepart, including a multi-eyed, multi-mandibled head. It was staring face-to-face with the renegade general.

A cluster of stingers shot out faster than seemed possible.

Krayper's screams reached Doc as he beat at the advancing jelly thing with the stick. It seemed to absorb each blow with little impact beyond a revolting quiver.

A sudden thought had Doc reaching to a pack on his belt, and he quickly pulled out several salt tablets and tossed them at the translucent monstrosity. Even better than the desiccation he'd hoped for, the thing began hissing in places as the salt had a burning effect. Eerily, it still made not a sound, though it finally ceased its attack.

Unfortunately, Doc continued to back away from it, and his next step touched nothing.

Not even the man of action-science had time to think as he tumbled down yet another slope. Only this one ended. It was a bluff. Off which Doc Armstrong dropped into space.

And landed on the unknown.

It was a narrow stream. Not a stream of water but of living things, all identical and mostly featureless, smooth and round and pale pink, like stubby worms the size of hogs, moving so fluently they seemed as one, with a uniformity of undulation that only added to the water analogy. The winding trough they ran down was a perfect fit, begging the question of which came first: was it a perfect fit for them? Or they for it?

Doc landed on his back, on their backs, and before he could even become aware of what or where, the most overwhelming sense of euphoria came to rest upon him. A numbness that removed all the anxiety and desperation and weariness and physical strain of his quest, replacing it with a higher sense of peace and contentment he had not felt in a long time. If ever.

Since his self-induced jungle exile, his return from bitterness and transformation, Dr. Paul Armstrong had questioned his purpose, questioned his very being. But he seldom stopped moving long enough to let it affect his work or his day-to-day life.

Of course, the scientist may have been able to deduce that the creatures beneath him, on whose backs he flowed, gave off some kind of natural chemical that induced such a feeling, for purposes unknown. But Doc was beyond such analysis, going with a flow he could neither comprehend, nor even be aware of.

There was no time. But he knew that. Even the scientist knew that. An illusion at best, and so-called reality its fragile enabler. Doc no longer thought of things. He only knew them, knew them on the stream. It flowed so smoothly that movement was negligible. Doc was not aware of lying there, staring up at the sky, as the snaking creature-stream wound its way around and through newly exploded nature like the miniature railroad he'd ridden as a child. Those tracks wove through snug tunnels of brush and trees, and Doc had always known it was a metaphor for something. Of course. It was a metaphor for everything he did not know.

The train wasn't entirely silent. There was a soft hushing sound as the featureless animals delivered him to an appointed and predestined unknown.

The first thing he actually became aware of was Betty, Betty's lovely face hanging above his own, facing him, as though she were riding parallel to him the whole way. Her progress mirrored his, and he wondered whose backs in the sky she rode upon. Not that it mattered. It was Betty. Doc might have smiled, he wasn't sure.

In his head he heard "Oh, Paul," and it was repeated again and again slowly as they went, in every possible connotation and inflection. If Doc were aware, he would have marveled at how many there were, and how many different reactions and feelings those subtle variations elicited.

The stream took a sharper turn now, into a darker, denser piece of wilderness. A brief tunnel. Then the canopy of trees opened up, and they flowed across an open plain.

Betty's face dissolved into something else. Something with blacker, deeper eyes and fixed grin. The laugh was a dead giveaway: that filthy booming arrogance. It shook Doc from his fog of chemically-induced calmness.

And hands. The hands shook him too.

He was able to see now, see that the stream of piglike worms was flowing right towards a hole in the ground, up ahead some fifty feet or so. Be there in a few minutes. If Doc had cared, he might have seen it as betrayal. After all, he trusted this stream. See if they'd get his business again. But they were heading right for that hole and there wasn't a dang thing he could do.

But the hands again. The hands wouldn't let him. They held on. And pulled.

Doc was yanked from the unearthly animal train and as he tumbled to the ground, more awareness returned. It was surprising how fast it did, once you got off of it.

He saw his benefactor beside him. He also tumbled. Mac did. The cookie-headed man came to a rolling stop and stood up, making sure Doc was okay.

Strangely, the scientist felt rested and got to his feet. He had needed that rest. He turned to thank the Macaroon-headed Man. But the strange fellow was gone.

He was, however, surrounded by a multitude of scrawny bulbous-headed gobblers.

Chapter 26

MEET THE RECONNOITERERS

The Sapisko J-21 Chippatoo helicopter sliced through the air like a funny cartoon dog slicing through a stick of butter. General Scottmanson had missed breakfast due to the urgency of this trip, but he saw no reason to completely miss a meal, so had provided foodstuffs for the journey. The helicopter made eating a bit of challenge, particularly the eggs over easy, but the veteran officer felt it was worth it. Whatever *it* was.

He still wasn't exactly sure. He was flying down to Viewton on a hunch, and General Scottmanson's hunches usually played out, like the thing with the buttons and the raccoon.

He had known Roostus Krayper since bootcamp, and even pantscamp, and he could tell right away by his voice that something was not right. Also, he once sat through *Loota and the Terrace People* with Krayper and his wife and knew for a fact that neither could stand jungle pictures: something he'd learned the hard way.

Soon they'd be landing, quietly and surreptitiously, at Viewton Airfield, and he would know one way or the other.

Nothing like a little surprise visit to catch people with their pants folded.

Scottmanson was also surprised he had heard no more from his friend Doc Armstrong, and had been unable to reach the scientist, whose phone was reported out of order. It wasn't like the detail-minded rock man to not keep him posted. He often thought, "If I had a lot more men like Armstrong, I'd certainly have a lot more." But it added to his overall suspicion that all was not right in this neck of the woods, though the specific location of anything like a "neck" remained elusive.

The pilot glanced over at him and pointed down. He was always doing things like that, and it could really make a trip annoying. He wished the man were more like those helicopter pilots who sing and tell stories, making the journey go so much faster—though that might have been in a movie. Scottmanson finally decided that if he simply stared hard enough at the man maybe he would cut that out.

But the pilot did it several more times, and finally the General got annoyed enough to look out the window of the copter. What he saw took his breath away and made him speechless for the words he didn't have.

There was no Viewton.

None that they could see. Where normally sat the pleasant city and its surrounding suburbs, there stretched a wide swath of green, as though they'd taken a right turn at the Amazon.

"Did you take a right turn at the Amazon?" yelled Scottmanson over the motor.

Whether the pilot didn't understand him or didn't want to admit to a mistake, the man would not answer and the General just let it go. He was wondering just how they would land when he saw the flying reptile with four horns on its head.

When Kro-Bar finally adjusted the transmutatron to a serviceable wavelength that would affect the cyclops, he and Lattis had hightailed down the street to catch up to the giant and the rest of their party. What they found was the one-eyed monster, lying with its head against some concrete steps.

"If I'd known Paul was going to trip it, I wouldn't have wasted my time," uttered the Marvan who actually seemed miffed.

"Do not sulk, my husband, it does not become you."

"Good. I would not want to become a sulk, particularly since it's a verb and not a noun."

"You've obviously never had a good sulk. How do you know Paul tripped the thing?" she asked.

"Please credit me with *some* science." Kro-Bar snorted slightly. " I see the pole. I know how Paul's mind works. Of course, you know that I am glad they're okay. Doc and the cookie man."

Lattis looked at him. "How do you know they're okay?"

"They're not here, my love. That is a good sign. I will answer no more questions."

"Come. Go," said the Marvan woman. "You waste time telling me you will answer no more questions."

They continued to scour the weed-choked streets in search of their companions. But with time wasting, it was inevitable they broach their only other option: continuing to the rendezvous with Guller Mobian.

"But if we arrive without the parchpyrus—" began Kro-Bar.

Lattis looked him squarely in the eye, both in fact. "Then we must search for the tube until we find the tube, for only with the tube can we make the tube trade for Betty."

"Let us hope we find Paul in the bargain," added her wise husband who usually never mentioned bargains.

General Scottmanson had been in hairy situations before. But the landing of the Sapisko helicopter in the jungle that was now Viewton ranked up there with the time he was accidentally locked in the duck decoy museum. He swore those things came alive at night, and proving it someday was on his list of "great things to do." Or the time he had to address a group of two hundred female veterans. He had never been so nervous in his life. But a helpful person advised him to simply imagine himself speaking to them completely naked: an unfortunate strategy that entirely backfired. By the end of it he was a total wreck. He'd have to remember just who that helpful person was, so he could give them a piece of his mind.

No matter. The pilot had found a reasonably wide flat area, and the helicopter swayed slightly as it descended. Finally, the Sapisko crunched down on a bed of branches and shrubs that had a road somewhere under it. It was the best they could do.

The General remembered the flying reptile, which he still couldn't believe he saw, and checked his army issue automatic pistol, packing extra clips into his jacket. He just wasn't sure what he needed to be ready for, so he decided to make himself ready for anything he might need to be ready for.

The pilot—Jopson, or Jodson, one of those kind of names, he couldn't remember which—climbed out with him, hefting a rifle. The two surveyed the wild terrain in the eerie dead silence.

"Which way, sir?"

The General paused, his eagle eyes scrubbing the horizon like a carwash professional. "Son... if I had the answer to that... we just might know... We just might know..."

And, despite the confused look he received from the pilot, General Scottmanson led the way.

Chapter 27

THE CROSSDIMENSIONALIZER

The surrounding horde of bulbous-headed gobbling things had not killed Doc. Of that Doc was certain. If they had, he'd be dead. Quite dead. And he wasn't. All of his breathing and moving and livingness was proof of that.

Instead, the savage little horrors herded him like so much porridge, if soft stuff like porridge or pudding could ever be herded, which was doubtful. He was vastly outnumbered, exhausted, and outnumbered. He remembered what one of his mentors, the Nuberian adventurer Captain M'Gugagong, had taught him about fighting monsters. He remembered the man's words like it was yesterday, possibly afternoon. "If there are more monsters than you, friend Paul, then count them and see just how many more. If it is a lot more, then try and determine if you have a way out, if you can avoid the fight, so that you might have another fight following this fight, perhaps on another day entirely. And if you spend all this time doing as I tell you, you will probably be eaten anyway, my friend."

In this case, of course, they already had him surrounded. But something in their demeanor—a tilt of the head, maybe a hint of coyness—told him that their intent was not to harm him, but simply escort him back. The scientist in Doc was instantly curious as to where these things, quite likely of limited intelligence, might want to take him, while, on the other hand, the homeowner in Doc really didn't care and just wanted to be someplace else. Then there was the barbecuer in Doc… But, as usual, the scientist won, and he went quietly. Fairly quietly: he did find himself humming at one point.

To many, this humming may have seemed a distraction to cover nervousness, or simply a fun way to pass the time in what was likely an uncomfortable situation. But Doc had started humming at an early age, listening to every barbershop quartet he could, getting close to bees, getting stung, until as a young man he had perfected over two-hundred million individual hums. He only estimated this, as counting that high could take a long time. Each hum had a distinct and unique frequency, far too subtle for the naked ear.

As Doc walked with the hideous little creatures he was, in essence, testing their responses to a variety of hums to see what, if any, effect it might have on them. He noticed subtle shifts and changes, imperceptible to the ordinary eye, but noticeable to Doc who had once spent a year painting clown makeup on spiders (non-toxic, of course, and he washed them off later). So honed to minutia were the scientist's peepers that he sometimes found it hard to unsee all the tiny things in the world (which is a whole whole lot if you really look).

The trained humologist became convinced that the creatures were under the control of a frequency of some sort, and he was betting beakers to Bunsens it was the same device that Guller Mobian used to control the rugmen.

It was an odd experience, walking in their midst. The little horrors seemed to swim about him, like a grotesque living pond that attached to the scientist without actually touching him—guiding him, moving as one: further evidence of that hive mind.

They were approaching the Sta-Mor-Down plant now, which stuck out like a agonized thumb, since there was not a single piece of foliage clinging to it—thanks no doubt to its master's control. As they neared the massive building, the whistle blasted again, much louder up close. The grinding of the arcane machinery that was based on countless carefully coordinated hedge balls followed, along with its resultant rumble. Doc saw the shimmer in the air that heralded shifting realities. Even he, as smart and scientific as he was, had to marvel at the dimensional hanky-panky that was going on. He had no doubt that Guller would fill him in in great detail: he was compelled to. Doc had discovered the hard way that smug accomplishment speeches were the number one common trait among megalomaniacal mad geniuses throughout the ages— from Cattakick to Elbin Pushcart to the Lost Skeleton of Cadavra. It was the reason they did what they did.

The commandeered scientist's short but bizarre escort paused before a large sliding door on the side of the building. As the gobblers seemed to expect, the corrugated steel door slowly rumbled open. When it came to a stop, they went inside.

It took some adjusting to the gloom, but much less for Doc. As a child he'd taped kaleidoscopes to his eyes and walked around for hours until his vision corrected all distortions of light and color. So heightened were his ocular muscles that it was said he could see a barn owl in a barn, at night, in a cave, underground, even if the barn owl had no business being there and was wearing all black.

Before his eyes could "strut their stuff" however, a switch was thrown and the entire opposite wall lit up. It consisted of an enormous mass of dials and lights and tape recorders and circuitry. Doc soaked in the vast machine like a goose in a wheat shop. Fifty feet high and a hundred and forty feet long, it dwarfed even the most ambitious of toaster ovens.

"Welcome, Dr. Paul Armstrong," came the shrill and grating little voice.

Doc looked up. He had never looked up at Guller Mobian before. The small mastermind stood high atop a lift platform attached to a hydraulic arm attached to a motorized bed, like an enormous version of a cherry picker truck.

Mobian worked a lever and the platform whirred right down to meet Doc, pausing just slightly higher for master villain's sake.

"What do you think of my little facility?" smiled the tiny-bodied genius. Doc saw he was wearing odd headgear: metallic bands crisscrossed his cranium from the forehead up.

"It's not little at all. It's enormous. I understand the irony though. Just as I appreciate the irony that these small gobbling monstrosities you're controlling remind me of you."

For a moment it looked like Guller might explode. He did. With laughter. And far heartier than one might expect, given his piercing voice.

"I thought so too, Doc Armstrong—at least, our proportions are similar. You refer, of course, to my mobiates, as I've taken to calling them. Useful little things, and easily controlled, just as the rugmen are, by my *mobion*," declared the egomaniac, tapping his headgear.

"Do you name everything?"

"Yes," came the quick and confident reply.

"It no doubt fills some deep-seated need."

Guller sneered. "You'll find mining the pit of my insecurities a lonely and fruitless occupation, Doctor."

That was enough verbal fencing for Doc. "Where's my wife?"

Mobian threw another switch. Above them, metal doors opened up, and the crazy rig holding Betty Armstrong slowly emerged. Though relieved that she was alive, Doc bristled when he saw his wife clasped in the absurdly complicated restraining device.

"Paul! I knew you'd come!"

"Betty! What have you done to her, you monster?" snapped the meteographer with the rage of a scrubbed test pilot.

"Relax, Doctor, she is unharmed. Most of that is for show." Guller smiled admiringly at his own handiwork. "Unless you try and free her, of course—that would prove fatal."

"Are you alright?" asked the concerned husband.

"Well, I've been waiting to try on a new dress, but the help in this place seems a little slow," smirked the unflappable Mrs. Armstrong.

Even in dire straits, Doc had to grin at his wife's pluck, and other parts. He made a completely untelegraphed move to lunge, but the mobiates surged right with him, and he thought better of it. Their goggly side-eyes shone with a light that indicated they wouldn't balk at a command to tear him to pieces. Which reminded Doc of something. He switched gears.

"General Krayper is dead. Unfortunate victim of one of the nastier byproducts of your foolish experiments," Doc snapped off casually.

"You of all people understand the sacrifices of science," argued Mobian. "It is inevitable, is it not? He served his purpose. Mostly running interference to delay military intervention. Which he did, rather famously. He also happened to believe in what I'm doing. As you might, once I've explained it all to you."

"He's been really looking forward to it, Paul," interjected poor aloft spread-eagled Betty.

"Yes, do let me. I've been so looking forward to it."

"I don't want to hear it."

"What?"

"I'm sorry, I'm just not interested."

"You're lying. You're a scientist. Of course you're interested."

"Free Betty and I'll listen with every ear on my head."

"Did you bring the parchpyrus?"

"It was lost in a little place called the road to hell— perhaps you've heard of it."

"You know my deal. Your wife for the parchpyrus."

"Should have thought of that before laying out the multi-dimensional welcome mat. Too bad you forgot the loathsome predator filter."

"What welcome mat? I have no— Oh. Sarcasm." Words oozed from Mobian like bitter worms. "The last resort of the noble scientist."

"I don't know what that means," said Doc.

"It just so happens there *is* a filtering process. It happens at intervals. You see, it's all about end results, Doctor Armstrong. I'm trying to save the world. I, and the brilliant unit you see before you, the crossdimensionalizer. Just as the Arradash did in 3000 BC when they created their city of Odarr, their paradise, so shall I rescue our world from the mechanization and industrialization of man and all its filthy residue. How much longer do you think this planet will put up with humans? A hundred? Two hundred years?"

"Can I sit down?" asked Doc.

"No. To make you fully understand I must first go back some twenty years."

"Do you have to do that?"

"Did you ever wonder why a reclusive and brilliant millionaire would settle in an insignificant little city like Viewton, make it his base of operations?"

"Well, our public schools *are* among the highest—" Betty got no further, as the determined madman went on.

"I was able to discover, through the use of scientific instruments, that Viewton, specifically Blendview, sits at the heart of an electromagnetic vortex, just as Odarr did in the Meegaw Valley near the Soot Soot Mound some five thousand years before. Prime conditions for inter-dimensional experimentation. I started out small—"

"Obviously." Doc had little patience for masterminds.

"Quiet," snapped Guller. "Several days ago I began testing out my process, focusing on small areas. Each time, this massive computer, my crossdimensionalizer, would record coordinates. And each time, in turn, I would send out my team of landscapers—"

"They're dead, by the way."

"Okay, thank you—to trim hedges according to the exact specifications on the parchpyrus, planting more round ones where necessary, so that the ancient blueprint—for that's what it was—was matched bush for bush in Blendview reality."

"That's when the people of Blendview started disappearing," chimed in Doc. "When you started testing, as you say, punching little holes, letting these bulb-headed freaks drag off my neighbors one by one," added the scientist with the gravity of a man who missed his neighbors.

"Bravo, Doctor. I see you've done your brain knowledge work. Neighbors. Bah. Small price to pay for a planet, wouldn't you say? Which brings me to the filtering process I alluded to a minute ago when I mentioned it. You see, essentially I am sifting through alternate realities, pulling from this world and that, with the crossdimensionalizer set to search out lush rich plant life that can thrive in our atmosphere —fruits, vegetables, pretty little flower things—but resilient enough to not be swept aside by humanity, not this time." Mobian grinned and it was not pleasant. "I've been 'cherry-picking.' Like shopping for home decor at an infinite department store—"

"I can appreciate that," offered Betty. "Sometimes they seem so huge—"

"It is like shopping, isn't it, Mrs. Armstrong. *Shopping at the shops of infinite realities.*"

"Is that a chain? I haven't—"

The self-centered Mobian cut Betty off again as he dramatized his reality shopping with a nauseating cuteness. "Oh, what have we here? This looks nice. I'd like one of these, and one of those. Do have this vine in red?"

"Stop pretending to shop," snarled Doc, who had no patience for people who acted out shopping sarcastically. "There's one thing I don't understand. Tell me, Mobian, how did you emulate the chanting of the Arradash? As I recall from the parchpyrus, their incantations were vital."

"Ah, I've saved the best for the last. I am most proud of that, Dr. Armstrong, most proud. For I was able to recreate the exact frequency of the Arradash chanting thanks to my patented mobian wave, which functions silently on small areas —as I first used it—but now comes in the form of a whistle blast for, shall we say, the larger operations of the next and final phase."

"You patented it?" uttered a mystified Doc.

"Just think, Doctor. A revolving door to other worlds, pulling in more and more, and each time the crossdimensionalizer makes note of the negative elements—"

"Why don't you just say monsters?"

"… thus eliminating most of them on the next round —the 'sifting' intervals in between—so that it's narrowed down to only those elements that will keep pesky mankind in check. After all, we had our chance. Now it's important there be *something higher* on the food chain. The perfect predator is one that will keep us subdued, but not eliminate us."

"And the crossdimensionalizer will tell you what that helpful monster is," interjected the savvy scientist.

"Exactly. Exactly, Doc Armstrong. I don't want us wiped out. I want us off the top rung. That, my friend, is paradise."

Doc stared at him. "You're mad."

"Be that as it may," continued Guller Mobian, "the good news is the crossdimensionalizer has accumulated all necessary data and we shall now begin the final phase, the final transformation. Thus, the longer intervals you're hearing. Soon, the lush heaven that is Blendview will spread its emerald glory across the entire planet, rolling out a carpet of green for our new apex predator—whatever it might be—and there will be no stopping it. There should be a name for this process… Terrafarming or terrarranging. Terramolding. No… Terradapting's not bad. Terrarigging? Ugh, no. Terradjusting, terracoercing—"

"They're getting worse," said Doc.

"Terramaneuvering. Terracquiescing—"

"I repeat, Mobian. You're mad," said Doc.

"You are the mad ones," served Guller with a side of venom. "Playing with a split atom like angry children with a toy, like um… one of those—um, those monkeys that play cymbals or—oh, it doesn't matter what toy."

"I won't argue with you about the great responsibility we all bear, in that regard. But what you're doing will open doors never meant to be opened in our existence. I guarantee you, the forces you unleash will be seven times worse than anything we might do to ourselves. I beg you to reconsider."

"Reconsider? Me? You might as well try and make a walrus wear jewelry."

"I would never do anything like that to a walrus," Doc spat back with the confidence of a man who knew he'd never do any such thing. He pressed on earnestly. "Mobian, please think about what you're doing before it's too late."

"I will not," came the affronted reply.

"Once you've looked into the face of the Great God Pan…"

Guller Mobian chuckled. "I know my Machen, Doctor. That was fantasy. This is reality. Multiple, in fact."

Doc Armstrong fixed the man with a look of steel and granite, possibly drywall. "What happened to the Arradash, Mr. Mobian?… Tell me that… No one seems to know."

"They probably got caught up in something—oh, look at the time. Almost ready for the final whistle, Doctor. It shall blast for one hour, one single hour, and then… New Odarr will begin to spread inexorably across the planet."

As if for emphasis, Guller pulled another switch on his platform and a slow rumbling started. The entire wall opposite the crossdimensionalizer began sliding up like a huge metal shade, revealing an enormous window.

"Here. You shall have a front row seat, Doctor."

Doc gazed at the almost panoramic view of much of plant-covered downtown as his captor grew thoughtful.

"You know, I still do not feel safe without that other parchpyrus in my hands, knowing someone else might acquire that knowledge. I believe I shall send out my mobiates to retrieve it. They're good little hunters you know." Guller put several fingers to the metal band around his temple, like a person concentrating or with a bad headache.

Gobbling erupted all around Doc, and, as one, the ghastly creatures scampered out the door with alarming speed. Doc was glad he wasn't that parchpyrus. But he also felt better about his odds in the mobiates' absence.

Guller countered by turning to his uniformed rugmen, and, with a similar I-have-a-headache gesture, mentally ordered the wig-wired automatons to trudge over and surround his scientist prisoner.

"And now—" began Guller Mobian.

Doc moved like a flashbulb, snatching a toupee off the head of one rugman and jamming it onto the head of another. The resulting sparks and smoke had a chain reaction through each of them, and a hissing, popping, flashing chaos followed, in which Doc was momentarily invisible.

Instinctively, Guller Mobian hit a lever and his platform began to quickly rise. Not quickly enough, as Doc leaped up and clutched onto the edge of it. Mobian saw this and began desperately stomping a tiny foot on one of the scientist's hands. But tiny feet often have little effect.

The platform was high above the floor now, and Doc began quickly pulling himself up. Mobian, feeling helpless, jumped up from his seat at the controls and—in a move that showed just how spry the little so-and-so was—leapt across to a catwalk not far from Betty.

Doc yanked a lever and stopped the rising platform. Then he also jumped across to the catwalk. Examining the complex contraption holding his wife, he drew on his ability to assess things at a high rate of speed, honed by years of watching beauty pageants.

"Careful, Paul. It might—"

Doc turned a small wing nut. All of the numerous facets of the complicated clutching device instantly opened as one, and Betty fell into his arms.

She let out a relieved, exhausted gasp as he held her. "I don't know if I've ever been spread-eagled *that* long before," moaned the tired housewife.

There was little time to moan over being spread-eagled, however, as shots started plinking around them.

"Come on!" shouted Doc as he took her hand, and together they jumped to the platform. "Hang on!" Doc also shouted, as he slammed some levers and started the motorized four-wheeled bed below that held the lift. It started moving quickly across the floor, lift extended and all.

"It's too late to stop me, Doc Armstrong!" boomed the voice of Guller Mobian over speakers, as much as his shrill voice could boom. "Too late!"

Rugmen still fired up at Doc and Betty high atop the platform, but the motorized bed plowed into them, and they didn't even try to get out of the way. Doc sped the vehicle towards the door now, lowering the lift as they went. When they reached the door, they were just low enough to jump off and run outside before the bowled-over rugmen could even react.

Behind them, the whistle blasted. This time it didn't stop.

Chapter 28

WHEN WORLDS COLLAGE

The man and woman ran side by side through the jungle with the furious and jittery incoherence of a nightmare. So exhausted were they, and at the same time exhilarated, that everything seemed drained of color. The ashen hothouse flew past them at hyperkinetic speed. Reality was in question, as it had been of late, and the piercing blast that filled the still air harkened to newer and more dangerous unknowns.

Each of them seemed to relive the past two days in a lightning speed loop that saw Blendview fill with greenery again and again, like the time-lapse nature footage they showed kids in school.

Betty had no sense of direction in her new extra-foliated town, but neither did she when she walked through her own living room. She trusted that her husband knew where they were going, as he always did, and that this frantic headlong plunge had purpose beyond simple survival, simple flight from madman and minions. She did not have to be a scientist to know that something dire and merciless was on the horizon.

She trusted Paul's common sense. Certainly, he loved science, second only to Betty. But, surely he would never allow it to go too far, farther than was ever intended. Surely, Paul's science had conscience. If anyone could stop Guller Mobian it was him. And maybe the high school gym teacher. He looked like he could take care of himself. But he lacked the science part. And right now that seemed like an awfully big part.

Doc felt the unreality too. It was similar to that first time he grasped quantum mechanics and felt the reality rug pulled out from under him. Once fully understood, there was no stepping back. Life and existence changed forever. Like getting your first apartment.

Humans come wired with a deep sense of what is supposed to be, and not supposed to be. Scientists have to step beyond that, or they're ineffective. But that didn't mean there was no vertigo at that next dizzy level, no bout of mental nausea to top the last. And no preparation seemed to prepare: they were always ready… and they were never ready.

He knew that Guller Mobian was wrong. What he was doing was wrong and dangerous. But he also knew deep down that the madman's tangled roots were born of something Doc often struggled not to think about. He could not help feeling in his heart that he was part of the problem, just as science was. If science was not immune from blame, then neither was Doc.

He also knew he could not let soul-searching distract him from his goal. And he had less than an hour before the mobian wave started spreading a computer-calculated and dangerous reality across the entire planet. That was unacceptable. Doc Armstrong didn't know if he could stop him. But he had to try.

They were past the heart of downtown Viewton now, though it was getting harder and harder to tell. Even the larger buildings—library, town hall, museum—were entirely covered. Doc reckoned they were close to the edge of Blendview, and he halted them so abruptly that Betty almost went flying, and would have if he hadn't been holding her arm. The scientist had just thought of something.

Betty tagged after Doc who seemed drawn to what was apparently one of the stores in the commercial district. At least, she guessed it might be, under all that flora.

"Paul. Paul, what is it?" asked his panting wife.

Before he could answer, a door opened in the plant-ridden mass and out of its shadows emerged Lattis, greeting them with a smile.

"Lattis!" exclaimed Betty with pleasant surprise. "Fancy running into you here."

"Hello, Betty. Hello, Paul."

"Is that the five-and-dime?" asked Betty. "Paul, how did you—?"

Doc smiled at Lattis. "So tell me… Is he having a good time?"

"Of course he is," replied Lattis.

Doc turned to Betty. "It was the one place Kro-Bar always wanted to have the run of."

"I had hoped you might remember that," said Lattis.

Under that thick mossy mat, with the electricity out, it would have been pitch black inside. But Joytey's Five-and-dime was illuminated by strategically placed candles, making it actually kind of cozy.

The first thing Doc and Betty saw, however, was quite unexpected, and Lattis had not prepared them. Off to one side, in an aisle, examining some plastic bow and arrow sets, was what appeared to be City Brad. Doc's elation that his friend—last seen heroically decoying the rugmen—was safe and sound, was tempered by the man's appearance.

City Brad was wearing animal skins.

Lattis stepped up beside the gaping couple and spoke softly. "So, there are several things I must tell you. He is no longer City Brad but Throwback Brad. He also claims he's taken a mate, but we have seen no evidence of her."

"When… when did this all happen?" Betty tried hard to make it sound delightful.

"We do not really know. This is what happened. When Kro-Bar finally got the transmutatron adjusted properly we ran after you, Paul, and found the dead cyclops, but not you or the others. We decided the best thing to do was to take shelter somewhere, somewhere we thought you might find us, so that we might regroup. Though we had some disagreement about this, Kro-Bar claimed the best store to find weapons in was the five-and-dime. That's alright, he's enjoying himself, and I knew that you would probably find us here."

"Paul! Betty!" the gruff but amiable tones were unmistakeable. General Scottmanson stepped out of an aisle.

Warm greetings were exchanged, and Doc quickly filled him in on both General Krayper's betrayal and demise, causing Scottmanson to wax philosophical. "I thought something might be wrong with him. Couldn't put my finger on it. Something in his demeanor, particularly making little napkin tents in the military cafeteria and lining up bacon. I always felt, of any of us, he would be the one prone to… outlandish ideas… however good his intentions. Like when he dressed up as a tree…" The General trailed off, lost in thought for a moment. "Did *not* think he'd get stung to death hundreds of times by a multi-eyed myriapod though… "

At that moment Kro-Bar came flying down the aisle on roller skates, right past them, looking like he was about to say something as he crashed into a display of tin robots.

In no time at all, Betty, with Lattis's help, arranged a sitting area towards the back of the store. She fussed over suitable tablecloth and place settings, until her husband convinced her it was fine. The only disappointment had been that there was no sign of Mac, their strange but pleasant macaroon-headed friend. Doc was particularly sorry. It was the only time a cookie man had saved his life.

As the group sat down to strategize, Lattis brought Throwback Brad over to join them.

"I will help," he said, speaking rather stiffly as he did now. "I will spread word of what is happening and tell my people."

"You have no people," said Doc.

Throwback Brad looked crushed and hung his head. Betty went to the proud but sad warrior, putting a supportive arm around him. "Now now, honey," she said, admonishing her husband. "Yes he does. City—I mean, Throwback Brad has us. We are his people."

"You are kind, She Who Bakes," said Throwback Brad softly. "But… with respect to the house-cleaning one, you are not my people."

"Right now we're the closest thing, sweetie, so let's forget all that silly stuff, okay?" chirped Betty as though talking to a child.

Throwback Brad stood slowly, proudly, taking all this in. "I hear your words and shall put what you say before the Council of Elders. It is for them to dec—"

"Okay, we have less than forty minutes," said Doc. "I don't think we can talk about this right now, Throwback Brad."

"Very well, smart brain," uttered Throwback Brad begrudgingly.

"The question is," declared Doc, "once begun, is the effect of the crossdimensionalizer reversible. Unfortunately, without the parchpyrus—"

General Scottmanson approached, placed something on the table and unrolled it. Doc stared.

For the next thirty minutes Dr. Paul Armstrong pored over the ancient scroll like a juggler selecting oranges. With the knowledge gleaned by his mentor, Professor Atroppasmirki, when he cracked the code of the mysterious artifact, Doc was now able to comprehend the strange markings, writing and symbols. It had only been good fortune that the General, having sent his helicopter pilot back for help since communications were down, proceeded towards the downtown area, upon which he stumbled over the tube containing the parchpyrus. Fortunately, no one was not hurt.

Betty was about to make coffee from various five-and-dime items, including flavor straws and wax tubes full of syrup, when Doc abruptly stood, rolled up the parchpyrus and announced that he was done.

There was no time to lose.

As Betty wrote later: "We were never to forget those minutes spent at Novelty House, as we came to call it, and would look back on them fondly for the rest of our days. We seemed so happy in the five-and-dime, with all its simple problems and useful notions and entertainments. The sound of Kro-Bar's happy play and Lattis's gentle scolding. General Scottmanson's soft snore in a cozy hammock display. Throwback Brad's soulful chanting of lost loved ones and great hunts and changing lands. And my own daydreamings of better times past, and still to come. Novelty House was an innocence the real world could never afford. Plus my husband is restless and must save the world."

The six who would save the world moved with a combination of speed and stealth matched only by certain golf pros. They were entering the stretch of downtown so recently like the Valley of the Kings, with its massive vine-strewn edifices. Now the manmade structures were invisible beneath deep layers of intricately knotted flora of unknown origin.

Throwback Brad was among their number, though he did not hide his great sorrow. He also insisted on bringing his mate, though, when it came time to leave, he was unable to produce her. Besides the animals skins—the origin of which eluded his companions—he bore a plastic bow with numerous suction cup arrows in a quiver on his back.

Likewise, General Scottmanson was packing his automatic, while Kro-Bar toted the transmutatron.

The group was passing what used to be the museum when the whistle stopped.

"Oh, Paul," gasped Betty with alarm.

"It's alright, Betty. Since I now understand the parchpyrus, I now know the effects of the mobian wave are reversible, even once they've begun."

"Did you ascertain that?" asked Kro-Bar.

"Yes, I did," replied Doc.

"I love that word."

"However, there is still a need for urgency, my friends. I have no idea the extent of the damage it might do."

And with that, they began running—no easy task through the mad jumble of nature littering the main street.

For a minute all they could hear was their own panting. Then Doc, who could actually hear the sound of a donut, became aware of a low steady pulsing hum. He wondered if this might in fact be the mobian wave. Was it in fact continuing? And if so, where was that blasting whistle? It had ceased minutes ago, and yet nothing seemed to be happening.

Doc suddenly entertained the enticing possibility that it had all been a bust for the tiny-bodied, normal-headed tyrant, that the mobian wave was ultimately a failure, or perhaps that the crossdimensionalizer's coordinates were off just a fraction, which is all it would take. Maybe he could go home and do science again. After some much needed landscaping.

The ground thundered so hard and so abruptly that the six running figures were almost knocked off their feet. And everywhere round things turned.

This time it was a cacophony. This time it felt bigger.

Everything shimmered with an energy unseen on Earth for five thousand years. There was a heightened and terrifying sense of the monumental, and the somehow obscene.

"Come on!" cried Doc, rallying the startled team, urging them on down the main street to Sta-Mor-Down.

As they ran, and as Doc had advised, they kept eyes straight ahead, ignoring any shifting movement on their periphery, lured as they were by a mixture of curiosity and dread. There was no escaping the activity ahead though: the wild roping tendrils and grasping brush, expanding and bursting forth with unconquerable might.

So loud were grinding hedges and trembling ground that the screeches and pops and squeaks and caterwauls of the new wildlife played second fiddle—the fauna supposedly handpicked by Guller Mobian and his crossdimensionalizer.

Doc could see the madman's Sta-Mor-Down plant a couple of hundred yards ahead, across the flat area still amazingly open, no doubt for Guller's convenience. Though safely away from the dark new plant masses, they felt vulnerable on the plain. But they could see more of the sky now, which appeared to subtly shift as ripples of energy passed over it. Something in the fabric of it changed, reminiscent of both bubbling and cracking, like a vast painting being touched up.

A shape ran out of the brush a ways up ahead, running perpendicular to their passage. Besides tall loping legs, there appeared to be little else to it. It continued, disappearing into the brush on the opposite side.

A long neck rose above some trees to their left and kept rising high above them, some three hundred feet. It had no head. Its sound was like a baby's crying. It merged with hundreds of other sounds: mewling and chittering and roaring. Each listener conjured different images of the grotesque, the unsettling, the inconceivable and the vile that this clamor suggested.

They were halfway across the plain when, as one, their attention was drawn upward again, up to that rippling sky. The strange shifting fragments in its dull yellows and blues had continued, but now seemed to swirl and rally, as though small cyclones were finally getting organized. Even running, knowing that they shouldn't, none of Doc's group could rip their eyes from it, for it felt somehow important: one of those things that required remembering where you were when it happened. Bits of clouds and chips of blue were gradually uniting with the very electricity from the air in a concerted effort of some kind. What could it be that worked in such a dangerous medium?

And while the group's eyes drifted, picking and choosing which of those trillion particles to follow in the unsettling manipulation, a form began to emerge. Though working from scratch, this potent and unknown resource was nothing if not thorough. And each of the witnesses wondered if they were seeing the same as their companions.

An enormous face was making sense of the sky.

Chapter 29

THE MOBIAN WAVE

"This way!" yelled Doc, veering to the side, diverting them from the open plain, but more from that sight in the sky. They were also closer to the Sta-Mor-Down plant and the scientist didn't want to risk Mobian spotting them. At a string of dark underbrush they took shelter and caught their breath. No one spoke.

What they had witnessed dwarfed the mastermind and the countless incomprehensibles cropping up in the jungles of New Odarr. Despite themselves, their eyes lifted again, returning to the immense face that must have stretched for hundreds of miles, though something about its scale seemed immeasurable. None of them could afford to look away.

"Who—who is it, Paul?" Betty broke their silence.

Doc shook his head. "I don't know, Betty."

"Do you think it's bad to look at?"

"I don't know. I'm a scientist, I look at everything."

Even while they gazed at it, more and more tiny particles of existence rushed and rallied to join its solidity, each bit of cloud and blue sky and wind and dust defining it more and more. It began to take on a grinning leer that chilled them to their very core, injecting a deep and dark terror more distressing than any monster the parallel worlds could conjure.

Doc Armstrong, the scientist, knew he could not identify this apparition, this piece of nightmare sky that he wished were mere fancy. Not without something, some hard evidence.

He only knew he had to stop it.

Guller Mobian was very high at this time. Not just in his lift platform, but in the crowning success he was basking in, if a tad early. All was proceeding according to his methodical and organized amateur scientist plan. And who better to hear all about it than his rugmen soldiers now in attendance?

Guller stood and addressed them. "All is proceeding according to my methodical and organized amateur scientist plan. It's a good feeling when hard work pays off, like that fence you always wanted to mend and finally got around to."

Dim faces looked up at him, wanting to comprehend but not having the first clue.

"Well, I was hoping to find a level you could relate on, but perhaps not. Price I pay for mind-controlled slaves I suppose. Might as well talk to myself. All I can say is, you'll be very glad you're in on the ground floor of this, believe you me. All of you will hold special places on my personal police force, making sure that anyone having a problem with our new world will be dealt with swiftly and fairly, and wait'll you see the uniforms. Alright, that's all I have right now, this isn't camp. Back to your duties. Send out more patrols. I see one returning now."

As the rugmen lethargically dispersed, Guller stared out the window at a group of six, in army uniforms, tromping across the flat.

The six plodded along, as any rugmen would, no doubt returning from patrol. They occasionally stumbled over the cluttered terrain, as rugmen will, even on a good surface.

As one did, their helmet almost got knocked off and they quickly straightened it. Not before a bit of Lattis's blonde hair spilled out.

The small group fell in with another converging on the large open door, and, when they arrived, yet another patrol passed by on their way out. Over all, the heavy pulse of the mobian wave never let up: a suffocating blanket of sound that covered everything, as the vegetation soon would.

Inside Guller Mobian's cavernous headquarters, their trudging steps merged with the whole, and the huge facility reverberated with the amplified plod of rugmen workers—like an oppressive symphony for the future of labor.

The six veered off from the others now, proceeding towards the massive wall that was the crossdimensionalizer, its lights and buttons and tubes and tapes humming with activity.

With a concentration too intense for rugmen, the small group marched straight towards a section of the lowest bank of controls. They were mere feet away when the sharp high voice from above slit the air like a letter opener.

"Halt!"

Rugmen closed in, faster than usual, like bees protecting a hive or visiting celebrity. Suddenly the six were surrounded by what appeared to be every available mindless minion in the plant.

A high whine of machinery announced the lift platform swooping down, down to meet them. Guller Mobian yanked a lever and came to a halt just above the trapped half dozen who now stood very still.

A piercing and triumphant laugh broke the tension. "How nice of you to come for the tour."

The six did not move.

Mobian looked annoyed. "I know you're not here for the tour—I don't even give tours. Yet. That was my sarcasm, don't you like it?"

Still they did not move.

The mastermind decided to forego the wit, for now. "Did you think for even one minute that I would not be expecting you? That I would not have arranged for almost all of my rugmen to be here to greet you? That I was not anticipating some... foolish strategy? To stop my crossdimensionalizer? Though not this obvious, perhaps—I did expect more from the great... *Dr. Paul Armstrong!*"

Still no response from the enclosed six.

"Doctor, I just gave you an opportunity for a dramatic reveal, why not rip your helmet off?" The mad genius was growing frustrated. "Come, come, the jig is up and I don't even know what a jig is. Let's not drag this out." And with that Guller touched the mobion on his head, and a rugman stepped forward and started knocking helmets off. First Betty's, then Kro-Bar's, Lattis's, Throwback Brad's, General Scottmanson's.

"It seems we've left the last for best eh, Doctor? How fitting." With that, the rugman knocked the final helmet off.

It wasn't Doc.

"Who?" Guller stared at the nondescript man in soldier's uniform. "One of my rugmen. But how—?" It was then he noticed that there was no toupee on the man's head.

"You know, it's a funny thing, Mr. Mobian," said Kro-Bar. "Without that horrid hair... they'll listen to anyone."

"Is it not funny, large-headed one?" scoffed Throwback Brad with quiet defiance.

"My head is *normal!*" screamed Guller Mobian. Then something dawned on him—something far more important than physical proportions—and he gaped at them, as though gaping were a new thing for him, and he did not handle it well.

"If... Doc Armstrong isn't here, then..."

Doc Armstrong was in fact staring up at the tallest building in Viewton. A building left surprisingly clean of encroaching vegetation: the reason for which had come to the scientist just a short time ago. Not simply because it was Mobian Towers. He knew there was more to it than that. The very existence of this building was vital to the diabolical millionaire.

His eyes went to the top, to the edge of the flat roof, then beyond that, up that tall radio tower ever-looming above the city. Radio tower. Transmitting tower. There was little doubt. That deep persistent pulsing hum known as the mobian wave was emanating from there.

Movement in the sky drew his attention, and he looked to that which he did not want to, that still-forming face across its vast expanse. It was clearer now, its saturnine features etched sharper. It seemed to look right at him, but he knew better, knew it appeared that way to everybody. That was its trick. But the leering presence served a purpose—it made him press on.

The man of science and several useful hobbies ran to the building at dizzying speed. As he neared it, rugmen guards spotted him and began to converge. Doc handily unsnapped his science gun from his belt—the science gun he'd just fetched from home—and fired on the run. Balls of U4Eon peppered rapidly, and down went the rugmen, feeling a lot happier. But inside, the lobby was packed with them, just waiting for him, behind thick unbreakable glass: certainly too much for a single assailant and his special gas gun.

But he never intended that.

Amidst strewn bodies of unconscious rugmen, Doc crouched like a panther at a wedding reception, whipping the pack from his back like he'd been whipping packs from his back for hundreds of years. As expectant rugmen watched numbly through the glass, out came the climbing gear he'd also brought from home, including skyscraper rope, grapnel and special rappel harness of Doc's own invention. His audience could do little as the man swung the grapnel high, caught a ledge two stories up, tugged on the rope and, with a snappy wave, jumped to the side of the building. Amazingly, he started to rappel upwards, pulling the rope furiously through his rigger's belt, clipping and adjusting at intervals. It was obvious this strategy was not covered in the gawking rugmen's instructions.

Doc continued his climb like a man who really wanted to get to the top of something. He managed two stories at a throw and continued his ascent pattern almost robotically. Somewhere an alarm sounded. Either the rugmen had thrown one, or Guller realized what was going on and was attempting a counter-measure.

Doc couldn't pinpoint when he'd first realized that the whistle on the Sta-Mor-Down Rug Company plant was a decoy. Not merely a decoy: its shrill blast covered the deeper tones of the mobian wave, camouflaging its true source, which was—as the scientist surmised—the transmitting tower high atop the tallest building in Blendview. He had to hand it to his clever opponent; it was a slick bit of misdirection. Doc was never above handing things, where things were due to be handed.

He had four of the high-rise's twelve floors left to scale and, already at the point of exhaustion prior to this assault, his arms were feeling the strain. Only Doc's daily regimen of doing physical things he didn't even want to do because they weren't science had kept him going this far.

He was two stories away when he paused to catch his breath. Instinctively, he hammered a piton into the concrete and hooked a rope to it while his inner-good-guy-strength recharged. He wished he'd brought water but was already loaded down and in a hurry, plus he remembered there was a bubbler inside which would be fine as long as lot of kids hadn't been using it, because you never knew.

Before another bubbler thought could pass through his scientific mind, Doc heard a sound he had not expected: a heavy clanking. It came from above, on the roof. The clank was rhythmic, steady and getting louder. Doc craned to look up, wondering what this unexpected noise could be.

His eyes were glued to the roof against the sky, and a shape suddenly broke its straight edge. Impossibly, it was the head of Guller Mobian. The eccentric villain stared down at Doc, and a grin twisted his features. Then, with two clanks, more of him came into view, and the scientist saw how that was possible. Mobian was seated in an automaton about three times as large as his Drydekker guise, when they first encountered him. Thus, no attempt to look human this time: all shiny metallic plate, like a large boxy mechanical man from the science fiction books Doc had enjoyed as a child. Except for the head sticking out. That was Mobian.

"Greetings, Dr. Armstrong. We meet again."

"Don't make this sound like a friendly lunch or something, Mobian," called Doc. "How did you get here so fast?"

"Did you really think I would not have an underground tunnel and fast railcar connecting my Sta-Mor-Down plant and Mobian Towers?"

"Yes. I did not think you would. You have obviously given this some thought," granted the scientist. Doc did not wait for a response. He quickly unhooked himself from the piton, threw the grapnel up and snagged another story. As he pulled himself up he heard whirring hydraulics as Mobian shifted in his automaton.

"Don't climb any closer. It won't do you any good to come up here. It can only mean your end. Oh, pardon me. I forgot to introduce the mechanical man I'm wearing. How rude. Allow me to present Hydraulic Henry, similar in basics to my Clyme Drydekker disguise, though without any subterfuge. And bigger, more powerful, also bigger... As you shall soon see."

Doc pulled himself up onto the next ledge. He was now one floor from the top.

"Give it up," spat Mobian. "That's as far as you get."

A crackling of energy sounded in the sky and Doc looked up from catching his breath to see the enormous face still forming, achieving greater definition by the second.

"Have you seen that, Mobian? Have you seen what you have wrought? cried Doc.

Mobian gazed up for just a few seconds. "Merely an atmospheric byproduct of the transformation. An illusion caused by my mobian wave and shuffling realities. Nothing programmed in my crossdimensionalizer is even vaguely like that. Nothing at all."

Doc tossed his grapnel to the roof edge, and a flexible tubular arm immediately swiped it away.

"What I *should* do is let it catch, then unhook it once you're climbing. But I'm a fair man."

Doc already had the grapnel flying up to a new location, several yards from the last. Mobian quickly clanked over and knocked it away just in time. "Really, you're forcing my hand. Just quit while you're ahead, Doctor."

But the grapnel was already returning, to yet a new spot on the ledge. Mobian again shifted over, frustration showing as he slapped it aside once more. "I see you're determined to give me a workout. Don't make me kill you, Armstrong. Don't be a fool. I'm giving you a chance. Why not give my world a try?"

Another clank as the grapnel hit, over to the other side. Mobian pounded his robotic frame over there. But before he could reach it another grapnel hit. Mobian was confused as he swiped at the first one, which had become lodged.

While the mastermind tried desperately to unhook that grapnel, Doc hurriedly pulled himself up the rope to the second one.

"Why make this difficult? Why can't you be more open-minded, Armstrong?" Mobian finally tore the first grapnel away, saw Doc halfway up the rope to the second one, and hurriedly clanked over. "You leave me no choice."

Guller Mobian yanked the grapnel loose as Doc was still several feet from the roof. Anticipating this, Doc quickly leaped for the ledge, grabbing it with both hands. Hydraulics whined as Mobian moved closer, raised one robotic arm and smashed it down right beside Doc's hand. It was only luck for the scientist dangling twelve stories that Guller Mobian's movements in the boxy metallic frame were neither swift nor fluid, but the best that modern—or even slightly advanced— science could provide. It was a mechanical effort each time that hard steel claw came down to crush one of Doc's hands.

But it was inevitable that Hydraulic Henry should connect and it did. Doc yelled out as the heavy steel claw pounded his left hand, and it took all his strength and determination to not let go. Again, the tubular arm raised up. The scientist's left hand could not take another blow, and that's where Mobian's claw was heading.

In a daring and possibly foolhardy (maybe even idiothardy) move that spoke of sheer desperation in elegant terms, Doc let go of the ledge with his left hand, quickly grabbing onto the "wrist" of the descending arm and claw with both hands.

Guller Mobian reacted instinctively by jerking the arm, but Doc held tight. Furious and frustrated, the twisted genius started moving the robotic arm up and down, in an effort to shake the scientist off and drop him about a hundred and thirty feet. Exhausted as he was, Doc Armstrong was not about to let go.

But he also knew time was on his opponent's side, and he couldn't hold on forever. Calling on his last ounce of strength, Doc began climbing inexorably up Hydraulic Henry's metal arm. Enraged, Mobian slammed the arm—Doc and all —onto the roof's edge. But the scientist held fast against the impact, continuing to drag himself up. Doc pounded his fist on the automaton's side, and though the machine was too strong to hurt by hand, the loud banging at least had the effect of disorienting its pilot.

Finally, in sheer desperation, Mobian whipped the automaton around at the waist, and the force flung Doc into the air. Fortunately, it was the air above the roof, and he landed hard in the gravel, relatively unharmed. The scientist's tenaciousness had paid off.

As Doc painfully got to his feet, he now had a better look at Hydraulic Henry, and his initial impression was confirmed: the eight-foot contraption might have stepped out of one of those old movie serials like *The Adventures of Crosh Donning, Spider Rockets of Moon Mars* or *High Planet Warning*. These had sparked little Doc's imagination, enough to make him become a scientist (and this reminded him that he had yet to build a robot).

Of course, technically this wasn't a robot since it did not function independently of the "driver." It also had no head, allowing Guller's noggin to stick out of the top, making it look quite small for a change.

All of this Doc absorbed in a third of a second, which was about all he had before Hydraulic Henry turned and started clanking towards him with ominous steady strides, the length of which made up for its lack of speed.

The roof was peppered with stacks and vents and fans, and the only two structures of note were the staircase housing and the big antenna itself which was Eiffel Tower style: steel latticework, wide at the base, tapering to a point a hundred feet up. A typical radio tower—in reality, the mobian wave transmitter. Doc, however, headed for the former.

As Hydraulic Henry continued to relentlessly pound its way over, Doc disappeared around the far side of the staircase housing and tried the door. To his relief it was not locked.

Guller Mobian throttled his contraption to the housing and brought it clanking around the corner. He halted. The door was open.

Stairs were tricky, but the stairwell was large enough that Hydraulic Henry could maneuver it. Mobian shifted some levels inside the "cockpit," and his machine stepped into the housing.

When Guller Mobian vanished from the Sta-Mor-Down plant, Betty and the others were still surrounded by the horde of rugmen. They weren't exactly sure where he had disappeared to, or how he was going to get to where Doc was. All they knew was, according to prearranged plan, they needed the mad genius out of the way. Without him, the rugmen would only be acting on previous orders. They did not think on their feet. Or anywhere else for that matter.

So the group waited for several minutes, long enough to make sure Mobian was on his way to the radio tower. And then five people moved like a well-oiled mackerel.

There was a slight hiccup when Betty tried an impromptu move inspired by something she'd done once before, coyly drawing up a trouser cuff, revealing a bit of leg.

But her army uniform disguise made it awkward and she dropped that ploy.

Lattis started the ball by feigning a sneeze that was really a yak. The force of the unexpected sound-punch knocked a group of rugmen back, punching a hole in the surrounding circle, through which Kro-Bar and Betty immediately bolted. When the sluggish rugmen started closing in, General Scottmanson and Throwback Brad stepped up and, like a four-armed machine, began a volley of furious punches. The rugmen, of course, kept coming, because that's what rugmen do. But the pair were relentless, stacking them like kindling, only kindling with eyes and facial features and limbs and uniforms and no wood in their physical makeup.

"This is my *general punch!*" snapped Scottmanson as he hauled off. "It's like a general court-martial, only with my fists!"

"I, unfortunately, have yet to name my punches, since Throwback Brad and his people do not possess that thing yet!" declared the valiant Throwback Brad as he swung mightily.

"You have no people!" Lattis called over her shoulder as she yakked her way to the big sliding door, her sharp yells knocking rugmen down like pins.

Kro-Bar and Betty were now on the lift platform, the latter conking rugmen on the head with her shoe as they tried to climb aboard. Kro-Bar mastered the controls like a future man, raised a lever and the lift swiftly rose. Betty saw two hangers-on and slapped her shoe on their hands, causing them to fall with the usual half-hearted ahhhs.

The platform reached the catwalk and Kro-Bar leapt to it, while Betty stood watch. He moved along the length of the crossdimensionalizer, referring to a paper he'd had in his pocket: a detailed sketch made from memory by the observant Doc Armstrong, who once recreated the Mona Lisa with trained aphids simply because he could.

Meantime, Lattis held the lever down and the big door slowly rumbled open. Rugmen continued to mindlessly come at her, and she kept turning to yak them away.

While Kro-Bar was making specific adjustments to the crossdimensionalizer, Betty spotted two rugmen climbing a ladder towards him. She looked at the lift platform controls and hastily tested several levers, resulting in some herky-jerky moves, until she got the hang of it. With a determination only a veteran of yard sales could muster, Betty swooped the lift down to them, slamming them against the ladder. With matching ahhhs, the rugmen dropped below. Thanks to the quick-thinking housewife, Kro-Bar safely continued to alter dials and knobs. Just then, commotion came from below.

Lattis was luring rugmen out the big open door.

At that precise moment, on the roof of Mobian's high-rise, Doc slowly raised his head from behind the radio tower base where he'd been hiding. The open door had fooled the madman. He was heading down the stairs. The scientist had no intention of leaving. Not without doing what he came to do. He had no choice. It was this, or concede to Mobian's dream of a New Odarr.

Doc climbed onto the base of the radio tower. Sure enough, close examination revealed that it was so much more. The low throb of the mobian wave was strongest here, and the scientist knew he had to work fast for many reasons, not the least of which being that—as with a talk show host—a person could only stand so much.

It didn't take a lot of searching before the clever meteographer found a hidden panel. Doc managed to pry it open, and his eyes danced over the newly revealed controls like an ant admiring his crumb collection. Grasping the science, he began making some adjustments that he knew would be really really neat. Doc worked feverishly, like a barber who knows his customer is dying.

Because of the near-deafening pulse of the mobian wave up close, he never heard the clanking feet. But he did feel the strong metal claws clutch him from behind. Doc was lifted like a rag doll, but a rag doll of a heroic scientist which was anatomically correct, which would be an odd thing.

Guller's head looked tiny protruding from that shiny steel box torso. The mad genius appeared pleased but annoyed. "It was a good trick, that open door, Armstrong. I was down a couple of flights when I paused to listen. There should have been noise of your footsteps reverberating in that deep stairwell. Did you suppose I never took reverberating footsteps in school?" He laughed, and it sounded like an insane clown's pet.

Mobian worked a lever, and Doc grimaced as the claws tightened. "Well, maybe he has some special non-reverberating shoes, I said to myself. I mean, he *is* a clever scientist." Again, Mobian worked the lever, again his prisoner flinched. "Then I realized the limited market for non-reverberating shoes, and I knew it must be a trick, a clever mischief-trick." His next words came luxuriously, like a large bubble bath especially made for sentences. *"Well… it will be your last… "*

Mobian's hand was on the lever. Doc, already in pain, knew that the next squeeze would crush him.

At the Sta-Mor-Down facility, Kro-Bar, seeming satisfied, looked at the sketch one final time and performed the finishing touch: he threw a large and important switch.

Before Mobian could work the lever that would make the claws crush Doc Armstrong, the omnipresent pulsing sound suddenly altered. It took on a different rhythm, less oppressive somehow, less malignant, in so many subtle ways.

Guller Mobian looked up at his tower, then down at his control box. His eyes went wide, and he looked incensed, like he might shoot flames.

Doc didn't wait for him to recover. The man-who-used-science-in-everyday-life lifted his feet and slammed them against the shiny bulky box of Hydraulic Henry's chest, then pushed off. Mobian's machine teetered backwards, releasing Doc who dropped to the roof, got to his feet and started running. With a long drawn-out scream, Guller Mobian pounded after him. Such was his unbridled fury, that one could never ever bridle it—even an expert bridler. The micro-madman throttled Hydraulic Henry as hard as he could. The contraption started smoking, but its powerful legs worked faster than ever.

Doc neared the far edge of the rooftop, then turned to look back. He was happy to see Mobian's emotions getting the better of him. The man was more concerned with finishing Doc than with any hope of reconfiguring his now skewed mobian wave.

Doc had nowhere left to go and stood there waiting in that heroic pose he'd used before, where his hands are in open ready position, just slightly away from his body.

Hydraulic Henry bore down like a fast freight, or even a fast freight train or a train that hauls freight. Wherever he went he would take Doc with him. The mad clanking came faster than it seemed possible as the metal monster rushed towards the edge. Doc and Guller stared at each other like roosters in a henhouse playing a game of kitchen. Only there could be no winner. In a henhouse.

At the last second, Doc hooked a grapnel on the ledge and dropped over the side, as Hydraulic Henry and its brilliant pilot, Guller Mobian, hurtled into open air without the benefit of Doc accompanying them.

The man of science could hear the whine of sophisticated hydraulics grow more and more distant, until the sound of a hard metallic crash finished it.

Dr. Paul Armstrong took a deep breath. And then he climbed back onto the roof. As he stood up, he turned towards that face in the sky. Its definition draining like air from a tire, the grinning visage was quickly transforming to something wretched and miserable before its final obliteration on the wind.

Chapter 30
ALL THE MATH THAT COMES AFTER

The world's greatest housewife exited the kitchen with the world's largest tray full of snacks. There were things for all tastes: baked kenters, sugar-diamonds, wokkles, some Nobin Creams, a bowl of binscopps and some cable bread and probably more things too numerous to mention.

The tray wound its way through a living room bright with sunlight from windows no longer covered in an excess of plant life.

There were strict landscaping laws in place now, most prominently, the Curtilage Grooming Act of 1963. Guller Mobian's tampering had seen to that. Restrictions mostly on hedge trimming: they could no longer be perfectly round. Rounded, yes, but not perfectly round. It seemed a small price to pay for public safety.

The tray landed on the coffee table, as it had so many times before, and several hands reached in for favored snacks.

"I was impressed with the speed with which things reversed, Paul Armstrong," said Lattis taking a nibble of a fruit carson.

"Two days. Not bad, considering," said Doc through a mouthful of wokkles.

"I do not understand the new landscaping laws," mused Kro-Bar as he went for another lemontroll.

"It's there to protect everybody," offered City Brad, now reverted from his temporary Throwback Brad persona, though he still liked to sit around a barbecue and tell tales of olden days and occasionally long for his mate. "It simply means that we can never enjoy hedges quite so round again, not perfectly round anyway."

Doc added, "They can still be ovals, ellipses, stadium shape is a particularly nice one—kind of an extended oval. There are plenty of options open to the imaginative gardener."

"Yes, but who decides what is too round in life?" queried Kro-Bar. "Is that not for each of us, each in our own heart, to decide for ourselves, if we are to be a truly free society that enjoys perfect roundness?"

"A society needs laws in order to survive, else there's anarchy and lots of confusing things," said City Brad. "Next thing you know, people are wearing strange things on their heads and dancing in the wrong places. I guess we can never be truly free can we?"

"They have a set of tools now for testing roundness, various calipers. I suppose Mobian pointed out what we needed to be wary of," observed Doc. "Really really perfectly round things. In a strange way, we should be grateful to him, twisted as he was.

"Hmm," thought General Scottmanson thoughtfully as he reached for another krole. "The atomic bomb is a round thing too, though not perfectly. So is the atom. Of course, that's something Paul and I have already been warning people about. And I'm happy to say that, thanks to our efforts, a new commission on Bombs That Are Way Too Bad is forming even as we speak."

"When did that happen?" asked Doc as he bit into a jimmy-wafer.

"Just this morning," said Scottmanson. "I hadn't even had a chance to tell you."

"See, honey?" said Betty, patting her husband's knee. "Sometimes things you *do* do, *do* do some good."

"That is a lot of do do, Betty," commented Lattis, and they all laughed.

"I said four do's!" giggled Betty, almost uncontrollably. "In a row!"

A hand that was different than any of the others reached for a macaroon. The macaroon spoke.

"Are do's funny? Because I don't know that," said the odd tinny voice of Mac, their macaroon-headed friend, seated on the couch, speaking through a cookie.

"They can be," said Doc, trying not to spit toodles.

"Two do's or more is hilarious, according to the Earth humor I've gleaned," added Lattis. "Three is very very funny. Four is unheard of. Any more and you might find me on the floor under such circumstances."

"Should I help you?" asked the cookie. "Should I help you off the floor?"

"No," said Lattis after a thoughtful pause.

"I may never understand things," said Mac.

"Well, since you are now able to come and go, back and forth, from your own reality to ours," observed Doc, "a happy byproduct of the crossdimensionalizer—you'll have all the time you want now to learn about do's and humor and, well, anything else you might want to learn about."

"Maybe I will also be able to explain my world to you sometime. As of now, there is no way to explain anything. The necessary words turn to nothing before they can even *pass through the cookie*, as they say. Earth simply has not the words."

"That must be so frustrating," sympathized Betty. "I know if I couldn't describe to Paul a sale or something a neighbor did, he'd go crazy."

Kro-Bar looked at Doc who shrugged slightly.

"Well, I have to catch a plane," said General Scottmanson, standing.

"Isn't it your own plane?" asked City Brad.

"Yes, but I still have to catch it," chuckled the General. "I can't just get on it any time I please. What kind of private plane would that be?"

Again, everyone shared a good laugh.

Scottmanson shook Doc's hand. "Paul, I'll see you at the opening of the Paul Armstrong Rugmen Rehabilitation Center next month."

"Yes," added Betty, nibbling on a scotia, "it's wonderful the work he's been doing."

"Well… we haven't started yet, hon," observed Doc gently, knowing all his wife had been through. "After the opening, then we'll start."

"Oh, of course," grinned his wife, almost spitting britto crumbs as she realized she'd made a bit of a *bon pain*.

Warm goodbyes were exchanged, and Betty loaded the high-ranking military officer up with goodies, though he reminded her that it was *still* a military plane, and there *were* some snack limits, and they were technically *not* requisition military treats. Nevertheless, he was weighted down with enough for three trips. As they bade farewell to their general friend, they knew it would not be too long before they saw him again. Any adventure worth its salt needed one general, particularly when engaging the unknown or *any* strange things, and there was none better for that than "Scotty" Scottmanson.

Saying goodbye to Professor Atroppasmirki had been equally hard earlier that day, but the venerable scientist had to return to his studies at the university. Doc's eldest mentor had been an invaluable help in cracking the parchpyrus, which Betty had framed on the living room wall—something her husband wasn't too sure about.

City Brad had to report back for duty. There was still help needed with the reorientation of the recently returned populace and that included the entire Viewton Police Force, save City Brad.

It had been quite a moment when the people of Blendview, and all Viewton, had returned en masse, once the effects of the mobian wave had been reversed. For some reason they all started emerging from the town hall, very slowly, walking down the steps in a daze, having no idea what had happened to them or where they'd been. Doc Armstrong surmised that it might all come back to them at some point. Or it may never. At any rate, they were all dressed as ancient Vikings, which was odd, particularly for some, like elderly Mrs. Toaspy who looked really out of place. They also had gift bags, strangely enough, which had Betty and Lattis complaining to their husbands how unfair it seemed that they didn't each get one, given all they'd been through.

The last thing each of the victims remembered was being dragged into the hedges by the gobbling little mobiates. The annoying and sometimes dangerous creatures had of course been returned, like everything else, to their original plane of existence.

"Do you really think Guller Mobian went with them?" Betty asked her husband.

Doc thought thoughtfully. It was a peculiar thing. But very true. When he had finally gotten to the foot of Mobian's high-rise, to his astonishment he found Hydraulic Henry empty. There had been no sign of the tiny normal-headed man. Upon examination of the automaton, Doc discovered that there was more than enough room inside to fit all of Guller, meaning he could basically duck down and quickly close a protective lid. He also found the bulky boxy robot-like torso extremely well-padded, with special gelatin-filled cushions. Enough to survive a twelve story fall?

Doc had no other explanation. For Hydraulic Henry was empty. And the little man was nowhere to be found.

It was surmised that the mad genius might have discovered a way to go with the mobiates to their own dimension: a place where he would be mighty, both of body and mind. Of course, it was all supposition. One of those mysteries you wonder about on a quiet night when you can see your own breath and have nothing better to do.

Doc excused himself to catch up on some much needed science work, and he left Betty to entertain Kro-Bar and Lattis and B. "Bunny" Bretterspitt and his family, as well as

Mrs. Toaspy and Anky Trayster and the Perrilsons and the Corters and the Reeters and just about everyone else in Blendview. Betty had remarked that they could almost call it a block party, if they had some blocks.

The events of the past few days had given Doc much to think about. Not only what too many plants can do, or some of the nastier things that apparently live in other dimensions, but the dangers of tampering: the great responsibility he and others like him now bore on the cusp of the cutting edge of the beginning of new technologies.

Maybe that's what the face in the sky was grinning about. The face that had never quite formed, for which Doc was grateful. Would he ever know what that face was? It was the only time the scientist could ever recall not caring if he got an answer.

He walked into his home lab, and it didn't seem quite as cozy as before somehow. Then he turned a lamp on, one Betty had put in there, and it was cozy again. Doc closed the door behind him and sat at his work table. He thought about Guller Mobian and what had moved the man to act as he did. He was mad of course. Genius, but mad.

But was he wrong? Was he so wrong? Not like arithmetic test wrong, or tie-choosing wrong. And not the way he went about it: that was misguided.

But what he tried to accomplish. Was he so wrong to want to do that? To want to do *something?* Wasn't it worse to do *Nothing?*

Doc opened his eyes and stared into the face of Science.

LARRY BLAMIRE writes, directs, draws, paints, and acts, making him an author, director, playwright, screenwriter, artist and actor, so it all actually fits quite nicely. His film THE LOST SKELETON OF CADAVRA has a cult following and inspired similar films which are similar. The first book of the graphic novel of his epic steampunk adventure STEAM WARS is now available, as is the absurd and ridiculous AUDIO ADVENTUREBOOK OF BIG DAN FRATER, VOLUME ONE. Larry's play ROBIN HOOD has been performed hundreds of times, worldwide. His painting tends towards the surreal, though it's hard to be certain since he has absolutely no idea what he's painting, but that's probably a good thing. This is his first novel, though he makes no excuses and in fact is threatening to write more.

Made in the USA
Middletown, DE
29 April 2017